Manu is a start-up tech executive with a passion to solve the global water crisis. He lives with his family in the San Francisco Bay Area. This is his debut novel.

All author proceeds will go towards solving the water crisis via the JalTara Save Groundwater Foundation (savegroundwater.org).

THE SCHOOLYARD BET
AFZAL AND FRIENDS VS. THE TERRORIST
MANU NAMBOODIRI

Published by Westland Books, a division of a division of Nasadiya Technologies Private Limited, in 2024.

No. 269/2B, First Floor, 'Irai Arul', Vimalraj Street, Nethaji Nagar, Alapakkam Main Road, Maduravoyal, Chennai 600095

Westland and the Westland logo, are the trademarks of Nasadiya Technologies Private Limited, or its affiliates.



ISBN: 9789360454364

10 9 8 7 6 5 4 3 2 1



Typeset by Ashutosh Jha

Printed at Manipal Technologies Limited, Manipal

*To*
*Tukaram Omble,*
*Sandeep Unnikrishnan,*
*and many other heroes,*
*known and unknown,*
*who sacrifice for the greater good.*

# Contents

# 1

# A Schoolyard, a Brawl, a Bigot

'… and that is why the Konark temple …'

Afzal could barely hear the drone of Mrs Gupta's voice. Unable to sit still, he fidgeted uneasily, his feet tapping. He glanced around the classroom anxiously.

The teenager's behaviour contrasted sharply with the serene demeanour of the other students. Except Beena. She sat in the next row over. Afzal smiled as he noticed her furtively glance at the clock above the doorway.

The bell would ring in precisely four minutes.

Except those four minutes dragged on for what seemed like four hours. When the bell finally rang, Afzal sprang up and sprinted out into the hall, followed closely by Beena. They rushed to the nearest exit and headed outside into their school's sprawling courtyard. Quite a few students were already gathered there, chatting under the shade of massive peepal trees.

Several boarding schools called Shimla home, including the one that Afzal and Beena attended. It motored along like any other Catholic school in India—punctual, strict and with no tolerance for drama. Tall stone buildings, wide corridors, expansive green lawns, ancient trees, children in grey and cream uniforms and dark-robed brothers and sisters of the cloth gave it a formidable and austere presence.

As if to say—safe, studious and boring.

As they reached the cool shade of the trees, Beena glanced over at Afzal. 'Is it still on?' She was a slender, athletic girl with straight dark hair, dimples and bright almond-shaped eyes.

Afzal huffed. 'You bet it is. No one insults my friends and gets away unscathed. This is war, Bee!' Afzal's lanky frame, mischievous grin, restless energy and unruly hair seemed out of place compared to his resolute demeanour.

Beena groaned. 'I can't believe he called me "chinkie" again. But that doesn't mean we go nuclear. Don't you think we're going too far?'

'Nope. Not at all. Parv started it. He was warned. Now he'll get what's coming. I'm sure the idiot would even call someone from Kerala a "kallu".'

'Hmm … in all the time I've studied here, Parv's the only one who's made fun of my looks.'

'And he'll never do it again after we teach him a lesson today. It is up to us to educate the idiot that India is a diverse nation. For heaven's sake, your uncle is a bloody officer in the Assam Regiment! What's more Indian than that?'

'You sound like Mrs Gupta: "India is a diverse nation",' Beena said, bobbing her head and laughing. 'Be careful or you will end up as her favourite student in social studies.'

'Social studies!' Afzal recoiled in mock horror. 'But hey, where's Rup? He's supposed to be here by now.'

He scanned the students still spilling out of the building.

Beena said, 'He'll be here soon. A drama buff like Rup will never miss a performance like we're about to see. But tell me, Afzal, how did you even find someone?'

'Arre yaar. Inside this boarding school cocoon, you sometimes forget this is still India. A few rupees can get you just about anything.' Afzal grinned, looking pleased with himself. 'She even agreed to make herself look as outrageous as possible. Cheesy make-up, messy hair, trampy clothes, you know—the works.'

Beena glared. 'Are you suggesting that I know how to make myself look terrible?'

'Possibly,' said Afzal with a wink, and then put his hands up in mock surrender. 'Kidding! You can never pull off trampy. You're welcome to try though.'

Beena snorted and shook her head. 'Nah, not my style. Honestly though, I feel this whole thing is a bit over the top.'

'Hey guys, over here,' a booming voice reached them over the students' chatter.

They turned around to see an excited Rupinder, aka Rup, waving at them. Rup was impossible to miss—over six feet tall and burly, towering over the rest of the students. Only his chubby face and twinkling eyes behind thin wireframe glasses gave his age away.

Beena and Afzal headed towards Rup as he swung a large backpack off his shoulder. He unzipped it, unpacked a tall tripod and set it firmly on the ground. As Rup affixed his phone onto it, he said, 'My phone can capture a wide-angle view from here. You both be sure to catch a few handheld shots with yours. Multiple angles, I'm telling ya. Multiple angles are the key to good drama.'

Beena checked her phone. 'It's almost time. Now, where's our target?'

'Don't worry, Parv will be here. With Yug, no doubt. There are a lot of students in this spot for them to torment.'

'Yeah, don't I know all about that.'

'I can't wait to see his face when ...' Rup's voice trailed off. 'Parv's here!' He jerked his chin towards the science department building.

Parv, a tall boy with long, straight hair, swaggered down the wide granite steps towards the courtyard, as if he owned the place. Accompanying him was Yug, a short, chubby kid. He pulled at his drooping trousers as he scampered to keep up with Parv.

Beena was more interested in scouting for the player than the mark. 'And where is …? Oh goodness …'

Rup and Afzal had spotted her too.

A tall woman in her mid-twenties sauntered into the grounds. She wore skin-tight, torn, blue jeans and a snug, skimpy, bright-red blouse that left little to the imagination. Her thick mascara competed with her heavy blue eye shadow. Her lips were a crimson pout, and her hair curly and unkempt, as if she had only just got out of bed. A jarring, colourful apparition that stuck out among the sea of plain, uniform-clad kids.

Afzal nudged Beena, grinning, 'She's perfect, no?'

Beena gawked at the woman. She stammered, 'Baap re … perhaps too perfect. I've a sinking feeling we're about to visit Sister Alisha's room of doom. Again.'

'It will be worth it. No one messes with you, Bee. Not while we're around,' said Rup as he rubbed his palms together and adjusted the phone camera.

The woman walked with slow ease, scouring the crowd. When she spotted Parv, she took a deep breath, adjusted her breasts and smoothed her tight-fitting top. Then she shook her head with flair and made a beeline for her target. She paid scant attention to swivelling heads and gasps as she weaved purposefully through the throng of gawking students.

Approaching Parv from behind, the woman's throaty voice rang clearly over the now hushed crowd. 'Parvy, sweetheart. Why haven't you called back? It's been days. See, I had to come here searching for you.'

Parv spun to the sound of the odd voice behind him, gaping when he spotted her. For a moment, the unexpected apparition rendered him speechless. Pale, he mumbled weakly, 'Wha … What?'

The woman continued in an even sultrier tenor. 'Parvy, don't pretend you don't know me.'

Parv backed away, stuttering, 'I *really* don't know you. You've got the wrong person. How do you even know my name? How did you get inside?'

Undeterred, the woman leaned closer, resting her palm on Parv's chest, and pouted. 'Don't be like that, Parvy. We have too much to throw away. Just talk to me, will you? We can push through our troubles together.'

Parv staggered, almost tripping, as he awkwardly shoved her hand away. 'Stop that! Don't touch me.'

A large group of students had assembled around the action. Yug stared quizzically at the strange woman, and then at Parv. 'Is there something you need to tell me?'

'With all we've been through, you can't even bear me touching you?' the woman demurred. 'You didn't mind being close the last time we were together.'

The crowd of students had grown. They roared with laughter.

Parv turned white as a ghost.

Then it dawned on him. His eyes sharpened, and he swung his head until he found the three of them doubled over in laughter, barely a dozen feet away.

'Son of a bitch! You did this, Afzal! I'm gonna …' Parv was so furious, words failed him. Sensing the rising tension, the strange woman decided her job here was done. Turning on her heel, she hurried off.

'What do you even mean? Did what?' Afzal said, chuckling. He sauntered over and stood right in front of the school bully, holding his phone chest-high. He jerked his face towards the woman, now rapidly disappearing into the distance. 'In my wildest dreams, I'd never have thought *that* to be your type, or I'd have been your wingman.'

'You bastard. You're going to pay for this,' said Parv, leaning in until his nose almost pressed against Afzal's face. Sweat gleamed on the veins popping out of his forehead.

Afzal shoved his phone into his pocket and shrugged, 'Not today. And another thing: keep away from my friends. Don't you dare insult any of them again.'

Parv's face darkened. He raised his fists and moved towards Afzal.

'Parvesh Singh, Afzal Pathan—you two, stop it!' an authoritative voice boomed from afar. It was Brother da Costa, the school headmaster, standing outside the doorway of the science department building. 'And stay right there! Don't you dare move.'

Afzal turned to the side and folded his arms smugly. 'We're done here.'

Parv grabbed Afzal's shoulder, hissing through clenched teeth, 'No, we're not. You pulled this cheap trick to send some kind of a message. You think you jihadis and your Chinese friends are better than us?'

'That's your best comeback?' Afzal asked, laughing and mimicking Parv in a singsong tone. 'Jihadis and Chinese friends … that's it?'

Parv sneered with contempt. Eyes narrowed, he continued.

'No, I got more. You think no one knows about your family's involvement in that terror attack in Delhi? Well, I do. And I think it's time that everyone hears about it—that you come from a family of terrorists.'

Afzal reeled, colour draining from his face. He gasped for breath as if someone had punched him in the gut.

'Aha! Don't like the truth coming out much, do you, *traitor*?' continued Parv, looking sickly pleased with himself.

'That's a lie. You take that back! You have no idea what those false accusations did to my family!' screamed Afzal, his voice turning hoarse.

'A false charge? Nope. A traitor's blood runs through your veins. After Delhi, none of you deserve to live in my country.' The bully's voice dripped with hatred. 'Why don't you go back to Pakistan and take your Chinese friend with you? That's where your true loyalties lie.'

With all the pranks they had pulled on each other, this was the first time Afzal had heard such venom in Parv's voice. He peered around at the students' faces crowding around them, felt their gaze. His eyes glistened, and his cheeks turned warm.

His voice almost a whisper, he said, 'I was also born here in India, and I'm just as patriotic as anyone. Definitely more than you.'

'Yeah, right. All I see is a whole family of traitors and terrorists.' Parv's voice was almost singsong. He was thoroughly enjoying himself.

'You want me to prove my patriotism?'

Parv chuckled, looked sideways at Yug and waggled his thumb at Afzal. 'I don't see how a moron like this guy can prove he's not a traitor.'

Afzal clenched his fists and took a deep breath.

'I don't need to prove anything, especially to you. But I will not have my patriotism questioned.' He'd regained his composure, his voice was calm and serious.

Parv leaned closer and hissed, 'Then prove it.'

'I *will*.' Afzal's voice was almost a whisper. 'Because I know I'm more of a true Indian than you ever will be. This should be easy.'

Parv sneered. 'Yeah, right. I'm so sure you can't do it. If you do somehow prove it, I'll shave my head and apologise. Right here. In this courtyard. That's how certain I am that you're a traitor.'

'Deal. Better get your razor good and sharp. You're going to need it.'

'Not in a million years. You did this whole slimy woman thing because that's how you and your people think.'

'My people? What does that mean? I set that woman up because you were insulting Beena all the time. Stop being a bigot. That's the message we were sending. Nothing more.'

Beena chimed in. 'Yeah. It's just payback for calling me "chinkie". You're such a dickhead.'

Brother da Costa finally made it through the crowd that had gathered around the two teenage boys. He glared at Beena, then grabbed Afzal's shoulder and spun him so he could lock eyes with the boy. 'Pathan, Maibam and Chauhan …' He turned to glance at the big teen behind the tripod. 'I see you over there, Rupinder Chauhan. Turn that thing off and get over here,' he barked. 'All three of you to Sister Alisha's office. Now!'

Afzal and Beena hung their heads as they waited for Rup to pack up and join them. As the three friends trudged off, side by side, Parv yelled, 'Filthy double-crossing traitor! We all know what you and your family truly are, Afzal.'

~

Sister Alisha knew how to wield a ruler to inflict a spanking. Maybe more than any human alive. Odd trait for a holy sister who taught things like 'love thy neighbour' and 'turn the other cheek'. But she and the other nuns had to somehow ensure sanity in a boarding school full of rambunctious teenage boys and girls.

Afzal, Beena and Rup stood in a line, slightly bent over to offer their behinds. Sister Alisha raised the ruler with a practiced hand and it came down fast—a smooth whistling blur. *Whack. Whack. Whack.* Afzal clenched his jaw and curled his fists.

Sister Alisha took a step forward. Beena was next.

'Sister, this is ridiculous. We're too old for … ouch! That hurts!'

'A ruler's supposed to hurt, young lady. You're not even sixteen. In my book, that's not too old for a good spanking, especially to remind you to behave.'

Sister Alisha then took another step to line up for Rup. 'It was a simple little joke. A prank to pay Parv back for disrespecting Beena.'

Sister Alisha sighed and said, 'I take no joy in this. You shamed Parv in front of half the student body.'

Beena rolled her eyes and shot back, 'Oh no. We can't have Parv experience a little shame, can we? Not with all his dad's donations to this school.'

Sister Alisha grimaced as she struck Rup, a bit harder than usual. However, his buttocks appeared to be more resilient than the wooden measuring stick, which broke on impact.

The sister waved the stub of wood at Beena. 'Donations have nothing to do with it, young lady. You cannot bring a strange woman to the campus and imply she has a relationship with a student. You know this. The parents will beat down my door when they hear of this, and quite a few of them will want you three dismissed. What a mess! Now, go to your rooms and think hard about what you did.'

On their way out, Rup whispered, 'How did she even know about the woman?'

Afzal rubbed his butt as he staggered down the hall. 'You know the sisters. They see everything, they hear everything. I think they are connected through some sort of hive mind. Maybe that's why ours may be the only school in the country that still gives the ruler treatment.'

Rup chuckled, 'With students like us, I can see why our parents don't mind an occasional dosage.'

'Sister Alisha does have a good arm-swing and follow-through,' Afzal said, wincing as he felt his behind.

'We're in real trouble this time,' Rup said. 'I hope she was only joking about the other parents wanting to kick us out. My dad will kill me if I'm expelled.'

'Well, at least your folks can afford another school in Shimla. Without my scholarship, I'll likely be enrolled in a nice government school,' Afzal countered.

'Maybe Sister Alisha was kidding. Oh c'mon, it was fun to see Parv's face when that woman put her hand on his chest,' Rup smiled wistfully.

Beena piped up, her voice soft. 'I dunno, Rup. We shouldn't have done something this extreme to hit back at Parv. Yes, his words were hurtful, but I should—*we* should—be better than him.'

Rup chuckled. 'Still, we got some entertaining video footage.'

'For you and your drama club group … was it really worth it?' Beena said, exasperated, then looked at Afzal anxiously.

'He publicly made these terrible accusations about your family, Afzal. I never realised your family went through something like that. How did Parv find out?'

Afzal's shoulders slumped. He paused for a moment and said, 'His father, most probably. You know Parv's dad hobnobs with politicians. But those accusations against my parents were proven completely false. Yet we were forced to leave Delhi, move to the coast. My dad's now a fisherman. I still don't understand why he threw that at me.'

Rup said, 'That's Parv. A junkyard dog's gonna bark.'

Beena nodded. 'What an asshole.'

Afzal was quiet for a moment before he replied. 'I'm not putting up with it.'

'No! No more stunts, revenge schemes or pranks,' Beena pleaded. 'Let it go, Afzal. Anything more now will just make it worse.'

'You sure? If we do nothing, he'll simply become bolder, and his friends will start saying awful things too. Yug already does.'

Rup scrunched his face. 'So, either way, it gets worse?'

# 2

# The Thin Line Between Crazy and Easy

Afzal lay on his bed, staring at the grey ceiling. It reflected his dark and gloomy mood. On the other side of the dorm room, Rup did the same. Neither moved more than was necessary to breathe.

Even the knock at the door failed to stir them. Without shifting, Rup said, 'Come on in, Bee.'

Beena entered and sat gingerly at the desk. 'How did you know it was me?'

'Who else is willing to talk with us right now?'

She leaned back and sighed. 'I'm not sure I want to talk to you either. But here I am anyway.'

'I'm glad you're here.' Afzal groaned as he tried to move. 'My ass stings. I got the worst of it. Top drawer stuff. Sister always does me first and gives me the best whacks. I suppose that means I'm her favourite. I should feel privileged.'

'She got a few first-class strikes on me too,' said Beena.

Afzal glanced at Rup. 'You got off easy.'

'It hurts me to see you two get hit. I hate that,' said Rup unconvincingly.

Beena inspected the big lad lying flat and motionless on his back. 'Why does the ruler always break on your ass? You do some special kind of bum exercises?'

'Nope,' Rup said with a grin. He turned over, adjusted his glasses and lowered his voice, as if sharing nuclear missile passcodes. 'Old-fashioned magazines. Topped with my kerchief for soft padding. We always get the ruler, thanks to Afzal's goofy stunts. So, I make sure I keep a couple of magazines handy and just shove them down the backside of my pants beforehand.'

Beena raised her eyebrows. 'What? Son of a bitch! That's sad, but ingenious. How the hell do you walk though?'

'Hey, it works. You should try it, Afzal. As you said, she always starts on you. If the ruler breaks on your ass, Beena and I needn't worry about getting whacked,' Rup said with a chuckle, then scrunched up his face. 'Well, unless Sister Alisha starts buying rulers in bulk.'

'Thanks for the tip,' said Afzal, unfazed.

'You're kinda lost in your thoughts there, buddy,' said Beena, studying the prone boy. 'You don't seem quite yourself.'

Afzal was silent, squinting as if considering whether he should proceed. He finally looked up and asked, 'Hey, Bee. Did I ever do anything to make you think I'm not patriotic? I love India as much as anyone. And no one in all of Shimla is a bigger fan of the Indian cricket team than me. Is this because my mom is from Kashmir?'

Beena shook her head. 'No. Parv was being a jerk, as usual. Don't let his nonsense mess with your head. He's just taking advantage of some fake news about your family—and the fact that it's not widely known here.'

'He meant what he said. I could tell.'

Rup sat up. 'I saw how deeply the remembrance vigil affected you. You did everything to console Beena and her family,' Rup said, then took a sharp breath and glanced at Beena. 'It was awful what happened to your aunt in Mumbai. Sorry for bringing it up.'

'It's alright, Rup.'

They sat without speaking for a while—the ceiling seemed to turn an even darker shade of grey.

After what felt like ages, Rup turned to Afzal. 'Really, Parv is a moron. He doesn't know you or Beena like I do. You mustn't let him get to you like this.'

Afzal pursed his mouth. 'I'm one of the few Muslims in this school. That's just a fact. But it's bigoted to say I'm loyal to Pakistan solely because of my religion. I was born here, and I love it here.'

'Like Rup said, Parv's a moron. Why do you let him bother you?'

'If he thinks it, I am sure other students do too.'

Rup walked over to his friend. 'Uh oh, I know that tone. Afzal, what are you thinking?'

'I can't stand anyone thinking that my family are terrorists. If that's what they think, I need to do something to prove I'm a true patriot. Plus, as a bonus, Parv shaves his stupid head.'

Beena chuckled. 'I'm sorry, Afzal, but one of your whacky stunts is not enough to change people's minds about something like that. Especially Parv's. He's filled with hate and thinks he's better than everyone else.'

Afzal rolled over and propped himself up on an elbow. 'It would take something really big, something a lot grander than our usual stuff. Something no one can ignore.'

Rup flopped back on the bed. 'Shit! I don't like the sound of that *something*.'

'Neither do I. Let it go, Afzal. We should be thankful we're not expelled.'

Afzal stared again into grey space as he considered his options. Then he stood and snapped his fingers. 'No, I need to act while this is fresh in everyone's mind.'

Rup sighed. 'I think I'll pre-emptively talk to my dad to see which other boarding school in Shimla can admit me. My future prospects do not seem that bright here in St Ignatius—nor does my behind!'

Afzal laughed, but his face was set. 'You're right, Rupinder. This is not over. We're only getting started.'

'Rupinder. He's even calling you by your full name. Next, he'll be calling you Mr Chauhan,' Beena rolled her eyes. 'I'm out. I put up with your stupid pranks because you're my friend. But I repeat, let sleeping dogs lie.'

Rup added, 'Me, too. Parv is a jerk, and I really, *really* don't care what he thinks. Especially about my friends.'

Afzal's head drooped. 'Neither do I. But he called me and Beena treasonous foreigners. If we don't push back, he'll continue doing it. My parents had to run away from Delhi because of those fake terrorism accusations. If I don't act now, I will need to do the same. One can't keep running away.'

'Alright, let's play this out. What will you do to make a statement?' Beena asked, her voice carrying more than a tinge of irritation.

'Volunteer for something or organise a charity for the fallen soldiers. Like the Assam Regiment. Beena's uncle can show us what to do. Helping others is always a good way to show your best side,' suggested Rup.

'Umm ... that's a cool idea, sure, but it won't sway anybody,' said Afzal. 'It will come off as fake. They'll think we're doing it to pull the wool over their eyes.'

'How about we hang a big Indian flag in our room? And you could wear a tricolour pin on your shirt.' Rup's eyes grew wide behind his glasses, as if he genuinely thought he had the answer. 'Or we could paint the flag on the outside of our door!'

Afzal's response was short. 'Nope.'

Rup frowned. 'So, you're saying there's nothing we can do.'

'Hmm, there has to be something.' Afzal chewed his lip, his frustration obvious.

Beena was listening with amusement. 'I love your determination, but we've other things to worry about. Like our studies. Remember? We're here in school to learn, which means there's homework. I finally got my Raspberry Pi kit, and my robotics project is due before the term ends.'

Rup tilted his head back and groaned, 'Ugh … I've so much homework. I'm screwed.'

'Rup, you're *always* behind on your school projects.'

'I *know*. If all I had was my performance art homework, or maybe some illusions, I would be all set. It is this stupid math and physics …'

'… and every other subject,' interjected Beena, chuckling. 'And if all Afzal had to complete was his chemistry homework, he would top the class too.'

'Well, not with that smelly glass he concocted a few months ago in the lab. I can't figure out how anyone could pull off glass that stinks. He would absolutely flunk there,' said Rup, chuckling and thumping his palms on his thighs. 'Or maybe he would top the exam—for achieving a feat no one else could possibly manage.'

He glanced at his friend, who was leaning against the wall with a thoughtful expression.

Afzal sighed. 'Rup, I don't feel like doing homework. The longer I do nothing, the worse my anger and frustration become. And Parv will continue saying bullshit in front of everyone. His hatred is like wildfire; it destroys everything in its path. We'll always be second-class citizens if we don't push back. We need to come up with a plan.'

Beena looked concerned. 'Look, don't do anything stupid right now, let things simmer down. We can talk about this again later if you need to. But try to let it go. Remember, nothing stupid, okay?'

Afzal smiled. 'You're saying I've gone too far?'

She huffed. 'I need to get back to the girls' dorm in time—don't want another whacking so soon. Plus, I've a big day tomorrow with my robotics project. We're wiring up a Hot Wheels car to navigate a steeplechase road on its own.'

'Wow, sounds pretty cool!' Rup was envious. 'We need to do some studying, too. But nothing as exciting as yours. Good luck with the project; I know your Hot Wheels will be the best.'

'Thanks, guys. See you tomorrow.'

~

Afzal sprinted into the school cafeteria, face flushed.

Beena gave him a once over. 'Didn't know you liked the lunch here so much. It's the same sabzi-roti-dal-chawal we get every day. Did you run all the way here for that?'

'Yeah, but that's not important. What's more important is that I got it!'

Rup tore off a chunk of roti. 'Got what? A better way than magazines to protect your behind from Sister Alisha?'

'No, you idiot. Something way better. I figured out how we can make Parv shave his head,' Afzal said with a grin.

Beena sighed as she spooned some rice into the dal. 'You were supposed to finish your homework and let this go.'

'No, Bee. I only agreed to wait and let things simmer down. And talk again later if I needed to. Well, now I need to.'

'Why?'

'Because, guys, I got it! It's the perfect plan and will be easy as pie. *Bahut hi saral kaam.*'

Rup eyed him dubiously, his mouth full of roti and sabzi. 'Okay, spill. What's this big idea of yours?'

Afzal leaned over the table, gesturing them to come closer. Then he spoke softly, but with a dramatic tone. 'We sneak into Pakistan, kidnap Rasheed Latif and haul him back to India to stand trial.'

Beena nearly choked. 'What the … we do what?'

'You on drugs?' Rup interjected, staring at Afzal as if he had suddenly transformed into a purple alien. 'I thought I heard you say you wanted to kidnap the world's most hated terrorist.'

Afzal hushed his big friend. 'Yes, yes, that's exactly what I said. Bring Latif to stand trial for terrorist attacks against India. And keep your voices down. This has to stay among us.'

'*Obviously* this insane idea has to stay among us,' Beena said, jabbing her fingers on the table. 'Not only that, this should never be spoken about again. This is crazy on another level. Afzal, you're losing it.'

'What do you mean? It is the perfect plan. If I haul Latif back to India to face justice, no one will ever doubt my patriotism again. And I'm sure I can pull this off.'

Rup shook his head. 'Did you slip and hit your head while taking a shower this morning? I'm sorry, but I'm with Bee here. You realise you have to be alive to prove your patriotism? What use is proving anything to an idiot like Parv from six feet under?' Before Afzal could answer, Rup continued. 'And your big plan is to break Latif out from a maximum-security prison in Pakistan and bring him to India? Across one of the most heavily guarded borders in the world? That is the dumbest, nuttiest thing you ever said. Expulsion from school doesn't seem like a big deal anymore.'

Afzal didn't let their lack of enthusiasm deter him. He pushed on, eyes shining. 'I know it sounds a bit out there. But that's what makes it so awesome. No one can ignore or question it.'

Beena's eyes narrowed, and she gazed into the distance. Her voice was low. 'I was only a toddler when my aunt was killed in Mumbai. I scarcely remember her now—except for a faint sense of smell and a hazy, warm sensation of being held tightly. I'm told she used to massage me with coconut oil before a bath. I'd throw tantrums and always insist on sleeping with her …' Her voice trailed off as she fingered a gold chain around her neck.

Rup put a big arm around Beena and gently squeezed her shoulders. Afzal looked across the table at her, his eyes misting up.

'I hate that I couldn't spend more time with her,' she continued. 'I hate that I don't have more memories of her. I hate that man Latif for killing hundreds of innocent people during that attack. And I want him to face justice more than the two of you combined. But what you propose is impossible. Not only that—it's dangerous and foolish.'

Afzal sat with his head bowed for a few moments. When he looked up at Beena again, his eyes were still glistening. 'I'm so sorry that you couldn't spend more time with your aunt. She sounds wonderful. You never shared this before; your unfinished memories and how she was unfairly taken from you.'

'And I don't want anyone else to be taken from my life. We should stop thinking about this dangerous idea right now.'

Afzal shook his head. He had a steely look on his face. 'We should be doing this *precisely* because of terrible losses like yours. This is a good plan because no one will expect it. I'm sure we can pull it off.'

'Pull it off? More like we will get our heads pulled off our bodies. I'm with Bee. This is madness.'

Afzal put up his hands, palms out.

'Listen, guys. I've been up all night, researching and planning. Did you know that Latif isn't in a maximum-security joint like you said, Rup? Where he's put up is more like a country club retreat with barely a few guards—a bloody travesty of justice. He's treated like royalty and no one expects him to escape because, well, he doesn't want to. He continues his dirty terrorism work from the inside, I tell you! Visitors walk in and out all the time. It would be easy for us to sneak in and kidnap him.'

'You really are nuts!' exclaimed Rup, then cautiously glanced around the crowded lunch hall. 'Besides, we shouldn't be talking about this here. If anyone overhears us, we'd progress way beyond wooden rulers.'

'Rup's right. On both counts. You are crazy *and* we should zip it,' said Beena, checking her watch. 'And classes start in four minutes.'

Afzal sighed.

She looked at his dejected face. 'Look, why don't we catch up in Rup's apartment tonight? After all, it's Friday. Compared to your shitty dorm room, we can have some food, and talk there freely, and I won't be forced to tour Sister Alisha's dungeon for sneaking into the boys' dorms at night.'

'Sounds awesome, Bee. *Mi casa es su casa*, my friends. Let's meet there.'

## 3

# If Opportunity Doesn't Knock,
# Break Down the Door

Rup's aunt had gifted him an apartment in a building she owned in Shimla. She was insanely wealthy, slightly eccentric and wanted her favourite nephew to have a place where he could escape to.

It's hardly ever a good idea to give a teenager his own apartment, but doting aunts think differently. And doting aunts with too much money are on an entirely different level.

Walking distance from their dorms, the apartment was little more than an empty space. The living room seating fixtures comprised a metal folding chair, a lawn chair and an overturned bucket. On the plus side, the makeshift table was also an overturned bucket, so it was a matching set piece. Sleeping bags and a rickety lamp rounded out the set-up.

Afzal and Rup arrived with takeout food before Beena. They tried to tidy up but she was punctual as usual, so they didn't make much of a dent.

Beena flew in, brandishing a shopping bag. She stopped in her tracks and sniggered. 'I see those crappy curtains are still here, as is the matching furniture. Even your dorm is like the Taj Hotel compared to this dump.'

Rup laughed, extending his hands and surveying his domain. 'Yep, these were always here. My aunt wanted to buy me new stuff, but I refused. I don't know why you'd think I would change anything—I love the aesthetic of this place.'

'Ha, bummer that the *Architectural Digest* missed Rup's apartment.' Afzal leaned forward, his eyes focused on the bag in her hands. 'What's that clinking noise?'

'Ah, this, my friends, is the surprise for the day,' said Beena and pulled two large bottles of beer out of the bag with a flourish.

Afzal's jaw dropped. 'I've no idea how you army types get— or, in your case, swipe it from those army types. Your uncle will kill you if he finds out you're pinching his beer and drinking with underage buddies.'

'Well, this is better than that crappy beer you brought last time. I had a headache after drinking that.'

'Ha! These do look quality compared to what I got. And best of all, you've got them without spending a paisa.'

'Believe me, I *shall* pay for it, if my uncle finds them missing,' quipped Beena. 'Let's hope that never happens.'

'Beer is important to generate ideas. Hopefully, good ones.' In a credible imitation of Amitabh Bachchan, he intoned, 'Michael *daaru peeke danga karta hai.*' He then disappeared into the kitchen, rummaging for glasses.

'We haven't had a sip and he's using awful voices already,' said Beena, thumping the bottles down on one of the inverted buckets.

'Glad to see you're in a good mood,' Afzal said and picked up one of the bottles. 'Wow, these are cold.'

'Yup, I stored them in our dorm mini-fridge,' Beena said. 'I want us to relax and have fun. You definitely need it, Afzal. I've been saving these bottles for a special event, and keeping you from getting killed qualifies.'

Rup returned, glasses in hand. 'Not to mention it's the end of a long, shitty week. Especially for you two weaklings with soft behinds, this beer is the balm you need. Thanks, Bee!'

Afzal filled the glasses before passing them around the bucket-table. 'Thanks for the beer, Bee, and thanks for hosting, Rup. Cheers!'

'Cheers! Don't down the entire pint. Just a little to relax. Afzal needs loosening up the most.'

'Hey, I'm always in a great mood,' said Afzal, chugging a big gulp, and smiling at Bee through the froth covering his upper lip. 'Damn, Bee, this isn't bad. It's making me forget that my ass still hurts, sitting on this plastic excuse of a chair.'

'Yeah,' Beena replied, 'but I can see you're still thinking about your ridiculous idea.'

'It's not ridiculous. It's the best idea ever in the history of the world. This is genius-level stuff, worthy of a Nobel Prize.'

Rup knocked back a swig with a grimace. 'So, Idea Man, tell me how you're going to get into Pakistan? There are tight restrictions on any Indian going there. You know you need to be in Pakistan to start this mission, right?'

'Ha, funny. I've been researching Latif,' said Afzal. He turned his laptop towards Beena and Rup. 'Like I was telling you, this article talks about how Latif is essentially living in a country club excuse for a prison. And here are dozens of posts from celebrities, politicians—some taking selfies with Latif, many from inside the bloody prison! Here is one outside Gate E of the prison. Check out @oily_boy, a social media kid. Even @oily_boy has a selfie with the man! It's as if all you need is a pulse and a selfie-capable phone to get inside that prison.'

'So, is your plan to pretend to be an influencer and sneak in? You're out of your mind. Latif is no idiot. He'll only meet people he knows, or if he gets something out of it.'

'Pretending to be an influencer is an interesting idea—something to consider. But I'm thinking we pretend to bring him business, or something else he desperately wants. It's all part of the research I'm doing.'

Beena put her hands on her head and moaned, 'Shit. Afzal's research will get us killed. Rup, pour another round. At least we can say we were drunk.'

'Shut up, you two.' Afzal hammered away at the keyboard, studying the screen. 'This is a straightforward job. Trust me.'

Rup slapped his thighs, laughed and filled their glasses. He held one out to Afzal and, imitating Arnold Schwarzenegger's voice, boomed, 'Drink!'

'Damn it. I forgot you banned me from saying "trust me".' Afzal downed the entire glass in one long swig.

'Remember your "trust me" from last year?' Rup asked. 'When we snuck out to listen to that terrible excuse of a rock band? And got caught? Trust me, my ass.'

'Hilarious,' said Afzal. 'Plus, that concert was an off-the-cuff scheme. This will be well planned and very doable.'

'Doable? Really? Indian diplomats have been trying to do this for years. Especially since that farce of a trial in Pakistan. Hell, even the Americans have tried to extract Latif—and they have a multi-million-dollar bounty on the bastard. You really think Afzal the Great can do what all of them couldn't?'

'Don't underestimate what a small, focused group can achieve when they set their minds to it. Some super smart guy said that. Not me.' Afzal then eyed his companions with a smug smile. 'You guys know about the Nazi war criminal Adolf

Eichmann, right? And how a tiny team captured and brought him back to stand trial in Israel?'

Beena reached over and smacked Afzal on the back of his head. 'Dude, of course we do. All the way from Argentina. But you are ignoring the details. That was a planned, well-thought-out retrieval involving the Israeli government, Mossad super spies, lots of money, guns and whatnot. With years of planning.'

'True, but the same principles apply here—even if the world has evolved. There's no way to send a bunch of agents to Pakistan and extract Latif. You need to be non-obvious and non-threatening to sneak under the radar. Besides, Mossad spent a lot of time searching for Eichmann because he was living under the alias Ricardo Klement. We don't have that problem. We know what Latif looks like, what his name is and *exactly* where he is.'

'That's my bloody point. Latif is *exactly* inside a prison. In Pakistan. With lots of guards, carrying lots of guns. You think it'll be a piece of cake?'

'Yes. Trust—I'm not going to say it.'

'Good. We won't have to hear Rup do any more of his silly voices.'

'Ha! He's impressive with those. His new grumpy old man voice sounds so real, I sometimes think he's Brother da Costa!'

Rup bowed his head to Afzal and used said voice. '*Dhanyavad, beta. Sukhi raho …*'

'Enough with your stupid impressions. Stay on topic and answer Rup's question. How do we get into Pakistan?'

Afzal avoided her gaze. 'That part I haven't worked out yet. But we should be able to figure it out.'

Beena raised her hands high above her head, the I-told-you-so expression clear on her face. 'We don't even have a beginning to this stupid plan.'

Rup interjected. 'Assume you solve it. You somehow sneak into Pakistan and break Latif out. Then what? You can't just stroll around, sightseeing the country with him. He's a famous, not to mention, dangerous terrorist.'

'Listen, you faithless little minions. You know how the Mossad snuck Eichmann out? Bundled in the boot of a car—which is exactly the right modus operandi for Latif.'

'We have to steal a car? And how do you plan to subdue Latif before you stuff him into a car's boot? He's a grown-ass man. Kinda big too, if I remember correctly.'

Afzal lifted up his beer glass and peered at his friends through it, smiling smugly. 'Knock-out drops, my friends. Chloroform. The basic ingredients of which are available with your friendly neighbourhood chemist. With the right dose, you can bring down a bloody elephant.'

'And after you bundle the elephant into a car and drive to the Indian border, then what? Do our soldiers invite us, including a terrorist, to waltz right across the border?'

'Absolutely,' Afzal replied, without missing a beat.

'No, shithead,' Beena snapped. 'That border has more soldiers pointing guns at each other than anywhere else in the world. And besides, the Indian soldiers won't know we're Indian. They'll assume we're Pakistani and shoot us dead before we can say namaste.'

'We'll take our IDs and wave them high.'

'Okay, smartass. And how will anyone see you waving IDs? Those soldiers will be hundreds of feet away.'

Rup gazed out the dusty window. 'I hate that stupid picture in my passport.'

Beena rolled her eyes. 'I don't think they'll mind a poor picture in the middle of a freaking international incident. Will you focus and help me?'

'I'm trying. But Afzal is in one of his moods.'

Afzal refilled their glasses. 'Look, guys. It's doable. That's why you're frustrated, Bee. You've been unsuccessfully trying to poke holes in my plan for hours.'

'According to you. You don't even have a bloody entry plan.'

'Pfft … I'll figure that out. But you're making it more complicated than it is. Here's the deal. The last thing Latif will expect is some teenager barging in to abduct him. We steal a car when we are in Pakistan, drive up north to Rawalpindi, break him out from his easy access luxury jail and scoot southeast to the Indian border near Jammu. Which is a just a couple hundred kilometres away. A few hours' drive—that's it. And we are home. Simple.'

'Really? Do you feel better now that you have a half-baked plan?'

'I do. Thanks for asking.'

Beena let out an exasperated moan and slumped in the lawn chair. Rup yawned. 'I've heard enough for one night.'

Beena moved over to Afzal and grasped his arm. 'Afzal, please let it go. You need to listen to your friends on this one. It's a nutty idea that'll get you in serious trouble—or, worse, killed. Proving anything to a shithead like Parv isn't worth it.'

'I can never live down Parv's accusation. A public allegation like that sticks and never goes away—and, besides, it tars my whole family. I'm glad my folks don't stay here in Shimla but are far away by the sea. They shouldn't have to relive what they went through in Delhi. This cuts too deep.'

'That's what makes you special. But can't you see we don't want you getting hurt or killed?' Beena asked. 'I let Parv's crude racist remark about me go. You should do the same.'

Afzal could see that Beena's face was filled with concern. 'I don't deserve you two as friends. But sorry, Bee, I can't.'

Beena winced like a mother watching a child learn the stove is hot. 'You've got us into stupid situations before, like that time we got covered in flour from head to toe, or the funky milk that turned everyone's lips blue. But I know you'd never put your friends in any real danger.'

Rup, in a poor imitation of Yoda, said, 'Hmm. Wise young Padawan, she is.'

Beena spun and glared at him. 'If you use one more stupid voice, I'm going to send a video of you drinking beer to Sister Alisha. There aren't enough magazines in the world to protect your ass from that whacking.'

After several hours of debate, the bottles of beer lay on their sides—empty. Rup's head flopped back as he sprawled in the folding chair, trying to ignore the banter between Afzal and Beena.

'Can we get some sleep now? I'm tired.'

Beena groaned, 'Rup's right. We've been up all night. The beer was meant to knock sense into you. It may have actually done the opposite.'

'This beer has given me some good ideas. Alright, here is the exit plan. Once we get Latif, we drive the short distance to Sialkot border, and then we hand him straight over to our border guards.'

'We heard the exit part of the plan, dumbass. You've repeated it a thousand times: "It's only a hundred kilometres—couple of hours." But you still don't have an entry plan. You have no idea how to begin!'

'I'm working on that. Maybe we drive up to Jammu and cross over?'

~

Monday morning came fast. Afzal barely made it to his class on time. Chemistry was usually interesting, but not today. He'd spent the night tossing and turning, unable to sleep as random ideas kept gushing through his brain. He sat at his desk, head in hand. With some effort, he managed to fight his drooping eyelids. Beena, seated next to him, helped with a sharp nudge now and then.

The teacher, Sister Chacko, wrote on the whiteboard with a dry erase pen in her right hand, wiping out what she'd written with an eraser in her left. The class scampered to take notes before she cleaned something they needed to remember.

All except Afzal, who was staring blankly out of the window.

The sister turned back to the class after jotting down a long organic chemistry formula and spotted Afzal's unfocused gaze. She knew that look; it was the vacant stare of a student who'd been needlessly awake all night and was now daydreaming. She swiftly swapped pen and eraser, arched her hand and flung the eraser across the classroom.

The whizzing projectile struck Afzal on his head with a muted thud. Shaken out of his dream, Afzal spun. 'What the …!'

Sister Chacko glared at him and pointed to the door.
'Sister Alisha's office, now!'

~

Afzal slinked back into his dorm room and sat gingerly at his small desk. Sister Alisha had been unusually kind and hadn't give him her full treatment—just a few sit-ups and a warning to pay attention in class. He folded his arms on the table and dropped his head.

Rup entered a few moments later, humming a tune from *Deewar*—the drama his group was staging in a few months. He was to perform an illusionist's card trick and an act with handcuffs to warm up the crowd before the show. Practice was intense.

Rup strode over and threw his book bag on his bed. Afzal hugged the desk a bit tighter and mumbled into his folded arms, 'At least one of us is in a good mood. How was the theatre club meeting?'

'My illusions are a disaster. I need to practice new card tricks.' Rup took in Afzal's crumpled posture at the desk and scrunched up his face. 'Forget about me. What's crawled up your bum?'

'My quads this time. So sore.'

'Sister Alisha? I told you to try the magazine trick. You should've listened.'

'What? Put *Playboy* magazines in my ass and risk Sister Alisha finding those too?'

'Ha! Funny. If you do accidently take a *Playboy*, please don't take Miss April—I can't afford to lose her,' Rup chuckled.

'Knowing my luck, she would absolutely find it,' Afzal sighed and raised his head to look at Rup. 'But this time she didn't give me the ruler treatment, just sit-ups. Those are murder on your legs.'

'Holy mark of the beast! What on earth's happened?'

'Oh, this?' Afzal rubbed his forehead. 'Sister Chacko drilled me with a dry eraser, like Jadeja throwing a cricket ball at the stumps. I tell you, she hits what she's aiming for. I would've appreciated her immaculate wrist action a lot more if I wasn't her target.'

Rup peered at the mark and laughed. 'Aha! I was afraid you had another practical joke go bad. Or you had undertaken some new religious pilgrimage.'

'Nope. Just a sister with a rocket arm.'

Suddenly, Afzal stiffened, and his eyes grew large with excitement. He leaped up and punched Rup in the arm.

'Rup, you're a bloody genius. You solved the biggest problem with the plan. A pilgrimage. That's how we enter Pakistan!'

'What are you babbling on about? What pilgrimage?' Rup stared at Afzal for a moment, and realisation dawned in his eyes. 'Oh, no. You mean Kartarpur? Are you nuts?'

Afzal had energy buzzing in his eyes. 'Kartarpur. Exactly. Don't assume anything. Hear me out. This isn't nuts—it's the answer we've been searching for.'

Rup raised a hand, 'Wait. I found out, not thirty minutes ago, the Chauhan family is going to Kartarpur in a few weeks. How did you …? Did my mom call you?'

'What? You and your family are going to Kartarpur? I didn't know, I swear. What a coincidence! No, a divine coincidence. The gods must really want us to do this. They're clearing the path for Latif to face some serious music on this side of the border.'

Afzal was striding energetically about the small dorm room, his face beaming.

Rup glared at his friend with a frown. 'I should never have told you that our family is going to Kartarpur. I can picture my new boarding school already—it's likely to be a military boot camp.'

'Oh shush, you big cry-baby. You don't have to do anything. Just let me come with you guys to the temple. Once there, I can sneak off.'

'I don't know, man. This sounds dangerous.'

Ignoring Rup, Afzal continued, 'And guess what? I know exactly how to slip out from the temple into Pakistan.'

'How?' asked a resigned Rup.

'Glad you asked, buddy. You know what they provide to pilgrims visiting the temple? Freshly cooked food. And that means food trucks are going in and out all the time—they must feed thousands of people every day. I climb into one of those and sayonara—I'm out of the temple and onto Pakistani soil.'

'And what do I tell my family when you disappear?'

'That I went to check out the place and we got separated or something. It's a massive complex, isn't it?'

Rup looked at his friend with concern in his eyes.

'You're going to get yourself killed. You remember that guy who crossed into Pakistan by mistake a few years ago? He was suspected of being an Indian spy and put in prison. Facing execution, if I remember correctly. No, no. There's no way we'll take you along.'

'Listen to me, Rup. Getting into Pakistan is the hardest part. Once I sneak out of the temple, I can easily blend in. I'll then go north to Rawalpindi, spring Latif from his country club and escort him back. Done! You come straight home from the temple with your folks.'

Rup wagged a finger in Afzal's face. 'No way! I'm not taking you with us. And that's final!'

Before they could continue, there was a loud, sharp knock on the door. Both of them froze. Afzal muttered to Rup, 'We'll finish this later.'

Before Rup could reply, the door cracked open slightly and Beena pressed her nose through. 'Get decent. Lady on the premises.'

'We're just chatting. Come on in.' Rup leaned over and hissed in Afzal's ear, 'No fucking way!'

Afzal's shoulders drooped, and his face lost some of its excitement.

Beena crept around the half-open door and peeked in. When she saw they were decent, she came all the way in and shut the door. She approached the seated Afzal and bent over him, staring at the mark on his forehead.

She smiled. 'I had to see it up close. That was so funny. You should've seen it, Rup—he almost fell off his chair'

Rup studied the blot on his friend's head. 'Sister Chacko does have good aim. And it looks like the mark of the devil.'

'I swear, the sisters must attend karate school to become a nun. No one can wield a ruler or throw things like that naturally.' Beena reached over and rubbed the black mark on her friend's forehead.

It didn't smudge and she giggled. Neither of the boys joined her.

She looked at their faces. 'What are you two so glum about?'

'Nada,' Afzal said, glancing sideways at Rup.

'Yeah, it's nothing.'

Suddenly, Rup's eyes went wide, and he rifled through his bag. 'Shit, I can't find my phone. I must've left it backstage. Be right back.' He squeezed past Beena.

As soon as the door closed, Beena pounced. 'You two were talking about your dumb plan, weren't you?'

Afzal mustered as innocent a face as he could. 'No.'

'You lie like shit. What were you two going on about?'

Afzal was too tired to resist. 'Well, the entry problem is solved. We figured out how to steal into Pakistan. You know the recently opened Kartarpur corridor? That connects to Guru Nanak-ji's shrine?'

'Yeah, I heard about it. It's an important pilgrimage for Sikhs, right? It was all over the news a few years ago, when they opened it up for easy access for Indians.'

'That's how I can sneak into Pakistan. Rup's family is visiting Kartarpur in a few weeks. I asked him to take me along, but he totally snubbed me.'

Beena punched Afzal in the arm. 'You idiot! I thought you promised to drop this silly idea.'

'Ouch!' Afzal rubbed his arm. 'I did no such thing! I said I would think about it. You assumed your speech convinced me. Plus, this Kartarpur thing dropped into our laps not ten minutes ago. It must be divine providence.'

'You're impossible. Divine providence, huh?' Beena huffed as she tilted her head to get a good look at Afzal. Taking a deep breath, she said in a clear voice. 'If you go to Kartarpur with Rup's family, I'm coming too.'

Alarmed, Afzal vigorously shook his head. 'No way, Bee. Too dangerous for you in Pakistan. Besides, how the hell are we even getting to Kartarpur? Rup has flat out refused to take me.'

Beena punched Afzal on his arm again. 'You moron, Rup has already agreed. You don't even know your friend. Didn't you see him all flustered—rummaging and lying about his phone being misplaced? I immediately knew that something was up. He's pissed that you got him in a spot. But he can never say no to you. He left to figure out how to convince his dad.'

Afzal glanced at the door. 'Shit, you're right. Rup is the greatest guy in the world.'

'Yeah, but you can't take advantage of his niceness. So, here's what we're going to do—I'm coming too.'

'Hold it right there, Bee. I can't take you—'

'I can travel with a girl from my gymnastics team. Her family has been planning a trip to Kartarpur for a while. But Rup can never find out.'

'That's silly. Why can't Rup know? Besides, it's far more dangerous in Pakistan for a Hindu girl than a Sikh guy like

Rup—especially someone who looks like you and walks around with a Ganesh gold chain around her neck. I've got to do this on my own.'

'Think, you moron. Your plan relies heavily on a car to get around. Your car driving skills are totally shit. You need me and my learner's licence. Not to mention my biggest superpower: I can wear a niqab, cover my entire body from head to toe and become practically invisible. Then I can slip into many places undetected that you cannot. And don't worry about my aunt's necklace. I'll hide it in my pocket.'

'I plan to steal a car, not rent it. You think I care about having a licence to drive a stolen car? I may drive like shit, but so does everybody. That reminds me … I need to learn how to hotwire and steal a car. I have a mechanic buddy in town—that's my homework for next weekend. But you got me on the niqab angle, I didn't think of that. It's clever and devious thinking.'

'I know. That's why you need me. Also, if for some reason you're asked for ID, it's easier to show them a licence. We can always say we got separated from the pilgrims, and a girl in distress always arouses more sympathy than a man.'

'Shit. I hate it when you're right. I agree about the niqab and the damsel-in-distress angle. But an Indian licence won't work in Pakistan and will get you arrested on the spot.'

'Forget the licence. I was stretching that strategy a bit,' conceded Beena, smirking.

Afzal paused and looked at her. 'You hated this idea from day one. Why the change of heart?'

'I still hate it,' Beena replied. 'But I realised something about you, Parv and this whole mess. You won't ever let this go. And it is better if you have someone sane alongside you. To … to stop you from getting killed. But the main reason is this: I'm dead certain you'll have second thoughts once you reach Kartarpur—

and I'll be right there to talk you out of this ridiculous plan, way before we're on Pakistani soil.'

Afzal let a small smile appear. 'I'm going to see this through. All the way. But you're as stubborn as me.'

'What did you call me? Stubborn? I'll kick your—' She grabbed Afzal's wrists, pulled and jerked him over her shoulders like in *The Karate Kid.*

Afzal flew over her, a windmill of arms and legs. He landed on his back on the bed and bounced a couple of times. Then he popped back up, wavy hair all over his face.

'Of course, the forty-five-kilogram girl with Asian features can toss a full-grown man. Just like Bruce Lee. How clichéd!'

'Are you making fun of me like Parv? And what's with the full-grown man remark? You're just a teen and barely heavier than I am.'

He held his hands up. 'I was only trying to make a joke. Besides, I'm sure you'll kick my ass—and my behind can't take any more punishment now.'

Beena smiled. 'Remember, don't tell Rup. He looks older and he's brawny, but he's a puppy at heart.'

Afzal laughed. 'I told him the same thing.'

'I can't believe we're going through with this nutty idea to prove something to someone who means nothing to us. It'll become real when we're in Kartarpur, and you'll realise that I'm right.'

'Maybe. Maybe not.'

'But once you realise it, we immediately come home. Promise?'

'Or maybe you'll see I was right. That it'll be a cakewalk.'

'You wanna bet on it?'

'Sure. What's the bet?'

She thought for a second. 'The loser goes to Rup's next play. Not for his card tricks or illusions. His drama enactment. And I don't mean we attend like we normally do and hang out in the back. The loser must sit through the whole thing in the front row. Start to finish.'

'Ouch.'

Afzal's eyes misted up. He smiled and said, 'Okay.'

Then they spat into their palms and shook on the deal.

# 4

# A Pilgrimage of One, or Two, Maybe Three

Afzal and Rup's family started early to make the eight o'clock departure for Kartarpur. Rup's father was happy to have Afzal accompany them and agreed to a day that worked for everyone. He filed the necessary travel applications for the group.

So, sitting in the back of the Chauhan family car, Afzal ran through the plan in his mind as they made the trip towards Dera Baba Nanak, the small town on the Indian side of the border from which they'd cross over to Pakistan.

Afzal and Rup watched from the back seat as the transit terminal appeared in the distance. Saanvi, Rup's little sister, squirmed between them, stretching her neck to take in the view.

From the front seat, Rup's mother said, 'I'm so excited to finally visit this temple. You remembered to bring your passports, right?'

'Why do we need passports, bhaiyya?' asked Saanvi, twirling her pigtails.

'Well, Bittu, because we are going to Pakistan, which is another country. You know Guru Nanak-ji, right?'

The girl nodded.

'Okay, come here. Check out these binoculars,' Rup said, lifting Saanvi onto his lap. 'What do you see?'

'Wow!' Saanvi peered through the binoculars. 'Is that big building where Guru Nanak-ji lives?'

Everyone smiled.

'No, Bittu, that's where Nanak-ji lived a long time ago. We're going there to pray because the Darbar Sahib Gurudwara is a holy place. It used to be hard to visit, but now they've built a special corridor for Indians to travel straight to the temple,' said Rup, balancing his sister as she leaned against the window, pressing her eyes to the binoculars.

They checked in, cleared security and boarded the bus connecting the two terminals between India and Pakistan. The ride across the border took less time than the whole security process.

As they approached the temple, Saanvi said, 'It's beautiful! Bhaiyya, I don't even need binoculars.'

Rup nodded, watching the gleaming domes of white marble filling the horizon. 'I know. It's magnificent. I can't believe we're here.'

'Neither can I.' Afzal's voice was more sombre. Looking at the grand temple, he felt uneasy and a bit guilty about using a pilgrimage as cover to sneak across. But he perked up thinking about the satisfaction the families of Latif's victims would feel when the terrorist was brought to justice.

The bus stopped and they exited along with the rest of the pilgrims. Rup adjusted his orange pagri on his head, making sure the turban was secure. Saanvi bounced in place as only a child could.

'I wanna go in!'

Their father smiled. 'Sure, Bittu. As soon as we get some Pakistani money. We'll need it to buy food, gifts and other things.'

'Uncle, why don't you and aunty go ahead with Saanvi? Rup and I'll convert Indian rupees to Pakistani ones.'

'Okay, sounds good.'

The group resumed walking, gazing around in admiration as they took in the immense complex with smooth white marble structures and archways gleaming in the morning sun.

After converting their money, Afzal and Rup hurried towards the entrance. On the way, Afzal couldn't help noticing an unexploded ordnance on display. He stopped to read the accompanying plaque. It stated that India had dropped the bomb during an air raid in order to destroy the gurdwara. The Sikhs knew this story was fake, concocted to increase tensions between the two countries. Though the Kartarpur corridor was now open, the exhibition was a reminder that India and Pakistan had obvious and serious differences.

Afzal rushed to catch up with his companions, and he accidentally bumped into a tall, sombre man dressed in a dark suit.

Afzal stopped, bowing slightly. 'Excuse me, sir.'

The man's eyes narrowed. 'Watch where you're going. You almost stepped on my toes,' he said irritably.

As Afzal backed away, he studied the steely lines around the man's eyes and mouth. This was a solemn, grumpy person who rarely smiled and seemed to take rules seriously.

'Sorry, sir.'

The man grunted and waved Afzal away.

The queue into the shrine was long, but they made it inside. Afzal was at the back of their group, and he let Rup and his family take the lead on their pilgrimage to the temple.

Rup said, 'Mother was right; it's a beautiful and spiritual

experience for us to come here. More would undertake the pilgrimage if they were allowed.'

Afzal nodded in agreement as he surveyed the milling crowd and the various areas within the temple complex. His mind was busy trying to figure out how to get to the food trucks. It was about time for him to find Beena.

Rup saw that Afzal was scanning the crowd. 'What or who are you looking for?'

'Nothing, but my bladder is about to burst. You continue into the temple. I'll catch up with you shortly.'

'You sure you'll be able to find us?'

'Absolutely. See you in a few.' Afzal dashed off.

Rup watched his best friend disappear into the crowd and muttered under his breath, 'Full bladder, my ass. How do I stop his stupid plan? I wish Bee were here to help knock sense into the idiot.'

~

Beena grimaced as she adjusted the red backpack on her shoulder. In it, she'd packed things needed for their mission. The distinctive red colour was to make it easier for Afzal to spot her amidst the large crowd.

Beena was friends with the family she was travelling with through the gymnastics team. She'd told them she needed to visit Kartarpur for a school project, almost the same story Afzal had used with Rup's parents.

Standing in the courtyard, she surveyed the massive temple complex. What stood out was the large contingent of soldiers with machine guns strapped to their shoulders. In addition to that, she was sure there were plain-clothes officers that she couldn't see. She wiped her forehead, acutely aware of her heart thumping against her ribcage.

*This is more dangerous than I thought. And where are all the bloody food trucks hiding?*

Observing the surroundings, she felt more confident than ever that Afzal would realise the sheer idiocy of his plan.

She wandered around the shrine, wishing they'd agreed upon a specific rendezvous point, when a hand fell on her shoulder. Her first instinct was to grab the wrist and pin the arm behind the nitwit's back. But this was a holy place, so she kept her cool and turned to find out who was being rude. As she did so, she heard a familiar voice say, 'Bee, you made it!'

'Afzal! You fool, I almost Bruce Lee-d you.' She pulled the heavy bag off her shoulder and dropped it on the ground. 'Of course I made it. How the hell did you find me in this crowd?'

He smiled and held up his mobile.

'I tracked your phone. Remember our plan? And the red backpack worked perfectly. I saw it from a hundred feet away.'

She felt for her cell. 'Ooh, I forgot we set that up.'

'I had to get away from Rup before I could search for you.' Then he raised an eyebrow. 'You alright? You seem kind of … nervous.'

'Have you seen the number of bloody officers around? With big-ass machine guns? I stick out like a big, flashing, warning light—especially with this stupid red backpack you made me haul. How did you convince me to lug this anyway?'

Afzal winked at her and gestured at the bag.

'You got everything?'

'Yeah, you moron. We have everything we discussed and more in this two-ton overstuffed sack. But do you see all the guards around us? I don't know how you can still go through with this stupid plan.'

Afzal snorted and waved a dismissive hand.

'Out here, guards and police are a government employment policy, not an instrument of law and order. These guys aren't well trained and are just looking to make their pay cheque. Don't worry about them.'

Beena released a deep breath, and much of her patience with it.

'Employment policy? That's top-drawer bullshit. I know you well enough to tell when you're making stuff up. Come to your senses, will you?'

'C'mon, the plan's working great. It's unreal that we're here. But here we are. We will not be expected, and that's why lugging Latif over to India will be as easy as getting wet in the monsoon. And you'll be glad to know that the food trucks are right around that building.'

Beena looked around. She saw the splendour of the shrine and the tranquillity of the wide-open spaces interspersed with beautiful domes. She jerked her head upwards. 'Instead of following this dumb plan, we should be experiencing this.'

Afzal ignored the vista. 'Listen, Bee, stop doubting me. We've kept things straightforward and simple so far. What can go wrong?'

Before Beena could spell out the million things that could go wrong, Rup's voice rose over the murmur of the crowd. 'Afzal, what are you doing over here? The bathrooms are that way.'

Rup ambled over. He nodded at Afzal, then glanced at the person alongside him and his mouth fell open. 'Bee? What are you doing *here*? I was about to call you for help to stop this crazy guy. And here you are helping him?'

Beena frowned. 'Shit. So much for keeping this quiet and between us.'

Rup turned a questioning eye towards his roommate and a look of guilt flashed across the latter's face.

'Rup, you weren't supposed to know.'

'You think I can't be trusted or I can't take care of myself, don't you?'

'No … Well, yes, not in Pakistan.'

Rup seemed to deflate. 'We're a team, the three of us. I didn't know Bee was in your corner. Why would you cut me out?'

'Because it's not safe for you. You'd stick out as non-Pakistani. Bee can put on a niqab and no one would notice her.'

'That's not fair,' Rup grumbled, pressing his lips together in a surly frown as he ran his hand over his bright orange turban.

Beena grasped his arm. 'Rup, I'm not in Afzal's corner. I was hoping when we got here that he would realise that his plan is nuts. I came along only to stop him, praying he would give up and return home with you. Did you see those guards—carrying all those AK-47s? I had no idea how far Afzal would take this, and it was better if you didn't know.'

Rup's icy stare was his only reply.

A high-pitched voice rang out. 'Rupi! Bhaiyya! Where are you?'

'Oh no, Saanvi. And my parents.'

Afzal grabbed Rup's arm and looked him in the eye. 'Rup, stay here. Don't worry, Bee and I'll see you home in Shimla in a few days.'

Rup shook his head. 'If Bee's going, so am I.'

Afzal shot an enquiring look at Beena. She said, 'Afzal, last chance to abort. Let's all head back to Shimla. We'll figure out another way to respond to Parv. What do you say?'

'No way. I won't get another chance like this. You both return home.'

'Not a chance. If you go, we go too. We're a team.'

'Bhaiyya! Bhaiyya!' Saanvi's voice punctured their back and forth.

'Shit, we don't have time to argue.' Afzal turned and pointed towards the rear of the complex. 'If you're coming, we need to move right now. If your parents see Bee, they will know something is up. Let's go!'

Rup started to move, following Afzal's finger. 'What are we waiting for?'

Beena grabbed the backpack and the three friends pushed towards the rear of the temple. They were reluctant to sprint through a crowd of slow-moving pilgrims as that would stick out like an ambulance blazing through slow traffic. But they still moved faster than anyone in the temple, pressing ahead into free spaces.

'Come on. Faster, faster,' Afzal urged them onwards.

As they streaked through the throng, Beena bumped into a pilgrim. The heavy bag slipped from her shoulders, tumbling onto the ground, and she skipped sideways to avoid it hitting her foot.

She blurted. 'Shit! This damn thing weighs a ton.'

As Beena reached down to pick it up, a large, veined hand grabbed one of the shoulder straps. She came face to face with a dark-suited man and his steely gaze. His voice was gritty. 'Oh. This is heavy.'

Beena froze, staring at the man's sombre features, then she forced a smile 'Books. Exams coming up, you know?'

The man forced a grin too, thin lips curling unnaturally around straight teeth. He lifted and held out the backpack.

'Good, good. Study hard. Knowledge is power. Have a nice day.' He stood tall and stared at all three of them, waiting for her to take the bag.

'Thank you,' said Afzal, waiting for Beena to reach out for the bag, but she hadn't moved, her hands clenched by her side.

Rup broke the awkward pause. 'Bee, I'll carry your books.' He grabbed the backpack and threw it over his shoulder. Afzal tugged at Beena's arm as they turned to leave.

The three friends continued at a deliberate pace.

Rup glanced back at the stranger. 'That man and his dark suit gives me the willies.'

'Yep, the dude is everywhere. I ran into Mr Grumpy earlier, tripped over him and almost kicked his shins.'

Beena took a quick peek over her shoulder. 'You playing football with his ankles is probably why he's still watching us.'

'Just keep walking. And stop turning around. He's one of those sticklers for the old ways; likes letting the younger generation know they should be seen and not heard.'

'I get the vibe that he's part of the security here. He seems focused on anyone who stands out—and right now, that's us. Mr Grumpy is the perfect description for him. I bet he hasn't been in a good mood for years.'

Afzal's palms were damp. He hurriedly wiped them on his jeans.

'What was that, Afzal? Are you sweating?' Beena's sharp eyes observed Afzal closely. 'I hope you're having second thoughts about this—especially with Grumpy there watching us like a hawk.'

Afzal waved dismissively. 'It's a warm day, guys. Nothing else to sweat about. Any security personnel out here will be bored out of their minds with this dull routine. A backpack falling on the ground is probably the most exciting thing that has happened to Mr Grumpy all day. Let's check out the food trucks and implement our exit plan.'

Still, he glanced behind them and sure enough, the odd man was still watching. Beena might be right about him being undercover security.

Afzal's mind raced—they had a schedule to stick to if his plan were to succeed. His original plan figured there would be food trucks and that one of them would work to hide Beena and him. Rup's presence meant the scheme needed to be more flexible; his team had grown by fifty per cent. The food trucks weren't big enough for three people—nowhere near big enough. Besides, everyone was starting to eat and there were teeming crowds around the trucks.

Too many people. Too many eyes. Too big a risk.

He felt a rising knot in his stomach. Should they split up and sneak into two separate food trucks? Too risky; they could end up going to separate locations.

Afzal looked beyond the gurdwara towards the rear of the facility. Putting on a brave face, he said, 'We must find a larger escape vehicle from a less crowded area.'

Beena followed his gaze. 'We're changing plans now? This is serious shit. You remember that Indian ex-naval officer, right? Stuck in a Pakistani prison cell. No trial and quite likely to be hanged as a spy. And he was merely wandering about and not doing anything shady. If they catch us kidnapping someone near their military headquarters, who knows what they'll do?'

Afzal shrugged, staring out towards the back of the temple. Tearing his eyes away from the horizon, he smiled and winked. 'We won't be caught. But right now, we need to think like a piece of trash.'

Both Beena and Rup were puzzled. 'What does that mean?'

'Follow me.'

He led the way to the rear of the shrine, with an array of loading docks. On the far side, they spotted a few larger trucks and vans. Afzal pointed at a cream-coloured van with fading Urdu writing on the side.

'There. See that produce delivery van? That's our ride.'

The two followed Afzal's gaze. A tall guy had removed a plastic crate filled with vegetables from within the van. He balanced deftly on one leg and shoved the large swinging door shut with his other leg before he approached the nearby building.

'Did you guys see him close that door with his leg? Like an expert.'

'Rup, what are you babbling on about his door shutting skills?' Beena turned to Afzal, 'How did you figure out that was a produce truck? You read Urdu?'

'Yup. There's a lot about me you don't know.' Afzal couldn't contain his cocky grin. 'Looks like he removed the last supply crate, so he won't be getting into the back of this van again.'

'How can you predict that? Maybe they'll fill it with garbage before they leave.'

'Rup's right. Also, this is a high-security facility. Won't they inspect the van when it leaves? Underneath, inside and everywhere?'

Afzal nodded. 'Almost definitely. That's why we needed a large produce van and not a small food truck. Think like trash. When they add in garbage or empty crates, all the better for us three to hide behind.'

'Or four,' Beena gestured at Rup and the backpack.

'Hey, enough of the big guy jokes now.' Rup smoothed the shirt fabric over his belly and rebalanced the backpack on his shoulders.

Afzal glanced back at the courtyard and at the crowd milling around the food trucks. 'Everyone is focused on eating. We've got to move before that man gets back.'

Rup said, nodding, 'Now is as good a time as any.'

'Alright, guys. This is it!' Looking around one last time for any guards, Afzal made a dash for the van.

Beena hissed, 'No!'

But Rup was already lumbering behind his friend, gesturing at Beena to follow. She hesitated for one last moment.

'All for one, one for all,' she muttered, and rushed to catch up with her friends.

Rup and Beena followed close behind Afzal as he made it to the van. He swung the door open, and they quickly hauled themselves in. It was dingy and dark, and the only light came from a dim bulb in a top corner. There were bags strewn around the floor and a row of empty, colourful plastic supply crates stacked in the rear.

'We hide behind these until we pass through security and off the gurudwara grounds,' Afzal said.

Rup held his palms up. 'We don't own a cloak of invisibility like Harry Potter. How are we going to hide here? Even behind these crate stacks, we may be seen.'

Beena grabbed her backpack from Rup, opened it and lifted out a roll of black plastic trash bags. 'These may help. I thought we might need something to hide Latif in the back of our to-be-stolen getaway car. Don't use them all up. Let's hide behind the crates and slip these on for extra cover.'

Afzal's face lit up. 'Wow, Bee! I don't remember planning garbage bags. You've packed a magic bag. Now we know why the bag is so damn heavy.'

5

# You Snooze, You Lose

The van rumbled down the bumpy road, bouncing the teens around on the floor inside garbage bags. Beena tore open her flimsy camouflage first. 'Afzal, when we get home, remind me to kill you. I almost suffocated inside this stupid thing.'

Hearing her, Afzal ripped his bag open as well. 'Yeah, but it worked, didn't it? Rup, how are you doing in there?'

Rup had been too big to fit into one bag, he had to use two of them. Beena giggled as he tried to slither out.

'How did the guards miss us?'

'They expected an empty van with empty crates and trash bags—and that's what they saw. These vans make a thousand such trips, so it becomes mundane and routine. See, I told you. This is going to be a cinch.'

Rup leaned on the side of the moving van to stabilise himself, almost as if he was mind-melding with the wall. 'The van is slowing down.'

'We jump out as soon as the doors open. Be ready.'

~

The van drove past an open-air market, turning into a small dirt parking lot. It headed directly for a large dumpster in the back.

After backing the van up to the dumpster, the driver got out, humming a tune as he made his way to the back. He threw open the swinging doors, his brain on autopilot.

But in a departure from his usual routine, three young people sprang out of the van like athletes competing in a steeplechase. One of them, a particularly well-built one, almost toppled him over. The surprised driver huffed and spun as they rushed by him. He waved his fists in the air and shouted curses as the three stowaways raced into the market and disappeared in the crowd.

The driver paused, conflicted.

*Should I call and inform the gurudwara authorities? They might sack me for transporting kids. Or they might sack me for the mess in the back. Or even for not informing them. Can't win.*

~

Beena glanced back towards the alleyway. 'Let's slow down. I don't think the driver is chasing us.'

They slowed to a walk as they entered the crowded market. Suddenly, Beena hissed, 'Rup! Give me the backpack!'

'What? Why?'

She snatched the bag from him, unzipped it and pulled out a dark, flowing piece of clothing.

'Shit, Bee's right. We must blend in. Also, this magic backpack has everything.'

Rup removed the orange pagri from his head. He surveyed the dusty little neighbourhood, the small shops and a banged-up vehicle nearby. No one seemed to be watching, and most of the women were covered head to toe in loose black. 'We're not in Shimla anymore,' he said, stuffing his turban into the backpack.

'Nothing to worry about. We'll be home in Shimla for dinner tomorrow.' Afzal patted his big friend on the shoulder.

Beena swiftly pulled the niqab over her clothes. She took out some cash from her trousers, stuffed it into the side of the niqab and made final adjustments to the flowing garment.

'This thing is hot. And I can barely see anything.'

'We'll be in a bus soon, the wind will cool us down.' Afzal scanned the area. 'Now, where do we catch the bus to Lahore?'

'I thought we're going to Rawalpindi. Isn't that where Latif is?'

'Yes. But to reach Rawalpindi, we go through Lahore. It's the nearest city, so a lot of buses should be going there.'

'How do we do that? Get to Lahore, I mean,' asked Beena, peering through her niqab.

As they walked, Rup's eyes flitted around. This was an odd, new place and he expected to find everyone staring at them, but no one seemed to acknowledge their existence. His shoulders relaxed. 'Alright, Urdu master, lead the way to Lahore.'

Afzal laughed, smacked Rup's shoulder and pointed at a faded green sign with peeling red letters. 'That says bus stop. It might be a clue, don't you think?'

'Well, aren't you Sherlock Holmes?' Beena examined the sign. 'Glad you can read Urdu. Does it say bus to Lahore?'

'Yup,' replied Afzal. He reached into his pocket and pulled out a stack of Pakistani rupees. 'I converted a bit of extra money at the temple for sundry expenses.'

Rup plunged a hand into one of his own pockets and pulled out a fistful of cash as well. 'I have some extra too. Will this help?'

'Ha! So, what could've been a chink in my blueprint becomes an asset. We have plenty of money now. Here, take mine too. You can be the official treasurer for our mission.'

Rup snatched the money and looked down haughtily at his friend. 'You should've let me in on your plans from the start. I'll keep track of every expense.'

'Rup, I'm glad you stumbled onto us. Now we're all together. That's the way it should be.'

'I really thought our adventure would end at the temple gates. I hate to say, but it has gone well so far,' Beena admitted grudgingly.

'What did I say? Easy-peasy. *Saral kaam.*'

Beena spotted juicy apples at a roadside stall near the bus stop, selected three and paid for them. She tossed them each an apple, 'Healthy snack for the ride to Lahore.' She scanned the surroundings one more time as they stood around at the dusty bus stop, but everything seemed okay. Maybe Afzal was right.

With full-throated confidence, Afzal said, 'The bus will be here soon, and we'll be off to Lahore. I told you this would be easy as pie.'

~

The steely-eyed man with the dark suit picked up his phone on the third ring.

'Qadir here.'

He listened for a moment. 'Three lost teens? Alright, got it. I'll come over and check it out.'

He pocketed his phone and cracked his neck. 'After years of spotless service, all it takes is to disagree with the wrong colonel and I'm babysitting brain-dead pilgrims,' he muttered. 'What type of morons get lost inside a closed facility?'

An officer in the Inter-Services Intelligence, or ISI, the Pakistani spy agency, Qadir Khan was posted at the temple to keep a watch on the crowd. If he saw an opportunity, he had orders to initiate contact with potential assets. A few disgruntled Indian citizens, given the right incentives, could provide a slew of valuable information.

It was important work, but far beneath a man like Qadir who had years of experience and a list of commendations in the Pakistani secret service. He glanced at the sky, then leaned forward and spat.

'Bloody idiot guards. They can't even reunite lost kids with their parents.'

Qadir entered the security office through the rear door and called out to the guard working the counter to join him. When the man appeared, Qadir asked, 'What's the situation?'

'We got two families with missing persons. A teenage girl from one family and two teenage boys from the second.'

Qadir nodded, 'Any descriptions of these missing teens?'

'The families filled out missing person's reports.' The guard handed a clipboard to Qadir.

He flipped through the pages. A line about the missing girl caught his eye. He read it aloud. '… carrying a red backpack.'

Qadir let all the pages fall into place and hummed before speaking—more to himself than to the guard. 'Two boys and one girl with a red backpack … from two separate families, you say? I'm sure these kids knew each other.' He leaned back in his chair. He'd had a feeling something was off with those kids, but he couldn't put a finger on it.

'Would they have got out of the gurudwara? If so, how?' he asked the guard pointedly.

The man shook his head and said, 'Not a chance. This place is bulletproof. They must still be somewhere here or they might have taken an earlier bus back to India.'

Qadir's eyes swept the outside of the building—the CCTV monitors showed the entire complex. A few police vehicles and food trucks were moving towards the rear gate.

'If they're still here, they'll turn up soon. If not … now that's an intriguing prospect. Then, either someone kidnapped them, or they left through that services gate in one of those vehicles,' he mused.

One of the guards rushed over, a phone extended. 'Sir, Mohammed, one of our produce truck drivers, wants to talk. Urgent.'

The guard spoke into the phone and stiffened with shock. He slowly turned around, eyed Qadir and said, 'The kids are not in the gurudwara—they stowed away in Mohammed's van. The three bolted when he got into town. He wanted to make it clear it wasn't his fault—even the guards at the gates didn't see the kids inside.'

Qadir smacked the table. 'I knew it. Seeing those snooty kids, it's likely they made a bet with their friends to sneak into Pakistan. Probably for a stupid selfie.'

'How were they not detected at the gate?' asked the guard aloud to nobody in particular.

'Your people don't check for shit,' said Qadir. 'What a mess. Let's not tell the parents anything yet. Have them wait in the lobby and, if it gets late, send them back to India. I'll pick up our uninvited guests and give them each a good thrashing before we return them.'

He got up from the chair, picked up his car keys and stepped out of the office. 'Where in town did Mohammad say he dropped them off?'

~

The trio dozed off on the swaying bus to Lahore. They hadn't realised how tired they were. The cool wind from the windows tempered the hot weather, making them all drowsy.

After a little while, Afzal stirred. He rubbed his eyes and glanced out. The open, brownish green of the countryside was starting to give way to the dull colours and tight, blocky shapes of a city.

Beena woke up next and took in the scenery whizzing past them. She nodded at Afzal. 'We're getting close.'

'Yeah. We should soon be at the Lahore bus station.' Afzal stretched and leaned back in his seat. 'Then it's one more bus ride for us to Rawalpindi. This is going to be epic.'

Rup popped up as if he'd been electrocuted. 'What the …? Man, that was weird. Felt like someone was giving me a massage.'

Beena turned around and sniggered, nervously adjusting her niqab. 'A massage? On the bus? Why did we ever think Rup would stick out? Calm down, buddy. We're either in a dream or a nightmare ourselves.'

The bus pulled into the dusty terminal at Lahore. The bustling space was filled with buses and theirs squeezed into a tight spot between two poorly parked ones. The door swung open and the three poured out. They looked around, taking in the crowded bus depot and the surrounding city.

Rup hoisted the backpack onto one shoulder and spoke with a hint of excitement, 'I hear Lahore has great lamb kebab.'

'Rup! Always thinking with your stomach.' Beena glanced at his belly meaningfully.

'Hey! Don't give me that look. You've got to admit a tasty kebab might be worth the trip.'

'Agreed, but it's fun to tease you.' She patted his tummy. 'That apple should hold you for a bit. Not sure we should splurge money for kebabs yet.' Turning to Afzal, she raised an eyebrow. 'Now what?'

Afzal walked over and consulted a hefty chalkboard with writing all over it. Obviously, a list of some sort. Rup shook his head at the smudged letters and illegible writing.

'That looks as readable as Saanvi's finger-painting ...'

'Yep, but I have a pharmacist's eye for squiggles.' Still, it took Afzal a few minutes before he eventually found the information they needed.

'This is it,' he pointed to a line on the chalkboard. 'The bus number and the time it leaves for Rawalpindi. We have about forty minutes.'

Rup jumped suddenly, then fumbled with his phone. His face went pale. 'Oh shit. My dad is texting me.'

Afzal winced. 'Don't answer, they'll be sick with worry. It's better to leave them in the dark for now—let's turn off our phones.'

'Okay.' Rup switched off and pocketed his phone.

'I need to use the toilet. It'll be a long bus ride to Rawalpindi, and I'm not sure of the facilities on the way,' said Beena.

'Makes sense,' said Afzal, pointing to a standalone small building at one end of the bus station. 'I think the washrooms are over there.'

They headed over to them. The men's section was on the other side of a larger dividing wall, and Rup and Afzal walked around it.

Beena was in and out quickly. Luckily, the women's toilets weren't as busy as the ones for men. She peeked through her face covering, taking in the sights.

Suddenly, she froze.

A tall lean man in a dark suit had stepped out of an official looking car and was looking around intently. *Oh no*, she thought, nervously pulling at her face covering.

*The weird man from the gurudwara. What's he doing here?*

The tall man waved down a passer-by and asked him something. The passer-by shrugged in response and continued walking.

*He must be looking for us. Why else would he be here?*

The man's serious gaze swept around the bus depot and came to a halt on Beena. After a short pause, he came striding towards her with an air of purpose.

Her heart stopped.

Before Beena could move, he was right beside her. She tugged at her niqab and checked her face covering once more. The now familiar raspy voice asked, 'Have you seen three teenagers around here? Two boys and a girl. Dressed in Western attire and carrying a bright red backpack?'

Beena willed herself not to turn towards the toilet wall—she couldn't give away the boys' location. With any luck, the men's queue was long and the two wouldn't come out right now.

'Did you not hear what I asked?' repeated the tall man. 'My name is Qadir and I work for the government. Those two young boys I mentioned? They kidnapped the third, a young girl. They were last seen getting on a bus to Lahore from Kartarpur. We are trying to rescue the girl. Have you seen them?'

'No, sir,' murmured Beena, from behind the anonymity of her covering.

At that instant, the man's phone rang. Qadir pulled it out, turning around. 'Yes?'

He listened before speaking again. 'So, the bus driver confirmed they got off at the Lahore depot? With a red backpack?'

After another pause, he spoke again, 'But why Lahore? Perhaps this is more than an adventurous bet by rash teens.'

The man went quiet, listening to the voice on the other side. Beena subconsciously inched a bit closer, her heart thumping a mile a minute. It pulsed so hard that her ribcage seemed to expand.

'I don't know about that,' continued Qadir. 'Let's find them before we plan any leverage against the Indian government. And let's not start calling them RAW agents or blame them yet for the bombing at the children's hospital.'

The boys appeared from behind the restroom wall. As they started to walk towards Beena, they saw her gesticulating wildly.

'Is the bus here already?' Rup started to jog.

'Stop,' Afzal hissed through clenched teeth, yanking Rup's backpack. They stopped and took in what Beena was gesturing towards. A tall, lean man in a dark suit—speaking on his phone. His back was to them, but he felt familiar.

'Shoot! That's that man! He must be a soldier or a cop. The news of our escape must have spread. Wow, prompt response indeed.'

'Quick, behind the wall. We can admire the reaction time of Pakistani cops later.'

They swiftly slunk back behind the safety of the dividing wall.

'But what if he wants to go to the toilet?' Rup asked.

Before Afzal could counter, a familiar voice came from the other side of the wall. 'You can come out. Mr Grumpy has driven off. But make sure the red backpack is covered.'

Gingerly, the boys came around the wall.

'Shit, he tracked us here. We must zip onward to Rawalpindi. I don't think they'll guess that's where we're going.'

'Did he speak to you? Who was he and what did he say?' Rup asked.

'Mr Grumpy's name is Qadir and he works for the government. He was looking for us, alright,' Beena said. 'And the red backpack.'

'Ooh, this backpack has turned into a red flag in the middle of Pakistan.'

'He thinks you two kidnapped me,' Beena laughed. 'At least that's the story he told me. Likely to appeal to my feminine nature so I would share something.'

Afzal added, 'Makes sense, because many folks don't trust cops or government officials.'

'Glad you warned us. If he'd seen us, we'd be in jail.'

Something caught Afzal's attention. 'Hey, that's our bus to Rawalpindi. We should board at once and keep out of sight.'

They watched a large vehicle lumber and pull into its spot. The door swung open on noisy hinges and the arriving passengers spilled out.

As soon as the bus unloaded, the three friends charged up the stairs. Inside, Afzal came face-to-face with a droopy-eyed bus driver.

The man didn't move. 'We don't board for another fifteen minutes.'

Afzal gestured at the empty seats with a slight nod 'I thought we'd wait on the bus. No?'

Rup stepped forward as though he was making a deal for black market movie tickets. 'I got this. My good man, we'll pay you right now for our ride to Rawalpindi, plus a few extra rupees for the best seats. What do you say?'

'How much?' The driver was obviously a man who didn't get paid much for long days of work.

Rup smiled and kept his eyes locked with the driver's as he confidently reached into his pocket. His fingers came up empty. He tried another pocket. Nothing there either. He opened his palms and groaned.

'Shit! I can't find our money. Did I give it to either of you?'

Afzal's face wrinkled as if he'd developed a bad case of gas. 'What does that mean?'

Beena winced, seeing Rup's empty palms. 'It's not hard to understand. Our money's gone.'

'Gone? How?'

'It's obvious. A pickpocket got to him when we were walking around. Or when he was dozing during the previous bus ride.'

Rup continued to empty out his pockets as he spoke, 'I had it deep in my pants. I don't know how someone stole it without me catching on.'

Beena was beginning to have a sinking feeling in her gut. 'They're pickpockets. It's what they do. They're experts at it.'

'But I didn't sense anything.'

'Maybe that's what startled you on the previous bus. Your dream massage was instead a real-life pat down.'

'Shit! We're screwed!'

Afzal grabbed the handrail as his knees buckled under him. Beena tried to control the *I-told-you-so* tone in her voice, but it was impossible. 'Still think this is going to be easy-peasy?'

# 6

# First Blood

The bus driver roared at the three youngsters, 'If you think this is funny, you couldn't be more wrong. I only have a twenty-minute chai break after a seven-hour drive. Now step off my bus or I'll mace you. Stupid little shits!' He started fumbling for something.

The three friends didn't wait to find out if he did have a mace.

As they hurried down the stairs, they could hear the driver talking to himself. 'Drive for fourteen hours a day, just for this goat shit? Where is that bloody mace when I need it?'

The three scrambled away from the bus, out of the depot and onto the roadside. A struggling Rup stopped not far into the run, bent over and threw up. After a few minutes of retching, he stood straight and wiped his mouth, leaning against the pavement wall.

'We're stranded!'

'No shit. We don't need Captain Obvious right now. Get a hold of yourself.'

Afzal was quietly staring at the sky. Beena turned to him, eyes shining through the slits.

'What's going on? What happened to all the confidence?'

'It snuck away. With a pickpocket.'

In a flash, Beena punched Afzal in the shoulder, whirled around and jabbed her finger in Rup's face. 'You two get your shit together. We can't just stand here and cry like babies. We're here in bloody Pakistan, *illegally*, and can't afford any unwanted attention. Get. Your. Shit. Together.'

Afzal rubbed his shoulder, grimacing. 'Thanks. I think.'

'Yeah. We gotta figure out what we're going to do,' Rup muttered.

'Calmly and without panicking. Any ideas?'

'Walk back,' Rup said. 'If we can't go forward, we must get back to the gurudwara as fast as possible. The only method of transportation we have right now are our feet.'

Afzal threw his hands up. 'So, that's it? One setback and we slink back to the temple, our tails between our legs? If we don't have money for a bus ride, this is the right time to steal a car.'

Beena snorted, 'Are you listening to yourself? Steal a car? When that Qadir guy, who I'm sure is an ISI agent, is hunting us?'

'Shit, shit. And things were going so well,' he groaned. 'I expected setbacks, but nothing like this. We'll never get an opportunity like this. We're already in Lahore; we can't give up now!'

Beena scanned the street. 'Look, I don't want to give up, but we must face reality. I only have a few rupees—not enough to buy bus tickets or anything useful. And stealing a car in this busy area will be tough.'

'We were always planning to steal one. Why not now? Just give me one chance. Twenty minutes to find a car. If it doesn't pan out, we think of Plan B,' Afzal said. 'I must find a car like the ones I practised on. An older model. Can I have the mini jimmy tool please?'

He walked up the road, hiding the tool in the crook of his arm. Rup and Beena followed a few steps behind. Ducking into a side street, they entered what seemed like a furniture and household goods open market, with cars parked on the streets.

Sofas, chairs and tables filled the sidewalks. A hawker on the opposite side of the road was trumpeting the benefits of his wares. 'Steel pots and buckets, best quality! Ten year no rust guarantee!' Afzal walked on the side of the road scanning the parked vehicles—a truck, a van, a taxicab, a small SUV …

An older model, a pale green Fiat sedan, caught his eye. He nodded to Rup and Beena, gesturing with his chin at the target. He casually walked beside the car and brushed against it—discreetly testing its door handles. It was locked. He looked around cautiously—everyone seemed busy, walking around and minding their business.

Afzal glanced over again at his companions, steeling himself for the task at hand. At that instant, Rup caught his attention with a wink. Gesturing at him to hold on, he crossed the road over to the hawker's stand. Rup reached over, seemingly to check out a bucket on the far side. As he did so, his elbow brushed against a tall stack of copper water pots, unbalancing them.

With a loud crash, the entire set tumbled over to the other side of the stand, making a loud cacophony as they fell, rolling around on the ground. The hawker leaped up, cursing Rup mightily, scrambling around to corral his rolling and clanging wares.

In the confusion caused by the noise on the other side of the street, Afzal glided the jimmy tool down between the driver-side door and window, and worked to pop the lock.

At that moment, a man carrying a package of groceries walked up behind the Fiat, staring at a bucket rolling on the street. Shaking his head and smiling at the hawker chasing the zigzagging utensils, he slid his keys in and flipped open the boot of the car.

'Afzal!' hissed Beena, tapping his shoulder.

Afzal jerked his head, catching the boot popping up and a man disappearing behind it. 'Shit,' he cursed. He tried to pull the tool out but it wouldn't budge. Afzal's hands began to sweat and shake, making it harder for him to grip the slippery tool. Panicking, he glanced at the open boot obscuring the man and gave it one final yank. No dice. The tool wouldn't come back out.

Clank! The force of the boot shutting reverberated throughout the car. The man stooped to lock it. Beena nudged Afzal sharply. He unclasped his fingers, let the tool go. Beena grabbed his hands and pulled. They continued walking, brushing past the car's owner as he approached the driver's side. Still chuckling at the hawker, he slid the keys in and opened the door.

'Damn. The jimmy tool is still stuck there,' Afzal whispered to Beena, glancing furtively back at the Fiat.

'Forget the stupid tool; that was a close call. A busy street is not where we should be looking to steal a car.'

Rup caught up with them, escaping the expletive-spewing hawker who was engrossed in restacking his wayward merchandise. He was panting. 'I didn't mean for so many buckets to fall. Thank God that shopkeeper is busy or he would've given me a proper hiding.'

'Good thinking, Rup. But bummer that your distraction went entirely to waste.'

Beena grabbed their arms, forcing them to slow down. 'We should return to the temple. It's not too far. Face it. We gave it a good shot and got further than I expected, but our luck has run out. Not enough money and now no jimmy tool either.'

Afzal had an unfocused expression. His lips were tightly pressed together.

Rup nodded. 'I agree. We should get back. No kebabs from Lahore then. It's going to be a long day.'

Afzal eyed the orange-tinged sky. 'You mean night. It'll be dark soon.'

'Thanks for the motivational words. We're so fucked.'

Beena looked over her shoulder. 'I'm sure Qadir also has local cops on the lookout. We can't be wandering the streets aimlessly. We either figure out our next steps or get back to the temple. Afzal, you agree?'

'Nope.' Afzal's voice was flat and dull. He didn't sound remotely interested in the question or in answering it.

Rup frowned. 'Then what the hell are we doing?'

Afzal kept ambling ahead.

'Hey, Afzal! Don't be an asshole,' yelled Bee. 'You had all kinds of ideas not thirty minutes ago.'

Afzal stopped, turning around to face the other two. 'I wasn't the one that lost our money.'

Rup waved his hand. 'There's plenty of blame to go around. You screwed up the jimmy …'

'Stop it!' Beena stomped her foot. 'You want another punch?'

Afzal bobbed his head and sighed. 'You're right, Bee. Sorry. You both came along to help prove my patriotism. You came for me and trusted my plan. I should be thankful. No more blaming each other. Now more than ever, we must stick together.'

'That's better. But no need to be thankful yet.' Beena flicked her head to her right. 'Look, there's a chai stall across the street. I have some last few rupees. What say we get a nice cup of chai, sit down and talk things out like civilised people. Figure out alternative transportation to Rawalpindi. If we can't, we abort and get directions to the temple. Okay?'

'A hot cup of chai sounds good,' Afzal said. He began to cross the street, weaving through the slow-moving traffic.

Rup and Bee did the same, and all three came together at the chai stall. Rup and Afzal went to use the washroom by the stall while Beena used the remaining money she had to buy hot chai and biscuits. By the time the two returned, the chai was ready. The trio settled on a rickety wooden bench. There was silence for a few minutes as they sipped their drinks, each of them contemplating what had happened and what they should do next.

'I can try again. This time in a less crowded area, with a larger car selection.'

'Where?'

'Not sure. There must be a parking lot around here someplace.'

'Do we wait until it's dark? Can you steal a car without a jimmy?'

Afzal was quiet. 'I can twist a bit of metal. I'm sure I can find junk lying around.'

'What? That doesn't sound convincing. Right now, we are better off getting back to the temple.'

Afzal didn't reply. He inspected the cup of tea as if it could provide answers.

Rup broke into his introspection. 'What if we go to the authorities, tell them we went for an adventure ride and got lost?'

Beena squinted at him. 'The police?'

'Yeah. We did get robbed. We could play the victims.'

Afzal was still staring into his chai. He shook his head. 'They're going to ask how we got all the way to Lahore. Or out of the temple complex. That's hard to explain.'

Beena nodded. 'Agreed. Besides, I didn't like what I overheard Mr Grumpy say. Something about using us as leverage. Hold on. Let me check something.'

She took out her phone.

'Aha, I was right. Our phones still work. Must be because we're close enough to the border. How about I let my uncle know we're in trouble?'

Rup nodded. 'Great idea. If anyone would know what we can do, it's him.'

Beena nodded again and started texting. She hit 'send' on her message and put her phone away.

Afzal asked, 'What did you mean about leverage?'

Beena cupped her chai and sighed. 'I caught a snippet of Grumpy's conversation. Not sure what it meant, but whoever Qadir was speaking to wants to use us to gain leverage against India. Not only that but also pin the blame on us for a bomb in a children's hospital or something. After they catch us, I mean.'

'Yikes. A bomb? Going to the authorities here might be a mistake.'

Rup closed his eyes and muttered a small prayer under his breath.

They silently sipped from the small glass cups and munched on the biscuits. A thin street dog approached them hesitantly. As Rup reached out, the dog warily twitched its tail and came closer, sniffing. Rup scratched its ear.

Beena eyed the skinny brown dog and grimaced. 'That thing is so dirty. You shouldn't touch it, Rup. It might have fleas.'

'She's not that dirty. Look at her beautiful brown eyes.' He scratched the other ear and the dog wagged its tail. 'See, she likes me.'

He took one of his biscuits, broke it in half and tossed it on the ground near the dog. The dog swooped down on it, and its tail wagged faster.

'You shouldn't do that. It might be the only food we eat for a while,' Afzal said, gazing into his cup.

Before Rup could reply, a sharp noise broke through the steady hum of activity on the busy street. A Jeep screeched to a halt in front of the tea stall. A gruff, broad-shouldered man exited and stood tall next to his vehicle as if he owned the place, stretching his limbs. A snake tattoo coiled around the man's muscular, tanned left forearm.

Rup continued to watch the dog, amused at its antics. 'She likes the biscuit. Poor thing—all skin and bones. She needs it more than me.' He threw the other half onto the ground and the dog eagerly ran for it.

At the same time, the Jeep driver made for the washroom and almost tripped over the dog chasing the morsel. He cursed in anger and growled, 'Filthy mutt,' then turned around and kicked the dog. The animal whimpered in pain.

Rup immediately popped up from the bench. 'Hey! Stop that. She's only trying to eat.'

The tattooed man turned around and eyeballed Rup. He sneered, 'And what are you going to do about it?' He drew up his right leg as if to kick the dog a second time.

'I'm going to make you apologise for hurting a defenceless animal,' said Rup and took a step towards the ruffian.

'Oh yeah, pig? Why don't you go fuck yourself?'

Before Rup could react, Afzal stepped in front of him. 'Hey, hey. Let it go, buddy.'

~

Qadir drove his car in an expanding loop around the Lahore bus depot and its neighbourhood.

*Where are those stupid kids?*

His bet was they'd take selfies and head back. It wasn't safe for a young girl dressed in modern clothes to be out in the rough back alleys of Lahore—even accompanied by male friends. They sounded like naïve, reckless teens, and trouble usually found such people—fast.

Time was running out and Qadir was keen to find them before nightfall. Three high-society Indian teenagers rescued from the dangerous streets of Lahore could mean a promotion for him and a better posting than this dead-end temple gig.

Navigating the crowded streets, he noticed a commotion near a roadside tea stall. A couple of big guys facing off. A dog barking. Dust being kicked up all around. Qadir smiled, amused. A typical day in Lahore. As he drove past, something familiar caught the corner of his eye. Qadir couldn't quite place it. He had to be seeing things. The stress was getting to him.

But after a mile, he braked hard. What had caught his eye was a familiar red—something he'd seen recently. Maybe a certain red-coloured backpack. It felt like too much of a coincidence.

Qadir spun the car around and sped back.

~

Rup shoved Afzal out of the way, adjusted his glasses and stepped towards the ruffian.

'And you'd know all about fucking pigs, wouldn't you?'

The muscular stranger lunged forward and threw a hefty punch. It just missed Rup's face. But the momentum of the man's swing caused him to lose balance and he stumbled over. As he went down, he flailed, grabbed Rup's shirt and dragged the teen down into a heap on the dusty street.

The tea-stall worker was not happy. 'Hey, you two! Knock it off.'

Rup lifted himself up, ready to pummel the man, but Afzal and Beena pulled him off. He got to his feet and watched as the animal beater did the same.

Beena glared at Rup. 'Stop it. Apologise, now!'

Rup paused and blew out a breath. He looked at the man and said, 'I'm sorry I knocked you to the ground.'

The thug eyed Rup, unsure whether to kill him or accept the apology. He shook the dirt off and smoothed his shirt. 'You didn't knock me down—I slipped, luckily enough for you. And you're doubly lucky I'm in a hurry to go to the toilet, or you'd be in the hospital. Watch yourself, pig fucker, or next time you'll get hurt.' He turned on his heel and continued towards the toilet.

Now it was Afzal's turn to be incensed. He started to say something but felt Beena's restraining hand.

'Let it go,' she mouthed quietly.

'You better make yourself scarce when I get back. Or else …' The threat hung in the air as the man disappeared into the toilet.

Beena closely watched as he stepped inside the toilet. When the rickety door shut, she sharply nudged a still-incensed Afzal with her elbow. He turned, his gaze lingering on the toilet door. She prodded him more vigorously.

'What?' he snapped, looked at Beena and followed her meaningful glance.

That was when he saw it—a shiny object on the sidewalk. It appeared to be shimmering, almost like a magical object floating above the dirty ground.

A ring of keys.

Afzal inhaled sharply. 'I don't believe it.'

Rup was dusting himself off. 'What are you babbling on about?'

Afzal nodded towards the ground. Rup followed his gaze and saw the keys. 'I don't remember bringing my keys. Is that yours, Bee? That's careless. You should keep it in the backpack.'

Beena rolled her eyes, tilted her head towards the toilet door and then towards the Jeep. Rup glanced back at the keys on the ground. His eyes lit up. 'No way. Must have fallen out of his pocket.'

'This Jeep puts us back on schedule,' Afzal said, his voice rising. 'Think about it. I was going to steal a car in a bit. Why not now?'

Rup shook his hand at Afzal 'No way. We're in too deep without stealing Rambo's Jeep. Did you see his tattoo? And his rippling muscles?'

'We can't give up now. Not with this divine opportunity staring right at us in the face. The gods are willing us forward. They replaced my jimmy with actual keys,' Afzal pleaded.

But it wasn't necessary. Beena moved fast—snapping the keys up from the sidewalk, she tossed them to Afzal in one smooth movement and rushed to the Jeep—hoisting her flowing clothes above her ankles as she ran.

Afzal immediately followed her, rushing to the driver's side. Rup remained rooted for a moment before he unfroze. He turned, grabbed the backpack from the bench and sprinted to catch up.

To his surprise, the stray dog was right on his heels. As he dove into the back of the Jeep, the dog followed. Boy and animal crashed into a stack of boxes piled on the rear seat.

Afzal started the Jeep, put it in gear and hit the accelerator. The engine screamed and tires squealed—the vehicle lurched forward.

And then it died with a harsh jerk.

Responding to the sharp sounds of a straining engine and burning rubber, the man came rushing out of the toilet. Afzal started the Jeep again and hit the accelerator. This time, the gears engaged and the Jeep jolted forward onto the road. They were off.

The ruffian ran after the swiftly accelerating Jeep, but stopped after a few paces and yelled fruitlessly at the dust clouds streaming from the vehicle as it disappeared down the road.

~

Qadir was almost at the tea stall when a Jeep whizzed past him. 'Idiots. They'll kill someone,' he muttered under his breath.

He pulled up to the stall. No sign of a red backpack. The only red he saw was a scarf on the tea-stall owner's shoulder. Was he seeing things? Had he mistaken this red scarf for the backpack? No sign of any kids either. Just a rugged-looking man standing on the kerb, yelling at apparently nothing on the road.

Just to be sure, Qadir approached the tea-seller and inquired about a girl dressed in modern clothes carrying a red backpack.

The man laughed. 'I've not seen a woman in jeans here in over ten years!'

*Well, a detour for nothing. I better get over to Rawalpindi and report these missing kids, otherwise those ISI idiots will assign someone else to this case. Finding these fools could be my only way out of the shit detail at the temple.*

# 7

# Sugar High

Mahen was besides himself. He'd gotten back from a run when he received a message from his niece Beena. A text that made no sense. He tried calling her back. No answer.

What was she doing inside Pakistan? He knew she'd gone to Kartarpur with her classmate, but how did she get to Lahore from there? Had someone kidnapped her? She was a capable girl, but Pakistan was a dangerous place, difficult for even trained professionals. Indians would certainly be viewed with suspicion, the default interpretation being that they were spies for the Indian intelligence agency, the Research and Analysis Wing, or RAW.

Mahen picked up the phone. The why and how would have to wait. Right now, he needed to find help. It rang three times before a blasé male voice on the other end answered. 'Why are you calling me after office hours?'

'Sir, we have a problem, and I thought you should know. Three Indian teens are stuck in Lahore. One of them is my niece. She went to the Kartarpur shrine with friends for a cultural project. Not yet sure how they got to Lahore from the Nanak temple—whether voluntarily or involuntarily. They're scared and trying to get home.'

'Sounds like a tricky situation, but this is why we have diplomats.'

'This could escalate into an international situation. We don't need any more tension with the Pakistanis. And the last thing we need is to give RAW another headache. With the recent skirmishes in Kashmir and new intel predictions of violence, I'm sure they have their hands full. They'll be pissed if we divert resources for a few lost teenagers.'

'That's true. I suggest you get the diplomats busy and work through formal channels. Since they're teenagers, there's no reason we shouldn't get them back unharmed. File a complaint about the misplaced kids and light a fire under those slow Pakistani asses. You know they'll drag their feet on this.'

Mahen took a deep breath. 'Yes, sir. I know the Indian ambassador in Islamabad. She should be able to help us.'

'I hope so. This doesn't bode well for your niece if it goes bad. Especially if the Pakistanis find out her uncle is a senior officer in the Assam Regiment. They will use them as bargaining chips, or worse.'

Mahen exhaled. 'I'm keenly aware.'

The tattooed ruffian from the tea stall jiggled the long steel wire he'd crudely fashioned into a slim jim. After about a half-hour's search, he'd opted to steal this pickup truck because it had plenty of horsepower and didn't stick out with its weathered grey paint.

As he tried to find the right spot for the door lock to pop open, another tattoo showed high on his upper arm. It read 'Tamir Kazmi'—his favourite television villain.

The click was soft but coincided with the lock post popping up. Tamir peered around, jumped in and shut the door. He bent under the steering wheel, ripped out the ignition wires and proceeded to hotwire the pickup with practised ease. The engine roared to life.

Within half an hour, he arrived at his shack outside of Lahore. He backed the pickup into the compound and pulled the gate behind him.

'Stupid bladder. That was the most expensive chai of my life,' Tamir muttered as he opened the door into the house.

He emerged shortly with a bag of supplies. Inside were two locally made pistols, shotgun, ammunition and clothes to change into. And a couple of phones.

Tamir loaded his gear and got in the pickup truck, settling into the seat. He took one of the phones, turned it on and opened an app. A map filled the screen, with a blinking red dot in the middle. He grinned, displaying stained teeth.

*I see you! Looks like they're getting out of town. If I were in their shoes, I would go through everything in the Jeep. That means they'd find the goods and—shit, the journal.*

His smile faded as he suddenly realised the import of strangers driving his Jeep.

*I must catch them before anyone realises what's going on. If that journal is compromised, it's a slow and agonising death for me.*

He looked again at the red dot blinking on the map, then picked up the pistol and checked the magazine.

'What are you fools heading north for? Islamabad?' He clenched his teeth. 'Well, your head start isn't big enough. If you stop even to take a piss, I'll catch you. You will rue the day, you fuckers …'

'I almost peed in my pants when the Jeep stalled!' Afzal exclaimed as he drove through the streets. 'This one has a weird transmission.'

'It's not the transmission, you moron. It's your driving,' Beena said with a laugh. 'I should've driven, but I'm glad you didn't panic and made a good recovery before Rambo pummelled us to mush!'

'I think we lost Rambo,' Rup chimed in from the back, patting the dog's head.

Afzal said, 'He would've reported the theft to the police by now. So, I think we should stay off the main roads. We'll take the N5 highway, not the M2, to Rawalpindi.'

Beena scrunched her forehead. 'N5? That's the longer and slower road, right?'

Afzal nodded. 'Yes, but not by much. The M2 has a lot of tolls and CCTV cameras, which the N5 doesn't. And looks like we've a full tank of diesel. Better be frugal, invisible and low tech. Safer that way.'

'Safe is good!' Rup was distracted, playing with the dog.

'Does Rambo have anything of value? Cash, maybe? What do we have in the glove box?' Beena popped it open.

A pistol fell out and landed on the floor with a thud. The three of them froze and stared at one another.

Rup leaned over the front seat. 'Holy fuck! Who is this douche bag?'

Afzal replied, 'You idiots are missing the most important question. Is it loaded?' Beena warily held it in her palms.

Rup reached out, gesturing. 'Gimme. I use a prop gun for my play. I think I know.' He took the gun from her and dropped the clip out. Eyeing the shiny magazine in his hand, he said in his best Gabbar Singh voice, *'Kitne goli hai? Che sarkar, che goli.'*

'*Aur aadmi teen*,' chuckled Afzal, getting into Rup's impersonation.

'*Aur ek kutta*,' Rup added, shaking his head at the dog, which was sitting on the bench seat gazing at him, pink tongue hanging out.

Beena glared at the two of them 'Stop your *Sholay* drama. So, it's loaded?'

'Yep, it's loaded.'

'Well, keep it back there with you and Rin Tin. I don't want it near me, especially with Afzal driving.'

'Wow. Thanks for the vote of confidence. Why don't you drive then?'

'Well, I would but I'm not sure how to shift that clutch with this loose clothing pooling around my feet. Might accidently step on the fabric.'

'I'm sure you'll be fine, but not sure if women in niqab drive in these parts. We don't want to attract any attention. But forget my wayward driving. You know Rup can unintentionally blast you from the back just as easily, right?'

'No way,' said Rup. He opened one of the boxes in the back and gingerly placed the gun inside.

'There—it's been put away. With the safety on.'

Beena studied the boxes in the backseat 'You should check those. If there is a gun in the glove box, what else does he have? And what is inside that camouflage backpack?'

Rup studied the boxes and bag, then squinted at Beena. 'I don't know. Isn't that infringing on the guy's privacy?'

'Bonehead. We stole his car and you're worried about his privacy?'

'I wouldn't want someone leafing through my room and finding my magazines.'

'Peek inside the stupid boxes, would you? Maybe there's food in there.' Afzal glared at Rup in the rear-view mirror.

'Good point. Those biscuits were a while ago.' Rup opened one of the boxes in the back. 'Hey, this guy is a sugar salesman. Look at all these bags full of it. Must be customer samples.'

Beena twisted to catch a glimpse. 'Samples? What are you on about?'

Rup took out one of the bags, opened it and stuck two fingers deep into the powder. Then he licked the crystals stuck to his fingers.

'Whoa! That tastes like monkey shit! That's not sugar.'

Afzal spun around in the driver's seat, checking the bag. 'Rup! C'mon man. Why would you taste some unknown white powder?' His brow furrowed. 'Oh, it's probably drugs.'

'Drugs?' Beena gaped at the open bag as Rup tried to scrape the remnants of powder from his tongue. 'But it makes sense, considering how Rambo was built, and his tattoos, not to mention the gun.'

'Shit, shit. This could become dangerous if we've stolen some drug dealer's car full of his stash. The stuff in those boxes could be worth lakhs of rupees,' Afzal said, trying to keep his eyes on the road.

'Drugs?' Rup finished cleaning his tongue and stared blankly at his friends. 'I've never even smoked ganja in my entire life.'

Beena glared, watching Rup's face. 'Let's hope they're normal, garden-variety hallucinogens and not some other hazardous chemical.' Then she turned serious. 'Stealing a drug dealer's car is the last thing we needed. We've made an already dangerous situation even more dangerous. But hey, on the plus side, Rambo won't be calling the cops about his drug-filled Jeep.'

'I guess we stole the perfect vehicle then,' Afzal said with a laugh.

'Perfect? I wouldn't say that,' Beena retorted. She looked at Rup, concern clouding her face. 'Even if they are drugs, you'll be fine. Maybe ...'

'Alright, stop teasing me. I won't taste anything else.'

'Just check what's inside the other boxes back there.'

Rup found more bags of powder. He opened the camouflage backpack and fished out half a dozen phones and an old leather-bound journal. 'Phones. Quite a few of them. But why is a drug dealer keeping a journal? You think he's an aspiring writer?'

Beena extended her hand to Rup. 'Give me that.'

Rup handed the journal to her and she flipped through it. Reading a few of the handwritten notes, she said, 'Could be business records, but not sure. I think some of the writing is in code. It certainly looks like the English alphabet, but no words I know.'

Afzal flicked his head. 'Those phones might come in handy. I think our phones don't work this far from the border. We haven't been able to catch a signal.'

Beena pulled her phone out. 'No signal. It would be better if we had one working phone. And we better power down our phones. They can be tracked—especially an Indian phone deep inside Pakistan trying to catch a cell signal.'

Rup picked up a phone from the backpack, turning it on. 'Yeah, this has bars. Cool, we have one phone.'

'Multiple phones with a drug dealer. Hmm. They must be burner phones, right? We should be able to use them without the authorities tracking us.'

Afzal chuckled. 'I'll admit we've had a few minor setbacks, but it would seem that the gods want us to catch this shaitaan.

They're supplying us with what we need—a vehicle, a full tank of diesel and even burner phones.'

'Ha! We're only back on track because I picked up the keys. You didn't even notice them on the ground. I can't believe you dimwits were so slow.'

'Is it getting warm in here?' Rup muttered.

'It's actually getting a little cooler. Oh damn, those drugs are entering your blood stream. How do you feel?'

'Right now, stupid. And a little bit sick.'

8

## A Sticky Wicket

After about twenty minutes, Rup was gazing ponderously at the back of his hand. *What is skin made of? Skin? But why, if skin is made of skin, is the palm skin different from the back of my hand skin? Someone should study this phenomenon.*

Beena squinted into the rear-view mirror. 'You okay?'

She was driving now, having taken over from Afzal, who was too erratic with the gears for anyone's liking. Beena was glad to take off the niqab and simply put on a headscarf instead.

'I can see the air around us. Pakistan has different air. Pink and purple, you can almost lick it, you know?' Rup waved his hand in the air as if he were playing with it and disrupting invisible puffs of smoke.

'We don't need Sherlock Holmes to conclude that stuff ain't sugar.' Afzal twisted in the passenger seat to watch his friend.

'You think he's alright? Should we make him throw up?'

'Hey, just because I spend time in the chemistry lab doesn't mean I know about drugs.' replied Afzal.

Rup, oblivious to all the concern about his drug use, was nuzzling the dog.

'Wicket likes being with us.'

'Who the hell is Wicket?'

Rup chuckled, holding the dog's face in his palms. 'The dog. She told me her name is Wicket.'

'Great. He can talk to animals now,' Beena groaned.

'What do you want me to tell Wicket?' asked Rup, as he scratched her ear. Wicket barked as though she also had a few points to get across to the trio.

'Tell her to keep quiet!' Beena said.

'What's the matter, Wicket? You want to play?'

'No! No playing. I'm trying to drive.'

'Don't be such a grouch,' Rup giggled as the dog licked his face. 'She likes me.'

Beena shuddered. 'Gross! That's a street dog slobbering over you, Rup.'

Rup ruffled her fur. 'Hey, did you guys even notice this white marking on her forehead? Shaped like a pagri. Maybe Wicket is Sikh too!'

Afzal laughed, 'Wicket Singh? Or Wicket Kaur?'

The dog responded by bouncing around in the back seat.

Beena thundered, 'Stop it!'

Wicket stopped, but not for long. She found something interesting between the driver's seat and the centre console. She wedged herself into the space, sniffing away. Whatever it was, she really liked it. And really wanted it.

Rup bent down. 'Good girl. What did you find?'

'Don't encourage it, Rup.' Beena removed one hand from the steering wheel and pushed Wicket back into the rear seat. 'Get it away from me.'

'She's not an *it*. Don't be dramatic, Bee. People carry screaming kids in cars all the time. Brats. Wicket's a dog. Ohh, what a good dog!' He ruffled her ears.

The dog had another try at whatever she was chasing. This time, she nuzzled her nose into the crevice. Afzal tried to get the dog to stop and return to the back seat, but she pushed back hard, sniffing loudly, bumping into Beena's seat.

Beena tightened her grip on the steering wheel and then, trying to calm herself down, exhaled gradually and half-closed her eyes. Unfortunately, she picked a bad time to centre herself—the road veered sharply to the right.

Afzal hollered, 'Bee, BEE!'

Beena snapped open her eyes, jerked upright, screamed and cranked the wheel to the right. The car swerved harshly, so she whirled the steering back to the left. The Jeep responded, screeching out of control. Beena wrestled for a few seconds, barely missing the road sign indicating the turn in the road.

Rup laughed and twisted to look at the road sign. 'Good save, Bee. But that sign is definitely pissed at us.'

Afzal wrinkled his nose. 'How the—'

The sharp sound of a tyre blowing out interrupted him.

'Son of a bitch! All that swerving's blown a tyre.' Beena thumped the steering wheel in anger. She glowered at the dog, and then at Afzal. 'I'm not changing it.'

She braked and slowly steered the Jeep to the side of the road. Afzal groaned as he peered to the rear. 'Rup's in no shape to help. You expect me to do it alone?'

'Okay, fine, I'll help. We do have a spare hanging in the back door, right?'

They got out and dismounted the spare. Afzal dropped the heavy tyre on the ground with a thump. The passenger door was open and Wicket spilled out to check on what they were doing.

Not far behind Wicket, Rup came staggering out. He gawked at the faint stars in the darkening sky, lifted his arms and started spinning in place. 'Look at that. The stars are making round lines in the sky. This is cool.'

'He does seem to like spinning,' chortled Afzal.

Bee watched him with a frown. 'I'm going to bolt him onto this wheel then.'

Rup stopped spinning and stumbled off into the roadside country. The dog followed closely, wagging its tail energetically.

'There he goes. Are you going to get him, or should I?'

Afzal replied, 'You go keep an eye on him. I'll change the tyre.'

Beena set off after their impaired friend. Afzal kicked the flat tyre, then clutched his foot, hopping in place. 'Shit, that hurt.'

It was dark by the time Afzal replaced the flat. Meanwhile, Beena had wrangled Rup back from the fields and towards the Jeep. Wicket followed Rup like a shadow. She loaded Rup into the back seat while Afzal tried to clean the grime off his hands.

Afzal sighed, 'I'm beat. Changing that damned thing was difficult.'

Beena nodded. 'Me too. Rup and his chamcha ran me ragged. What do you say we catch some sleep before we continue?'

'But where? This main road doesn't seem safe.'

'How about that side street?' Beena pointed ahead at a road sign, faintly illuminated by the moonlight. 'We can rest for a few hours and still reach Rawalpindi by morning.'

'You're right. We've had enough excitement for one day.'

Beena climbed into the passenger seat. Afzal asked, 'You don't want to drive?'

'Not anymore. The driver's seat is stuck; it doesn't move back. I knew you'd want to be a gentleman and deal with it yourself.'

Afzal huffed. 'You assume a lot.'

'Yeah. But I'm right a lot, too.' She let her head fall back and closed her eyes.

Afzal frowned and slid into the driver's seat, pressing a lever to recline it. *Ugh.* It was stuck, just as Beena had said. He pounded the steering wheel, making Wicket jump.

'Go back to sleep, you flea-ridden moocher. My exercise for the day is all your fault.' He started the Jeep, eased it off the main road. The headlights revealed a narrow, tree-lined lane. Afzal drove a few hundred metres down the quiet road and parked. He switched the engine off and settled in to sleep.

It was quiet off the main road. The minutes passed sluggishly as he fidgeted, trying to get comfortable. Eventually, he managed to doze off.

Hours later, a low growl from Wicket stirred Afzal. When he opened his eyes, he noticed a pair of faint lights behind them. They were at some distance, but in the rough lane, the mild rocking of yellowish, twin beams was quite noticeable. He jerked up straight.

*Who is this?*

Afzal examined the lights. They grew larger, though it seemed that the approaching car was moving slowly. Wicket growled again.

*Please don't be the police.*

When the beams got to about fifty metres from them, the strange vehicle slowed to a crawl, its tyres crunching on the gravel. Wicket let out another faint rumble—her curved canines visible in the low light. Afzal leaned forward and felt for the keys.

*Shit. Wicket doesn't like this. I'm getting a bad feeling.*

The strange vehicle stopped about twenty metres behind them. He could see the faint outline of a pickup.

On a hunch, Afzal turned the ignition. The roar of their engine kicking to life stirred Beena. She glared at him. 'Damn it. I was sound asleep.'

'Something doesn't feel right. Wicket growled and woke me up,' Afzal whispered. He glanced in the rear-view mirror, pressed the clutch and placed his hand on the gear shifter. Beena peered out the back, the lights from the pickup illuminating her face.

'Why is he not passing us?'

All of a sudden, the pickup's door opened and a big man got out. The truck's headlights revealed a pistol held at arm's length.

'Fuck! It's Rambo!'

Afzal threw the Jeep into gear, spun the tyres and bolted. In response, the man let two rounds fly. The rear window in the Jeep shattered, shards flying everywhere. Wicket whimpered and nuzzled into a sleeping Rup.

Beena saw the man dive back into the pickup truck and chase after them. It steadily closed the gap and loud cracks sounded as more bullets whizzed through the air.

Beena clutched the dashboard. 'Do something, Afzal!'

'Do what? Can't see a damn thing and I'm going as fast as this stupid Jeep can move.'

But, in fact, he did do something. Accidentally.

The narrow lane ended in front of them and instead of braking, Afzal launched the Jeep straight through a short walkway and into an open field. They thudded onto the earth, the four-wheel-drive vehicle shooting forward.

The ground was lumpy, rugged, as though the harvest had just been done. In the dark, the bumps were impossible to see, but the three friends and dog were bouncing into the air with every jarring thwack.

Beena peeped out from the hole where the rear window had been once. 'He's still on our ass,' she informed Afzal.

'I can see his bouncing lights in the mirror. Too close for comfort.' More gunshots sounded. 'I can hear him too!'

Jostled about by the rough terrain, Rup finally popped his head up, clutching at Wicket.

'What? What are we doing? This is a funny road.'

Beena and Afzal shouted in unison, 'Not now, Rup!'

Afzal turned hard, ploughing through a spot in the fence and thundering into another field. They were bobbing inside the car like human ping-pong balls. Beena clutched the door handle and roof, straining to keep her balance. Rup held onto Wicket, while searching with his free hand for something on the floor of the Jeep.

'Hold on!' Afzal turned hard, this time to the left, and roared through a tall, wire mesh fence. There was a sound of crunching metal as they tore through it and into a field filled with white-tipped plants.

Meanwhile, Rup found what he'd been looking for—the box where he'd stashed the gun. He took out the pistol, aimed at the pickup through the broken window and fired. The sharp kickback sent the weapon rocketing back towards his face. He barely hung on and was lucky to avoid being hurt.

'Are you kidding me?' Beena glared at Rup, her tone loud enough for him to hear over the commotion.

'You're right, Bee. Bad idea,' Rup said, as he hurriedly placed the gun back.

'Where are we? And what the heck are these?' Afzal glanced at the white-tipped plants in the field, swerving to avoid making the Jeep an easy target.

Rup took in the crop, lit up in front of them like little waving lamps. 'They're kind of beautiful in their own way. Shame to be running over them.'

'I think these might be poppy plants,' said Beena. 'What's with this drug connection we're caught up in? Chased by a drug dealer through a field of poppies? If the grower finds us, he'll kill us and Rambo back there too.'

Rup crouched low and peeked out the back. 'Hey, I think he's trying something new.'

The blast was loud—all three of them instinctively slapped their hands over their ears. It was a double-barrelled shotgun. After a pause, there followed a second ear-shattering boom.

Rup wheezed, clutching his chest. 'We're going to die!'

'Not yet, we're not. Hang on tight!' Afzal scanned the poppy field as a few more explosive shots rang out. The field was narrowing, and they were running out of space on either side. He spun the wheel and sent the Jeep through the tapered path, straight towards the only building in the area—an old barn, dimly lit by the moon and their bouncing headlights. The building's exterior looked like a patchwork of faded tin sheets.

'That barn looks ancient. So, fuck it!' Afzal floored the pedal, gripping the wheel. The vehicle accelerated towards the old building.

'Afzal, no!' Rup's eyes were wild, his face colourless. He clutched Wicket tightly to his chest.

'Oh shit!' yelled Beena.

The Jeep crashed through the wall, cutting through it like butter.

The inside was quite another story.

It was full of shiny industrial equipment, lit with bright white lights hung from the ceiling. There was an acrid smell of cooking, tar and chemicals. Stainless steel tables, vats and machines were laid out in rows. Three enormous tanks sat against the opposite wall.

The Jeep had the advantage of momentum. It thrust the tables aside and blasted right through the equipment. But there was no time nor space to turn. Rushing towards the opposite wall, Afzal tried to steer away from the large tanks. He was successful—for the most part. As he threaded the fast-moving vehicle through a narrow gap, it glanced off the side of one and smashed out the other side of the barn—back into the open fields.

'Shit, we nicked that stupid tank! It spilled its guts of some ghastly liquids. That stink reminds me of your lab, Afzal.' Rup laughed hysterically.

'That odour, my friends, isn't Chanel Number 5,' shouted Afzal, as he manoeuvred the Jeep. 'If I'm right about the smell, you better hold on. Shit's gonna blow!'

Rup looked back just as their pursuer zoomed through the gaping hole made by the Jeep. The pickup truck was dragging metal, sparks flying behind it. There was a slight lull, a flash of fast-moving flames and then the entire barn exploded. The sky lit up like an orange balloon, ejecting shards of wood and metal everywhere.

Afzal stared slack-jawed at the explosion in the rear-view mirror. 'Do you think …?'

Rup watched the bright explosion in dazed silence while Beena stared ahead with a set face at the wild shrubs they were careening though.

It was clear no one was going to answer, so Afzal continued, 'I'm fairly sure the main road is in front of us. We'll find it and then we'll be fine. We'll be back on track.'

Beena turned to stare at the driver sitting next to her. 'We destroyed a gang's poppy harvest, got shot at and blew up a drug factory. Tell me, in which way are we back on track?'

Afzal kept quiet, concentrating on steering the Jeep. Rup scratched Wicket's ears. 'You're shaking. But it's alright. No one's behind us anymore.'

However, Rup's optimism was misplaced. The pickup came bursting into the field, framed nicely by the burning barn and trailing flames from the lit cargo in its bed.

'Shit, he's back! That guy isn't Rambo, he's the Terminator. Nothing can stop him. Does that pickup look alright?'

Beena turned around to watch their pursuer through the missing back window and, out of the blue, she started laughing.

Afzal glanced at her. 'What?'

'Nothing. But I don't think we need to worry about speed anymore.'

'What do you—'

A thunderous boom sounded behind them. Afzal glanced at the rear-view mirror as the truck's headlights swerved from side to side, flickered, then disappeared.

'What the hell?'

Beena chuckled, 'His engine was on fire. The hood blew up onto the windshield and I don't think he could see where he was going. Chanel Number 5 must have burnt right through. Or Rup hit Rambo's engine with his only shot. Whatever the reason, he isn't going anywhere for a while.'

'Definitely my shot,' Rup proudly claimed.

'Well, I'll take it, no matter what it was.' A relieved Afzal slumped forward in the driver's seat.

After a few minutes, Wicket started wedging herself between the driver's seat and the console again.

Rup patted the dog's rump. 'What in the world has you so interested?' After a bit of a struggle, Wicket surfaced with what seemed to be a long-lost potato chip.

Beena gagged. 'That's gross.'

Rup laughed as the dog gulped down its prize. 'Now we know what Wicket likes. Biscuits and chips.'

'We got a flat and nearly got killed because your dog was trying to eat a stinking potato chip?'

'I guess. Wicket gets what she wants. A potato chip. It's kind of funny if you think about it, don't you think?'

'Maybe in ten years we'll think it's funny,' said Beena, glaring at the animal, its paws contentedly extended onto Rup's lap. 'If we live past the next few days that is.'

'No harm, no foul,' Afzal said. 'We're all in one piece and the Jeep seems fine. Why don't we drive for a bit?'

# 9

## Break-out Formulae

The sun had been up over Rawalpindi for a few hours. The locals completed their morning ablutions by the thousands, under a clear blue sky that allowed the sun to bathe the city in warmth and light.

At Adiala Jail, one of its most famous 'guests', Rasheed Latif, was also conducting his morning routine. As every Indian knew, Latif was responsible for planning and executing multiple, horrific terrorist attacks across India. They hated him for what he'd done.

But in Pakistan, many didn't believe it, or viewed it differently.

Latif sneered at the prison orderly standing in front of him. 'This mooli paratha is cold. There's no achar. And the dahi is all mushy.'

'I'm sorry, sir. The breakfast travelled far to get here.' The delivery boy bowed his head and stared at his toes.

'Throw away this sorry excuse for a breakfast. No tip. You should've kept my food warm,' Latif said and shooed the orderly away with a wave of his jewelled hand.

After the boy left, Latif leaned back in his chair and checked the missed calls on his phone. 'What does the idiot want now?' he muttered as he hit speed dial, flipped on the television to catch up with the news and waited for the person on the other end to pick up.

'Hello, beta?'

'Haan, papa.'

'Why are you calling me so early? *Kya kaam hai?*'

'Well, have you thought about my birthday gift, the Mercedes G-Class SUV?'

'Not the stupid Mercedes again! Why do you need such a vehicle in Pakistan? Why don't I buy you a nice BMW SUV?'

'Anyone can buy a BMW. The G-Class is what I want. I'll look regal driving around in it. The least I'll settle for is a Range Rover.'

'Beta, I cannot discuss this trivial matter right now. We must find you a bride first, and Haneef has someone in mind.'

Latif hung up and returned to the news.

The TV showed a building that was burning; the fire crew was trying to douse the flames. As smoke swirled up from the smouldering structure, the news ticker at the bottom of the screen read: *Suicide attack at children's hospital kills dozens.*

Latif smiled, his thin lips parting to show stained teeth. Without taking his eyes from the TV, he barked, 'You! Get in here!'

A squirrelly man wearing an ill-fitting prison uniform rushed in and stood erect. 'Sir!'

'They're still talking about the bombing after three days. That's good. I need maulana saab to prepare our message. Tell him I need a relevant verse to explain the reason behind this attack and its significance for jihad. Fetch him.'

'Yes, bahut acha.' The nervous man hurried off.

Ten minutes later, the maulana arrived—a droopy shouldered man with a henna-stained beard. Behind the maulana, the nervous man stayed in a corner, trying to remain unseen.

'How can I serve you, Latif saab?'

Latif replied, 'Find me a passage from the Quran or Hadith for the hospital attack. Make it clear that we were justified and restrained in our response.'

The maulana nodded. 'Understood. I've the perfect one. Give me half an hour.'

'Okay, this better be good. All involved did well.' Latif turned to his lackey in the corner. 'Make sure they get bonuses.'

'*Theek hai, saab*,' the lackey replied. He paused, fidgeting.

Latif growled, 'What?'

'The boy's family is here,' stammered the man. They have been waiting outside since yesterday.'

'What boy? Which family? I've a massage coming up. I don't have time to meet anyone,' Latif said, shifting his attention back to the TV.

'But saab, this is the family of the boy from the hospital.' He gestured meaningfully to the TV.

Latif scowled. 'What terrible timing, just when I was looking forward to my massage. Oh, alright. I think I can spare a few minutes.'

A few minutes later, a middle-aged man and woman, a young boy and a toddler girl entered the room. All four were dressed in soiled, oversized clothes draped shapelessly over their skinny bodies. Their pale faces were blank with grief, eyes drooping.

Latif, seated expansively on his chair, raised his hands and smiled. 'We're appreciative of your boy's sacrifice. Allahu Akbar. He took honourable action for our holy cause.'

The family didn't move. Their despondent facial expressions remained unchanged as they stared silently at the fat, bearded man.

Latif continued, 'You have our gratitude. Our people understand the sacrifices we all must make for our noble cause.'

The middle-aged man took in the open, well-lit space with lavish rugs on the floor, expensive liquor sitting next to hand-cut crystal glasses on a minibar and silk sheets on the bed. 'Yes, sir.' His voice was flat, like that of a man who had lost all hope in life.

'I'm sure your son is in Jannat right now. You, young man— you should follow your brother's example, eh?' said Latif, speaking to the boy, maybe about ten years old, half-hidden behind his mother, holding onto her worn out niqab.

The mother pulled her son close, shielding his ear with a flat palm. 'Actually, we're hoping he'll be a doctor,' she said dully, out of habit. 'He is very good in school. Got hundred per cent marks in math and science.'

Latif examined the little boy, and smirked. 'School? No need for that. Why become a doctor when you can serve Allah in a better way? You should join me in a greater cause. I'll send for you next month, and I'll take care of you.'

The family was quiet.

'But now you should leave. I've urgent business to take care of—we must deal with the kafirs using a firm hand, no?' He glanced at the door and roared, 'Get in here!'

The squirrelly man reappeared. 'Yes, sir.'

'Make sure these people have bus tickets to reach home.'

'Yes, sir.' The nervous man began to escort the grieving family out.

Latif raised his hand, freezing the lackey in place. 'And where's that masseuse? Why is he late? My neck is killing me.'

'I'm terribly sorry, sir. I thought the boy was expected in

the evening. Let me find out if he can come immediately, Commander Latif.'

'Good.' Latif closed his eyes and exhaled, 'Off with you.'

~

It was late in the morning by the time Afzal drove the banged-up Jeep into Rawalpindi. They drove through the city towards Adiala Jail. The trip had left them exhausted, but reaching their destination caused a surge of excitement. They pulled into the parking lot surrounding the imposing concrete prison building. There were tall grey walls topped with barbed wire, with watch towers at regular intervals.

Rup's eyes were wide as he surveyed the structure. 'I can't believe we're here. What now?'

'We get on with what we came here to do. No dilly-dallying,' said Beena.

'Now?'

'Yes, Rup. Now.' Afzal found a place to park about fifty metres near the entrance and brought the Jeep to a stop. 'Here we are. Gate E. Based on what I dug up about Latif, the prison is easy to slip into, especially if we act as though we're part of his sleazy business.'

Rup surveyed the sky as if it would impart wisdom to him. 'So, what do we know about Latif's business, other than he hangs out with @oily_boy?'

'My uncle once told me about him,' said Beena, scratching her nose. 'Like most terrorist leaders, he's very paranoid. No business on the phone, so he likes to meet in person. They go in and out of his jail cell, as if it's a business office. Apparently, the guards turn the other way when he has visitors for his …

questionable business and immoral personal dealings. They call it plausible deniability …'

Rup laughed. 'So, if they don't see it, it didn't happen?'

Afzal nodded. 'Kind of, I guess. And he often indulges his carnal needs.' He paused. 'I was thinking about that. We might be able to come up with an excuse to get one of us into the prison.'

Afzal's eyes bounced between Beena and Rup.

Beena stared back quizzically. 'Only one of us goes in? No way. Neither Rup nor I am going in there by ourselves. You go in alone if you think it's such a good idea. Right, Rup?'

'Why can't we all go in together?' asked Rup.

'All of us traipsing in there would draw too much attention. This isn't *Amar Akbar Anthony* where three people with questionable disguises can sneak into a villain's lair.'

Afzal studied his hands for a moment, then turned to Beena and mumbled.

'I thought maybe you could pretend to be an escort and go in.'

Beena jerked up. 'What? Are you out of your fucking mind? An escort? This is your big plan? I thought you were researching his businesses for a way to get in.'

Afzal started to say something.

But Beena powered on, her eyes blazing, 'I should've never shared what my uncle told me about Latif's sordid lifestyle. I see now where all the supporting statements about his carnal needs came from. You want me to dress like that woman you set up for Parv?'

Afzal was defensive. 'What else do we have as an excuse to go inside? The plan makes sense based on what your uncle told you—you see that, right? We need to dangle something that Latif wants, in front of him.'

'And that's me?'

'We don't know enough about what he likes besides the obvious—escort girls, ladies of pleasure, whatever you choose to call them. Besides, you're the toughest among us three. Unless, you've a better idea of why Latif would want to meet any of us.'

'I hate this man for the pain he brought my family. But there's no way I'm walking into that prison alone to seduce and kidnap him. You nuts? And anyhow, solely to play this out, what would I do if I did slip in?'

Rup snorted. 'That's a good question, Afzal.'

'And I have a good answer. We use the knockout chloroform drops that I developed; Bee has it in her backpack, inside the small wooden case. You slip some of it in his drink and bam—he's out like a light.'

'Wonderful, and then I sling the fat-ass over my shoulder and lug him out?'

Rup snorted, 'Beena, two. Afzal—zip, zip, zippo.'

Afzal sat back in the driver's seat. 'Not zip yet. Rup will follow a few minutes later to assist you. He can tell the guards he has an important message to deliver to Latif.'

Rup grumbled, 'I guess I should've kept my mouth shut.'

Beena shifted in her seat. She thought for a moment, and eyed Afzal.

'That's the only thing you've said that comes close to making sense. Latif would have couriers bringing messages in person. Why don't we do that instead of me going in dressed like a sleazy call girl?'

Afzal's eyes got a little brighter. 'A messenger will deliver a letter and not interact much with Latif. We need someone who can get close and slip something into his drink. We send you in with the knockout drops and one of Rambo's burners. As soon as he's knocked out, call us, and Rup comes in to wheel him out. I'll keep the Jeep warmed up and ready to go.'

'Are you out of your stupid mind? A girl can't waltz into a prison like that all alone.' Beena scowled. She shouldn't have to tell him this fact.

'Girl or not, you're the best suited among us to do this,' Afzal said. He grabbed the red backpack and took out a small wooden box. 'Here, check this out. We've packed handcuffs and the knockout drops are in this case. Open it and use this vial, the one with the black cap.'

'What are the other vials for?' asked Rup. 'You're making this kind of confusing. And why are we lugging your chemistry experiments around?'

'Don't worry about those other vials. Concentrate on the one with the black cap. I didn't leave any of my stuff in our room. Someone could have found it and thought they're drugs.'

Beena snorted. 'That's because they technically *are* drugs. And there's no way I'm going in alone. We should've figured out this part of the plan back in Shimla. It is too late to be sitting outside the prison, improvising escort disguises and multiple vials of weird and unknown formulas.'

'Formulae,' corrected Rup, 'not formulas. Formulae.'

'Hmpf! Formula, formulas, formulae; makes no difference.' Beena folded her arms and made an odd noise that made Wicket whimper and cock her head to one side. 'I need fresh air. This last-minute escort nonsense you're throwing around is giving me a headache.' She opened the door of the Jeep, adjusted the hijab around her head and stepped out.

Beena walked out of the parking lot into the surrounding street, strolling aimlessly, taking in the people going about their day. The loss of her aunt in the Mumbai terror attacks had been devastating to her entire family. She hated the terrorist that Afzal had set his sights on, but she'd never imagined she would have to take such risks.

*How could Afzal think a girl would be safe in a Pakistani prison?*

She needed to think.

*How else could they break Latif out of prison?*

She saw a bus stand and wandered over to it. Leaning against it, she closed her eyes and took a deep breath. A vision of her aunt swam before her eyes and she instinctively wrapped her arms tightly around herself. Tears welled up behind her closed lids. She let out a long sigh and wiped them away with the back of her hands.

*Was she being cowardly for not taking this opportunity for justice? Afzal was right about one thing; she was more than capable of taking care of herself. In fact, better than most, and certainly better than either Rup or Afzal. Logically, she would be the right person to go in.*

Beena nodded, steeling herself for the task at hand. As she started to step away from the bus stop, she heard a low sniffle. She involuntarily looked around for the source of the sound.

A family of four was huddled on the other side of the bus stop's glass wall. A father, a mother, a young son and a toddler daughter. All distraught.

Beena immediately felt her chest tighten, as if she shared their pain. She stayed quiet and unmoving, pressing her back against the glass partition. She didn't know why she had stopped, or why she cared—but it didn't take long to make out what they were saying.

The mother wailed, '… that he's a monster! Our son was a good boy, and he brainwashed him into doing such a horrible thing. Did you see those terrible images? I cannot live with myself. That's the same hospital where our son was born. And that's where he died, taking so many with him.'

The father took her hand, his face was lined with sorrow. 'We didn't know this is what they'd planned.'

'You heard the guards talking. Latif used him to satisfy his perverted needs, filling his mind with all kinds of twisted hate. He convinced our boy to do the unspeakable.'

'There's nothing we can do about it now.' Her husband tightened his grip on her hands. 'And we still have two children to raise. We must focus on them now; work to make them doctors, who save lives as penance for the damage their brother caused.'

The mother hugged the young boy, wiped her tears and looked up, seeking divine assistance. 'But now he wants to send for this little one too.'

At that moment, her eyes landed on Beena staring at them through the glass.

Quickly, the mother collected herself and picked up the young girl. 'We must be careful. People are starting to stare.'

Beena felt her face flush with embarrassment for violating a grieving family's privacy. Backing up a few steps, she turned and hightailed it back to the Jeep, jumped into the back seat and slammed the door.

She was quiet, breathing hard and looking down at her clenched hands. Both Afzal and Rup realised something was up. They looked at one another, waiting for Beena to speak.

After a while, Beena collected herself. 'Um. I think I saw the family of the boy who blew up the children's hospital. You remember that terrorist attack from a few days ago that was on the news?'

Afzal spun to lock eyes with her. 'Yeah. It was horrible. Many were killed. But how do you know you saw the bomber's family?'

'Because the mother of the boy said so. The whole family was at that bus stop right there, and I happened to catch a part of their conversation. It sounded like they'd just met with Latif inside the prison.'

'Whoa. Are you sure? Or maybe you're simply imagining things because we're on a covert mission?'

'No, I'm not. Also, the mother said something very strange about Latif. She said she heard the guards talking about how he used their son to satisfy his perverted needs.'

Afzal gasped. 'Oh, snap. Bee, what did the mother say? Exactly.'

Beena shrugged. 'Almost word-for-word what I told you.'

Now it was Rup's turn to gulp. 'The man is much worse than I thought!'

Beena felt the bile rise in her throat and she gagged. 'I never imagined … he's the worst. And apparently now he wants the kid's younger brother. I saw that little boy with them. He didn't even look ten!'

Rup grimaced. 'What do we do now?'

'About a terrorist asshole who is a pervert that takes advantage of innocent young boys?' Beena couldn't suppress the disdain in her voice. 'If that's the angle we must play to sneak inside, we only have one person to do it. We send Afzal in.'

Afzal reeled back as if hit with a bolt of electricity. His eyes became the size of saucers. 'What? Me? No fucking way.'

'You were okay with sending Bee in,' Rup said. 'Why are you—?'

'We could send Rup, who is the actor,' Beena interrupted, tapping Rup on his shoulder. 'But he doesn't look like a cute boy. Unless Latif likes wrestling with a burly guy, you're the only logical play we have.'

Rup gazed meaningfully at Afzal and added, 'She's right, as usual. If you want a quick lesson on how to sway your hips as you walk, I'm your guy.'

'This little escapade gets worse with every passing moment, but we can use this new information.' Beena reached over the driver's seat and ruffled his wavy hair. 'It means you're up, pretty boy. You, your vials and your formulae.'

Afzal turned pale. 'I can't do that. And I ain't pretty.'

Beena glared at him. 'Objectification does not feel very comfortable, does it now? Unless you are not keen on proving your patriotism. If that is the case, we can abort right now. If not, well, it's your turn to show some balls. Your lean figure, big brown eyes and wavy hair will come in handy to trap the worst person on earth. You just need to be pretty enough to slide by a few bored guards.'

'And maybe you should pick up tips from @oily_boy and pack massage oil. We should've guessed, with a handle like that,' added Rup.

Afzal buried his face in his hands. After a moment, he pushed his hair back with a quick motion and looked up at their expectant faces.

'Shit! I hate it when you are right. Hand me the backpack and a phone before I change my damn mind and back out of this entire thing.'

'Sway away, buddy. Rock those hips. And undo the top two buttons of your shirt.' Rup was generous with his acting tips.

# 10

# The Difference between
# Black and White

Afzal approached the two prison guards. One was tall, bald and sweaty. The other was short with a bushy beard. He had come a long way, so he mustered all the courage he had left and said, 'I've an important message for Latif saab.'

'Message or massage? Ha!' laughed the short one, pleased at his own joke.

The tall guard frowned. 'It's Commander Latif for little shits like you. Respect your betters.' He examined a paper in front of him. 'Aren't you supposed to be coming later?'

Feeling his mouth dry up, Afzal cleared his throat. 'This is the time I was told to come. I'm sorry. It's my first time delivering an important message.'

The short guard eyed Afzal up and down and chortled. 'A young man like you should be nervous around Latif. To get to his quarters, follow the signs to the warden's old office.'

'Wear this badge,' said the other guard, and handed over a yellow plastic card strung on a green ribbon.

'Thank you, sir.' Afzal grabbed the badge and moved on past the guards.

They didn't give him a second glance as he went inside. The rumours about the prison and Latif seemed true. Visitors could walk right in.

The old prison was a maze of dingy corridors, flickering lights and the smell of bleach. Signage was sparse, but Afzal finally found the warden's old office. There were no iron bars, only a large, polished wooden door behind a small, beaten-up desk. He came face to face with a thin, pointy-faced and defeated-looking man wearing a guard uniform two sizes too big.

Afzal walked over, displaying his badge. 'Is Commander Latif in? I've got something for him.'

'A message, huh?' He smirked and gestured at Afzal to go inside. 'He's ready for you.'

Afzal found himself inside a spacious suite with floor-to-ceiling windows, a plush sofa, a dining table and minibar on the side. Rich tapestries hung on the walls next to a flat-screen TV.

The warden's old office had been converted into a luxury suite.

Latif stood at the edge of the dining table: an obese, bearded man, bent over, snorting a line of cocaine, wearing nothing but a cream-colored kurta and lime green underwear. Next to the drugs, Afzal spotted a stack of colourful magazines. Photos of naked men graced the cover. Afzal gasped, turning bright red.

Latif glanced up, white flecks caught in his scraggly, stained beard. He laughed at the blushing boy and nodded at the magazines.

'First time?'

'Never seen those types of magazines. Mainly pictures and videos on the internet.'

'Hmpf, internet,' the man snorted. 'Take one when you leave. Anyway, you came right on time. My dick has a mind of its own today.'

Afzal's cheeks flamed. He'd never imagined a situation like this. But in a flash, it hit him. An opportunity. The perfect segue.

Looking meaningfully at Latif, he said, 'I've something with me that should put the steel back in your hammer.'

Latif patted the front of his stringy underwear with one hand. 'Sometimes, it takes some help to extend the pole to support the tent.'

Afzal shuffled through his backpack, grabbing a vial. 'Put this in your drink. It's magic. Last week, the minister used it and was very happy'.

'The minister should know,' said Latif. He took the small bottle while grabbing a crystal glass from the bar. 'This bottle of good American whiskey should do nicely.'

He squeezed a few drops into the glass and placed the vial on the bar. For the first time since entering the prison, Afzal felt a burst of confidence.

Latif poured a shot of whiskey. He swirled the drink, held up the gleaming glass and said, 'Cheers.' He tilted his head back and tossed the concoction down his throat in one quick motion.

'Done! How long does it take to work?'

And that's when Afzal froze, his gaze zeroing in on the vial sitting on the bar. Its cap was white, not black.

*Oh fuck! Oh no!*

His confidence evaporated in an instant.

'It takes just a few minutes, I think,' he stammered.

Afzal had a general idea of the effects from the white-capped vial's contents—but he wasn't sure how fast it would affect a large man like Latif. The chemistry nerd in Afzal came alive, eclipsing his fear for a short moment. He leaned forward, his eyes peeled to observe this experiment on a full-grown human.

'Well then, what shall we do as we wait?' Latif lifted the top of his tiny underwear. 'Nope. Nothing yet.'

Afzal shuffled his feet, fear overriding his curiosity. 'Um, I don't know.' He scanned the room, a single thought racing through his brain.

*I need to get out. This man is crazy.*

'Lighten up. Let's have fun. How did it work for the minister? You should take off your … Ugh!'

Latif abruptly bent over and grabbed his stomach with both hands. He stared at Afzal, his face turning pink.

'What did you give me?!'

'Exactly what the minister uses. He gave me those vials.'

'Fuck the minister!'

Latif switched to grabbing his ass. After a few loud groans, he darted for the toilet. Awful sounds emanated, amplified by the porcelain bowl and the hard tiles within the small room.

The squirrelly man came rushing in. 'I heard yelling. What's the problem, sir?'

'I'm shitting my organs out, you dumb donkey,' Latif moaned, his sweaty face turning a shade of beet, veins popping out from his forehead.

Then, his body went limp and he flopped onto the floor, splayed halfway between the toilet and the room.

The guard took in the sight with bulging eyes—and stepped back. 'Is he dead?'

'I don't know.' The colour had left Afzal's face. *These drops seem stupid strong.*

'It smells like he's dead. That's rotten shit.' The guard fanned the air with one hand. 'What did you do to him?'

'Me? Nothing! He said his stomach hurt, then this happened.'

The half-naked Latif moaned. 'Oh! He's still alive and needs a doctor.' The lackey turned around, examined Afzal for a moment and stroked the length of his arm.

'You are too delicate to be involved. Leave right now if you don't want trouble. In return, I'll ask for a massage later.'

Afzal rushed out of the luxurious place of depravity faster than a comic book superhero.

*Was everyone in this prison a pervert?*

Back in the Jeep, Wicket was napping in the rear seat with her feet in the air. Rup and Beena sat in the front, each with an expectant eye on the phone when they spotted Afzal rushing towards them.

'Um, this doesn't look good. I thought he was supposed to call us to pick him and the bastard up.'

'We've seen way too much of "this doesn't look good" lately.'

The rear door flew open. Afzal scrambled to get in, but caught one of the backpack straps on the Jeep's door frame. He was in such a hurry that the strap ripped clean off the bag.

Afzal slammed the door shut, as if zombies were chasing him. He looked at the two anxious faces and exclaimed, 'I think I might've killed the fucker!'

'What?' Beena examined Afzal, head to toe, 'What the hell happened?'

He gagged. "This whole thing just shit the bed!"

Beena blinked a few times. 'So … I guess we came all this way for shit then.'

'Shit. You've no idea how right you are.'

Rup chuckled and pointed at an ambulance racing up the road. 'You think that's coming in to pick up Latif's body?'

Afzal settled down a little and took deep breaths. He stared at the rushing vehicle. 'Of course they called an ambulance. It's probably taking Latif to the hospital. We should follow.'

'What on earth did you do to him?'

Afzal smacked his forehead. 'I gave him the wrong drops. The bastard was standing there, virtually naked with piles of porn magazines and cocaine strewn around like candy. I was sweating and couldn't think straight. In my hurry, I took out the white vial instead of the black one.'

'Fuck! The white vial?' whistled Rup.

Beena smacked him on the shoulder and motioned Afzal to continue. 'Then what?'

'Then? He drank it. His ass exploded and he collapsed on the floor. As you said, we came here for shit. And there was plenty of it. Shit in the pan, on the walls, on the floor, down Latif's legs, everywhere!'

Rup couldn't stop laughing. 'He just shat all over? This white vial is better than knockout drugs. You should've mixed them both up and given it to him, just to be sure.'

'That's repulsive! I don't know why boys find potty jokes funny,' said Beena. 'I'm glad it wasn't me in the room.'

'I had developed the white vial for Parv. It was one of my stupid plans. I didn't realise the laxative was this strong.' Afzal shuddered.

'You should sell this formula. Call it a super laxative. "Super-lax makes your bowels relax." You can make a buttload of money.' Rup guffawed. 'A buttload …'

Beena managed a chuckle, imagining the terrorist with severe runs. 'Okay, we follow the ambulance to the hospital. And what do we do then? Finish him off?'

'No. We can still kidnap him from the hospital.'

'At least he'll be lighter to move, with all the shit out of his system,' Rup added, still sniggering at his own jokes.

'Enough, Rup. C'mon, we've work to do.'

Beena shrugged. 'We've come this far. What's a few more miles? We don't have to sneak him out of a prison. A hospital could be easier.'

'That's a kickass plan.' Rup was on a roll.

'Oh, shut up, will you?' Beena snapped. 'The ambulance is here. Focus. We must make sure they load Latif into it.'

Two technicians jumped out of the ambulance and sped inside, pushing a rolling gurney. After a few minutes, the gurney re-emerged with the squirrelly man running alongside, holding a man's hand.

Afzal said, 'Bingo. That's Latif. And I'd recognise his shady assistant anywhere. Don't lose that ambulance, Bee.'

Rawalpindi's traffic could be a nightmare to most. But Beena had driven on the congested roads of India which prepared her well for a very unique job—following an ambulance in a crowded city ferrying a dangerous terrorist leader shitting in his undies.

She navigated the Jeep as though she'd been born for the chase, but as they neared their destination, she thumped the wheel. 'Shit, just our luck. It's a military hospital, just like a prison. Out of the frying pan, into the fire.'

'Military or not, it's primarily a hospital,' replied Afzal. 'It should be easier. Let's find a place to park.'

# 11

## Fat Man Has Left the Building

Afzal, Beena and Rup sauntered into the hospital lobby pretending to be deep in debate. Over his shoulder, Rup carried the backpack with the torn strap dangling like a streamer.

A lone nurse sat at the reception desk, boredom etched into her face. When she looked up, Afzal said, 'We were here earlier, but I forgot my book in my father's room.'

The indifferent nurse waved them on and they walked past her. Once out of earshot, Rup said, 'For a military hospital, I expected more questions or at least a sign-in register. This is like walking into a restaurant.'

'How about we split up?' suggested Beena. 'We'll find our man faster.'

The three set off in different directions, each with a burner phone from the drug dealer's stash.

After ten minutes of searching, Afzal's burner rang. 'Yes, Bee?'

'I think it's room 342. There's a man in an oversized prison uniform outfit standing outside the door. I'm sure he was the one escorting the ambulance gurney.'

'That's it! Sounds like Mr Squirrel Guy. You found Latif's room. Let me get Rup. We'll be right there.'

In minutes, the three of them were huddled in a corner of an intersecting corridor. Afzal peeked into the hallway and confirmed the target with a nod. 'That's him!' he whispered. 'Squirrelface!'

'How do we slip past the guard?'

'That's only one of our problems. We can't sit here in this corner twiddling our thumbs. There are doctors, nurses and other employees wandering around here.'

'I'm thinking.' Afzal rubbed his temples.

Beena spotted a nurse walking into the nurses' station down the hall. She peered around—the hallway appeared clear.

'Fortune favours the bold,' she muttered, stood up and ambled over.

The lone nurse was busy, her focus buried inside a large terminal. Beena waited for something to happen as it always does in a hospital. There was a beep and the nurse darted to check a blinking notification. As soon she was gone, Beena swung around the counter and opened a closet.

'Bingo,' she breathed.

She re-emerged within a minute, walked back over and smiled at her two friends. 'How do I look?' A white nurse coat and a clipboard had transformed her, making her look official.

Afzal grinned. 'Shit, you scared me. For a moment, I thought a nurse had caught us sneaking around.'

Rup examined her uniform and nodded approvingly. He smiled, reading off the name tag on her white coat. 'Nice to meet you, er … Ms Rahima. You look like you were born to stick extra-long needles into people. I always suspected that's what you secretly wanted from life.'

Beena adjusted her hijab and smoothed down the coat, sniggering. 'Well, that's what you get when you are born into a family with half a dozen nurses. You learn the lay of the land inside a hospital and a nurse's station. They're the same everywhere.'

Rup pointed. 'Is that a real clipboard? Won't that patient miss it?'

'An empty one. Could be janitor cleaning logs. No one will be the wiser,' she said. 'Wait here for a second.'

With that, Beena made her way around the corner and paraded down the corridor as if she owned the hospital. Rup whispered, 'Damn. She's enjoying it. I must convince her to join my drama group. She's awesome.'

Afzal nodded nervously as they watched her approach room 342.

Beena walked straight to the lackey guarding the door. 'We must rush this patient to the operating room. He may be poisoned and we must pump his stomach immediately. Nasty business, if you ask me. You don't want to be close by when we extract his shit.'

'I can't leave him alone. This is a prisoner, you see.'

'And this is a military hospital. You can wait in the dining hall downstairs. They have free food and chai. And you won't be in our way when we do what we must do.'

The lackey quickly peeked through the small glass partition on the door and turned to her. 'But I must know when he's out of the operating room.'

She then turned around and pointed. 'Come by that nurse's station in about an hour and I'll have an update for you.'

'Okay. I could use some chai,' the squirrelly man said and shuffled off to find the dining room.

When he disappeared behind the elevator doors, Beena gestured at Afzal and Rup, grinning like the Cheshire cat.

The two teens came out of hiding and joined her outside the room.

'Awesome, Bee,' Afzal said. 'Let's do it. This time with the right vial.'

'Okay. You still got the bottle with the knockout drops?'

'Yeah. In Rup's backpack. All we need are two drops. It's technically a vial, not a bottle. Knockout drops vial.'

Beena rolled her eyes. 'Doesn't matter what it is technically. Just give it to me and make sure it's the right one.'

Rup opened the knapsack and Afzal carefully fished out the black-capped vial. Armed with the knockout drugs, Beena moved along the corridor and stopped at room 341, peering inside.

Rup asked, gesturing at the number on the door, 'Did you not say he's in room 342?'

She huffed and rolled her eyes again. 'I'm looking for a decoy. Duh!'

'A what?'

'We need another man to knock out first. Someone about the same size that we can put in Latif's bed so no one will realise he's missing—it'll give us extra time to escape.'

Afzal slapped his knee. 'Genius! You think of everything, Bee. We should all search for a decoy.'

They moved swiftly and checked the adjacent rooms until Rup found another chubby man, maybe a little shorter than Latif—a possible decoy. He waved to his friends, and they rushed over and peered through the small glass square in the door.

'Check him out. This guy should do nicely.'

Beena nodded and palmed the vial. 'Give me a minute. I'll tell him he needs additional medication.' She entered the room and closed the door.

Standing outside the door, Rup whispered, watching Afzal, 'I hope this works. Sometimes I don't trust the stuff you concoct. You sure Bee has the right drugs?'

Afzal avoided Rup's gaze and peered through the small glass pane. 'I'm fairly sure. But we'll soon know, won't we?'

A few nervous minutes later, Beena opened the door a few inches and stuck her head out. 'It worked. He's out.'

A relieved Afzal said, 'I told you it'll work. Hang on, let me get that wheelchair I saw in the other room—easier to move him.'

After a quick minute, he wheeled it in. As he did so, he noticed the patient's trousers hanging on the door hook. He grabbed them and started to check its pockets.

'What are you doing?' hissed Beena.

'We need a new ride. Something has been bugging me. How did Rambo find us in the middle of nowhere? He must have a tracker on the Jeep. We're almost out of diesel anyway. Plus, I saw people checking out the bullet holes and a missing window in the Jeep. It's too hot for us to continue driving.'

He shook the pants and they jingled. He fished out a set of keys with a car security fob. 'Bingo.' He also took out the man's wallet and grabbed all the cash in there. 'Not a lot, but it'll be useful to buy fuel and food.'

Rup noticed a military ID card hanging from the belt. 'This might come in handy too. A military hospital does have its benefits.' With one quick move, he removed the card and pocketed it.

'Alright, enough of this petty theft. Let's get down to business.'

Beena approached the bed and pulled the blankets off, revealing a portly man in a hospital gown wearing white socks.

'Okay, you guys wheel him over to 342. I'll go on ahead and slip Latif a few drops from the vial, exactly like tubby here.' She left the room.

'Be careful. That's a super dangerous terrorist—' Rup started, but Beena was already out of earshot.

'Rup, give me a hand getting this guy into the chair.'

Neither of them had moved a limp body before, especially a heavy pear-shaped one. But they managed to load the unconscious man onto the chair and wheeled him towards room 342. The two peeked in through the small glass pane on the door. Beena was standing beside the bed and nodding to the patient.

Latif.

He was propped up on his pillows, drinking something.

Afzal and Rup stood in the hall waiting for Beena's signal. As luck would have it, a doctor rounded the corner and headed straight for them. When he was about ten feet from them, his eyes narrowed, taking in the scene.

Thinking fast, Afzal spoke aloud to the unconscious man in the wheelchair. 'Papa, I *know* you're only pretending to be asleep. Stop it. You're being rude.'

The doctor relaxed and broke into a smile. 'Be understanding, beta,' he said as he neared. 'It's hard when you become old and have to rely on others.'

Afzal patted the decoy on the shoulder, looking dejected. 'I know. We were really hoping to get him some fresh air, but looks like we're pushing it.'

The doctor nodded, walked past them and disappeared around a corner down the hall.

Beena's voice was faint through the door. 'Move! He's under.'

Afzal opened the door and Rup wheeled in the knocked-out stranger. They transferred the decoy onto a chair. Meanwhile, Beena reached into the backpack and took out an electric trimmer. It switched on with a deep hum. Within a minute, Latif's facial hair was gone, revealing patchy, pale skin underneath.

Afzal admired her handiwork. 'Wow, Bee. He looks like a completely different person.'

They lifted Latif out of the bed to place him in the wheelchair, but Latif was heavier than they expected. He slumped, slipped out of their grip and crashed to the floor, face first.

Rup cringed. 'That had to hurt.'

'He won't know. He's out cold.'

'Doesn't matter. He must have felt that.'

'Can you stop empathising with his pain and help me get him into the chair?'

Rup and Afzal were barely able to hoist Latif into the wheelchair. But his body seemed more comfortable in a horizontal position—it slid leisurely down the chair, onto the floor.

'Are you kidding me?' Rup prodded the prone lump of flesh.

Beena glared at Rup. 'Give me the backpack. You two get him back in the chair and hold him there.'

The two boys hoisted Latif back into the chair. Beena took out a pair of handcuffs from the backpack and latched him to the armrests. Then she ripped the dangling strap clean off the bag and proceeded to tear off the good strap too.

'Hey! That's my favourite backpack.'

Beena chuckled, 'Not anymore buddy. This magic red backpack is about to perform its final trick. Ze grand finale.'

With Afzal and Rup holding Latif tight, Beena tied the two straps together around his chest, lashing Latif to the chair. His head lolled forward, strings of saliva dripping from his mouth and down onto his chest.

'There you go. A little short, but he's staying put.'

Afzal placed the strapless backpack in Latif's lap. 'There!' He stepped back, admired their handiwork and beamed at his companions. 'You're a genius, Beena. There's no way I could've done any of this alone. I'm glad you are both here with me.' The confidence in his voice was returning.

'Hold on. Something's missing,' Rup extended his palms as if directing a movie—focusing on Latif's lolling head.

He sprinted out the room and reappeared in a few moments holding a woman's wig. Beena blinked at the hairpiece. 'Where did you find that?'

'An old lady sleeping in a nearby room. I noticed her earlier when we were looking for the decoy.' He placed it on Latif's head, adjusted it, stepped back and cocked his head to one side—as if measuring the scene for a wide-angle shot. 'There. Now it'll be even harder to recognise him—or her.'

Afzal chuckled, at the wigged terrorist and at Rup. 'If you say so.'

'Okay, are you two morons done? We need to get out of here.'

They headed straight for the ground floor. As they stepped out of the elevator, they froze. A group of three or four soldiers lounged around in the reception area, talking to the nurse.

Beena swallowed. 'Getting into the hospital was easy. But sneaking a patient out—a known terrorist—taped and tied to a wheelchair and wearing a bad wig, through what seems like a full battalion of soldiers? That's going to take something special. We need a distraction.'

Rup cleared his throat. 'I got this. Be prepared to move.'

He fumbled with the backpack on Latif's lap and took out a matchbox. Then he headed towards the reception desk. Beena glanced at Afzal, her face wrinkled with worry.

'Give him a chance. Rup doesn't act that confident unless he has a good idea.'

'I hope so.'

They watched as Rup walked towards a bulletin board, filled with notices. He stopped at the board and grabbed several flyers. Afzal smacked his head.

'I know how I can improve Rup's plan. Not super special, but special effects!'

He reached into the backpack and took out another vial— one with a red cap. Meanwhile, Rup crumpled the papers into a loose ball and placed them in front of an air vent. Sliding open the matchbox, he took a match, struck it and held the flame up to the kindling, which rapidly caught fire.

Afzal strode towards Rup and the small ball of fire. 'Dude, awesome idea. Let me make it even better. Step back and hold your nose.'

He unscrewed the vial and sprinkled its contents right onto the fire. The blaze intensified and thick, dirty, yellowish smoke rose up, smelling strongly of sulphur and other unknown chemicals. It filled the air and wafted towards the lobby.

'I can barely see through this haze. Woah, this stinks. I now understand the source of your smelly glass skills.' Rup scrunched his nose. Then he took a deep breath and sprinted into the lobby, signalling at Afzal and Beena to follow.

His voice resembled Han Solo as he shouted, 'Fire, fire! This whole place is going up! I've got a bad feeling about this!'

Noticing the heavy smoke billowing towards the lobby, the nurse at the reception desk screamed and jumped out of her chair. 'Fire!' she cried out. 'Everyone, get out!'

The two people waiting in the lobby ran out the front door. The three soldiers, on the other hand, rushed towards the source of the fire.

Pushing the wheelchair and holding their noses, Afzal and Beena dashed past the incoming soldiers. Rup gestured towards the door, huffing.

'Path is clear. Let's go!'

They cut through the lobby, making a beeline for the exit. After a minute, they were well clear of the building. The three rushed to the parking lot. Afzal took out the decoy's keys and pressed the horn button. A marked green sedan, not far from them, chirped. Rup was impressed. 'No way! Last time we stole a drug dealer's Jeep, and now we have keys to a military vehicle?'

Afzal locked the brakes on the wheelchair and picked up the strapless bag. 'I need to grab the other knapsack from the Jeep. This one's no good anymore.'

Rup gave a sharp nod. 'You guys stay here. I'll grab Wicket and Rambo's bag with the phones.'

Beena winced. 'Why are we lugging that dog around with us? We've enough to deal with.'

'I can't leave her here alone. Besides, she's an excellent guard dog. Remember how she warned Afzal last night?'

Rup ran towards the Jeep while Afzal and Beena checked out their new ride. It was a fairly new and spacious sedan with a large boot. With difficulty, they manoeuvred the wheelchair to the rear of the car.

'Let's hope the boot is clean,' Afzal said. He opened it and found army uniforms inside a dry-cleaner's box. 'Shit. More boxes. What is it with boxes in cars on this trip?'

'Don't complain. We can use those,' Beena said. 'I still have this nurse's disguise on. If you and Rup are dressed as army men, driving a military car, it'll help us blend in.'

'Good point. You're taking on Rup's characteristics—all about them disguises.' Afzal took out the box and put it in the back seat.

Rup returned with the camoflage backpack and Wicket in tow, puffing hard. 'Got it.'

Without delay, they unhooked Latif from the wheelchair, trying to stay as inconspicuous as one could while loading a wanted terrorist wearing an old woman's wig into the boot of a car. Fortunately, the hospital complex and the area around the lobby was abuzz. They blended with the chaos of everyone responding to the mysterious smoke and smell of strong chemicals in the lobby.

The large boot helped. However, Wicket's sudden barking at the terrorist did not. Beena grimaced and scanned the surroundings. 'Hush, Wicket!'

Afzal and Rup turned their attention to the uniforms in the dry-cleaning box. Afzal said to Rup, 'Right then. Time to become military men.'

Rup pulled out one uniform; it seemed a bit small for him. The clothes Afzal pulled out were the same size as Rup's, but a bit large for him. And one military hat, which seemed to be a free size.

Afzal shrugged. 'They'll have to do.'

Standing on the other side of the sedan, the young men hurriedly changed.

As he removed his pants, Rup said, 'Bee, no peeking.'

She laughed and got in the car. 'Are you kidding me? That's your concern? Not the world's most-hated terrorist, drugged and knocked out in our boot?'

12

# Seeing Red

Qadir listened to the Bluetooth earpiece in his right ear. The voice on the other side was direct and crisp.

'Khan? Are you in Rawalpindi?'

'Not yet. But I'm close.'

'Did you see anything that might help us at the hospital?'

'Help where with what?'

'Rasheed Latif is missing. He might have escaped. A nurse found another man in his bed, drugged unconscious. We think it happened about an hour ago at the military hospital in Rawalpindi. How could you not know? They even set a chemical fire in the lobby to escape.'

'What? That's big news,' Qadir said. 'I just drove into Rawalpindi—I've been pursuing missing Indian teens from the Kartarpur temple. Besides, is Latif not in Adiala Jail?' He pressed his foot down on the accelerator and the car leaped forward.

'I thought so, but it seems he was at the hospital when he went missing. In any case, screw those teens. You need to investigate this. This is the only case that matters. You're the only senior ISI officer in the neighbourhood. The others are in Karachi for a training exercise.'

'Understood. Any initial hypothesis?'

'It must be those Indian RAW agents we previously got intel about. It's the only thing that makes sense. They've wanted to put Latif on trial in India for years now.'

Qadir frowned. 'You sure it wasn't one of Latif's accomplices? That prison is too relaxed; Latif could've easily arranged an escape. The ISI might be under the assumption that we have a mutual understanding—but these idiots always have an agenda of their own.'

'I don't think so. He was living the good life. If he's out there, the US bounty becomes attractive to many people. He's safer in prison and he knows it. We extract some work out of him as well. Everyone is happy when he's in custody. I feel it's an abduction.'

'I'm fifteen minutes away. I'll investigate.'

He dropped the call. 'What a mess! If this is true, and someone has kidnapped Latif, this will spin the brass into orbit. They'll be intolerable. And anyhow, it sounds like solving this Latif case might be better for my career than finding those stupid kids.'

Qadir drove straight to the hospital and walked right up to the front desk. Looking at his ID card, the nurse at the desk asked, 'ISI? Is there a problem here at the hospital?'

'Can you show me to the security office?'

She rose and led the way, instinctively knowing not to be curious about the who, when and why of the request. The less she knew, the better.

Qadir felt a sense of urgency, but none of this made sense. Trained agents would use the cover of night for something like this—not broad daylight. The facts didn't add up.

*Indian RAW agents couldn't possibly make it to Rawalpindi without us getting a whiff of it, let alone sneak into a military hospital and extract a patient in broad daylight. How had they known Latif would be in the hospital and not in prison?*

A few minutes later, Qadir stood in front of a door labelled *Hospital Security*. The nurse hurried off and Qadir knocked firmly on the door. No answer. He tried the doorknob; it turned easily and the door swung open. Shaking his head in disgust, he let himself in.

*Dumb, irresponsible shits—leaving the security room unlocked. And no one on duty here to monitor anything.*

The room was full of blinking electronic equipment. A massive television console dominated the wall, displaying twelve squares of black and white video streams. There were dozens of switches below the console. Qadir sat down at a computer and pulled up a few video files. Before he could view them, the voice in his ear came alive.

'Qadir! You there?'

'Yeah. What's up?'

'HQ has learned the identity of the decoy. You won't like it one bit. It's your boss they drugged and put in Latif's bed. RAW targeted a senior ISI officer to rub salt into our wounds.'

'What, my boss? How could that even have happened? And right under our noses. What was my boss doing here anyway?'

'He was there for minor arthroscopic surgery on his knee. This is a dead serious situation. Let us know what else you find.'

His earpiece went quiet. He went back to the list of videos and started with the corridor outside Latif's room. The quality was poor, but he could make out three operatives from the grainy images—two men and one nurse.

Then he tried the camera outside his boss's room. Again, the quality was poor, and Qadir muttered under his breath, 'Did they buy this security equipment second-hand?'

He squinted at the screen. 'That big guy seems familiar. But it can't be. Two guys and a girl? Hmm …'

He replayed the video multiple times, peering closely at each frame, watching them enter the room with his boss and exit with a wig-wearing Latif.

Thirty minutes later, he lifted the phone to his ear.

'HQ, any indications that Indian agents have crossed the border? Or activities in any Pakistani city with potential connections to RAW activity?'

'Not to our knowledge.'

'RAW agents make no sense then. But I've a theory. I've been watching the CCTV footage frame by frame. This might seem a bit crazy but hear me out. What if the kids that went missing from Kartarpur did this? One of the perps in the CCTV footage has a similar build and gait.'

There was a pause at the other end. A long pause.

Then the voice back at headquarters roared with laughter. After a moment, it said, 'That's preposterous. Three stupid teenagers could never pull off something like this. Latif would've gutted them himself.'

'It's a big coincidence, don't you think? A day after those kids go missing, we lose Latif?'

More laughter poured through the earpiece.

'Drop this stupid theory if you don't want to be demoted. How did they make it to Rawalpindi without being discovered? Have you even seen their photos? They're school kids.'

'You're right. Let me check the security cameras in the lobby. I'll let you know what I find.'

Qadir thought for a moment, then took out his phone. He punched speed dial and the phone was answered on the first ring.

'I've been expecting your call,' Qadir's former assistant replied.

'Yeah. Seems a lot of shit just hit the fan.'

'Tell me about it. The wires are going wild.'

'Buzzing wires is precisely why I'm calling. The security cameras in this hospital are like tits on a bull. Useless. What have you heard?'

'Everyone is scrambling around, but none of it makes sense.'

'Why was Latif in the hospital and not in prison? Have you heard anything about RAW being active in this?'

'Not specifically. Lots of people are sure it must be them, but nothing has been confirmed yet. Apparently, Latif was moved to the hospital that morning with a stomach issue.'

'Thanks. Keep your ear to the rail. Someone's bound to reveal something.'

The phone went dead. He put it away and muttered, 'Let's see what the lobby camera caught.'

He found the files and opened the first one, watching as an image sprang to life on one of the monitors. Pausing the video, he studied the image. Then, Qadir's jaw dropped and he banged the desk with one hand.

The three teens stared back at him from the screen—entering the hospital lobby.

'Holy shit! How did you kids get all the way up here to Rawalpindi and do this? I bet if this screen was in colour, that backpack would be red. Stupid black and white monitors. Hmm, let me try something.'

He paused and fiddled with the controls, isolated a video clip and saved it as a separate file. Then he attached the video file to an email and sent the message to himself. Taking his phone out, he played the video clip.

It displayed perfectly, in full colour.

'The red backpack!' Qadir said. He leaned back in the chair and muttered, 'What the heck am I going to do with this? No one in HQ is going to believe me.'

~

The store in New Delhi sold electronics, and they were the biggest in the city. Kids loved the huge flatscreens on display.

But today, every channel displayed the same thing: breaking news. The bombastic anchor was having the time of his life. He adjusted his glasses, waved his hands for emphasis and shouted, 'Three innocent Indian children are missing from the holy Sikh shrine in Kartarpur. Indian intelligence is sure that Pakistani agents kidnapped them. Pakistan denies this and insists they don't know where the kids are.'

The anchor paused for effect, staring at the viewers. 'And my question to our viewers tonight is this: do you believe that? I don't. This is a classic Pakistani manoeuvre. They have taken our children and I know they're being brainwashed to hate their homeland. The Pakistanis intend to send them back as ISI spies. It's an outrage.'

One of the young kids in the crowd asked, 'Where are the cartoons?'

An older woman hushed her. 'Quiet, sweetie. This is sad. We want to know what happened to the missing kids.'

The anchor's voice boomed from the numerous screens. 'This is an indignation that India cannot stand. We demand the return of our children now!'

# 13

# Up is Down, North is South

As Rup drove away from the hospital, the mood in the car was ecstatic. They'd caught the terrorist. Now all they had to do was bring him home.

Afzal sat in the passenger's seat, adjusting the stiff military clothing. 'The hard part is done—it's easier now. We drive southeast and we cross over the border near Sialkot in a few hours. Should be smooth sailing.'

Beena was occupying the back seat along with Wicket. 'Yes, yes. You've repeated that part of your plan a thousand times. Rup, put Sialkot into the navigation system.'

'Sounds good,' said Rup, fiddling with the phone. 'Funny. There are lots of places ending with "kot" in Pakistan. Sialkot, Samirkot, Balakot. "Kot" must be like "pur" in India—Rampur, Haripur, Palampur.'

'Enough with the geography lesson, buddy. Just put the destination in.'

'Alright, hold your horses.'

'That decoy plan was genius, Bee. That gives us extra time to escape. See, I told you we could do this. We'll be back in India before they even know Latif's missing.'

'I believe your exact words were "easy-peasy".'

Afzal grabbed his chest like someone had knifed it. 'Ouch, Bee. I know we had some hiccups, but you don't have to rub it in. We worked it out.'

She laughed. 'I don't know how. But yes, we did.'

Afzal turned to Rup. 'Just follow the map directions to Sialkot, alright?'

Mimicking Commander Jean-Luc Picard, Rup replied, 'Make it so,' and saluted.

Beena yawned. 'Rup, I don't know who that voice is, and I'm too tired to figure it out.'

'I do, and you're not missing anything.' Afzal looked at Rup. 'You watch way too much American television.'

'They have many wonderful shows and awesome actors to learn from.' Rup hummed the *Star Trek* theme.

'That lullaby is making me sleepy. And we haven't slept all night. Stop with the humming, will ya?'

'That's no lullaby. That's from *Star Trek: The Next Generation*—the best sci-fi show ever.'

'No wonder it's putting me to sleep,' said Beena with a wide yawn.

Afzal yawned too. 'Stop it, Bee. Your sleepiness is contagious. We can't afford to nap now. But if we're too tired to drive, maybe we should pull over for a bit?'

'Nope. Let's get to India as soon as possible,' Rup said. 'Why don't you two take a quick nap? You've been up all night, driving. I got sleep yesterday in the back. If you want, I can hum the music from *Star Wars* too.'

'I can't keep my eyes open. I hope I didn't ingest some of that black vial stuff when I was dosing Latif. Maybe a quick fifteen-minute nap,' said Beena.

'How about thirty minutes?' Afzal asked. 'Not a minute longer. When we wake up, we'll switch drivers, and you can catch some sleep, Rup.'

'Sure,' Rup said. 'I got this.'

~

Afzal's eyes opened when he felt the car bump over something. He stretched and lazily glanced outside. Then he jerked upright, fully awake.

'Shit! How long were we asleep? Rup, you were supposed to wake us up.'

'Yeah. But you guys were fast asleep, so I kept going. To get us home sooner.'

The conversation stirred Wicket, which roused Beena, who rubbed her eyes 'We there yet?'

'Nope, but we must be getting close. I've been driving a while.'

Beena looked outside. 'Wow, it's dark already? Thirty minutes sure goes by fast.'

'Try ninety instead,' snorted Afzal, looking at his watch. 'But thanks, Rup. I needed that snooze—I feel refreshed. We should stop a bit before the border. Make sure we have our documents and all that.'

'Sounds good. You know where we are now, Rup?'

The headlights hit a road sign and the lettering glittered like a diamond on black velvet. Rup read it aloud. 'Abbottabad. That's what it says.'

Afzal's face turned red, swivelling fast to look at the signpost. 'What? Abbottabad? That sign said Abbottabad?'

'Yeah,' replied Rup. 'Is that close?'

'No! Not even in the same universe! If that sign said Abbottabad, we're heading north. We were supposed to drive south out of Rawalpindi. Oh shit! What did you do, Rup?'

'I was following the navigation. See? It says we are on the right track.'

Beena groaned softly, her head in her palms, 'No, no, no. Don't tell me we were driving all this time in the wrong direction! Did you not put Sialkot in the navigation? Sleeping in moving vehicles is killing us—first the pickpocket in the bus and now this?'

Afzal snatched the phone and stared at it. 'Shit, shit,' he moaned. 'The navigation is set for Balakot, not Sialkot! With all the talk about "pur" and "kot", you input the wrong endpoint.'

Rup looked at them beseechingly and stammered, 'Shit. Sorry, guys. I'll turn back around, and we can get back on track.'

Beena was livid, but before she could say anything, something moved in the boot. Wicket went wild and barked, staring at the backrest of the rear seat.

Afzal laughed mirthlessly. 'Shit. When it rains, it pours. Our guest is up. We can't drive south at this point. We've to traverse double the distance and go through Rawalpindi again. That's a military HQ danger zone. If they've discovered the decoy, they'll be on high alert.'

Beena folded her arms and sulked—not saying a word.

~

Qadir returned to HQ from the hospital.

With a sense of urgency, he darted towards the ISI's version of a war room. He burst in. 'Anything new on Latif?'

The lone junior analyst shook his head. 'No. The training session has been cancelled. Everyone, and I mean everyone, is out turning over every rock to find something. Come to think of it, why are you here?'

'Because I think I know who is behind it. There's no evidence RAW is involved. However, I can't confirm until I've got more proof.'

'That's … weird. Well, you're alone in your hypothesis. Our dominant theory is that RAW is responsible. Some of the agents think it's the Americans, but that's a long shot.'

Qadir took his phone and played the surveillance footage again. 'I came here to give you this video. Three youngsters who entered the hospital right before the kidnapping. Can you identify them?'

'Is that who you think did it?'

'I'm not sure if they did it by themselves, but they're involved somehow.'

'We're short on manpower. It might take a while to get to your video.'

'This is urgent. Can you not prioritise this?'

The analyst was stubborn. 'I have many satellite images queued already. The borders are closing, and agents are manning every escape route, including the airports. They're fearful of an air extraction near the border. We have the army and air force involved, and most analysts are on eye-in-the-sky duty.'

'Shit! This little incident has turned us all on our heads. Up is down.'

'And sideways. But no matter; the country is on lockdown. This could embarrass us worse than the bin Laden incident. None of this is public news yet—Latif's kidnapping is a strictly internal military and ISI matter.'

Qadir pressed his lips together, turning the phone's screen to watch the video one more time. His mind raced.

*These three kids keep popping up. It must be them. But if I tell anyone without undeniable proof, or if I'm wrong, I'll be laughed out of my job.*

The analyst studied Qadir. 'You seem lost.'

'No. You're right. I need to be out in the field. I was figuring out where to start.' He turned and left, planning his next steps.

~

Tamir paid the mechanic. The wrench turner smiled. 'Thanks. You're lucky that I had the right radiator and hoses for this pickup. You could use new ignition wires too. I can have everything here tomorrow.'

'What? Tomorrow? Nah. I must get back on the road immediately.'

He took the keys from the mechanic and climbed into the driver's seat. *Smells like a stinking oil refinery.* He rolled down the window and took out his phone. The red dot on the map was still blinking—but it was stationary.

*Still in Rawalpindi? Hmm, military HQ. Those three kids must be military brats, thinking they can get away with anything. Including stealing my Jeep. Guess I'll have to teach them some harsh life lessons. I'll enjoy watching the assholes suffer, slowly and painfully, for putting me through this shit.*

He gritted his teeth and hit the accelerator.

After long hours of non-stop driving, Tamir pulled into Rawalpindi. He headed to where the tracker had located his Jeep—a military hospital.

'Good,' he muttered, looking at the building as he drove up the road. 'When I beat you up, the doctors can fix your broken bones.'

But upon arriving, he couldn't get inside. The entry gate was blocked. Fire trucks flashed their lights and firefighters were crawling around everywhere. The military presence, too, was overwhelming. Soldiers were posted at every one of the hospital's entrances, and a helicopter buzzed not far overhead.

Tamir stared. 'What the fuck happened here?'

# 14

## Sheep in Tiger's Clothing

The thumping and screaming in the boot got louder. Beena stared at the back as if she had X-ray vision. 'Your knockout formula is shit. It didn't keep him out very long.'

Afzal shrugged. 'A few hours. For a large tub of lard like him? That's not bad.'

He gazed out of the windshield, his eyes narrowed. 'Also, Latif being awake is not our biggest problem now, is it? This isn't a pleasant neighbourhood to be driving around with one of the world's most infamous terrorists in the boot.'

Beena snorted. 'Yeah, people here hero-worship him. Abbottabad is smack in the middle of what used to be Al-Qaeda country. The nap just might be the death of us.'

'It's Jund-e-Khasir, or JeK terrorist country now, so it's even worse than Al-Qaeda.'

The pounding from the boot continued.

Afzal exhaled. 'Let's stop. He's making a racket that even a deaf grandma across town could hear. We've to figure out what we're going to do, and we need to shut Latif up or we won't be able to think.'

'Agreed. We need to regain control,' said Beena. 'Rup, can you pull over there?'

Rup stopped on the side of the road, close to a dim streetlight. He turned off the engine and looked at them both.

'So, how do we do this? This isn't some random criminal. This is bloody Rasheed Latif, and he's pretty riled up back there. We must be super careful.'

Afzal grabbed a water bottle and the vial with the black cap. 'We'll offer him a drink of water. I'll doctor it, and while he thinks we're caring for him, he takes his nighty-night medicine.'

Beena glared at her two companions.

'I can't believe I'm travelling with two of the biggest dorks ever. You know Latif is right behind us and can hear us talking, right?'

'Shit!' Afzal glanced at the vial in his hand, then lowered his voice to a whisper. 'You got a better plan?'

'It's too late now to have a silent plan. Let's try yours first. If he doesn't drink, then we improvise.'

The night was silent except for the sound of an occasional vehicle whizzing by. The streetlamp cast its feeble light onto the back of the car. The trio and Wicket piled out and headed for the rear.

'Be careful. This is a dangerous terrorist,' whispered Afzal. 'A tiger caught by the tail. If he does anything, shut the boot immediately.'

Rup held the car keys in his palms and paused, steeling himself before approaching the boot. Impatient with the delay, Beena snatched the keys from him, inserted it—and in one swift move, popped open the lid.

The beam from the streetlamp streamed down on the man inside the boot. He blinked several times and squinted at the three teens with bloodshot eyes. He was sweaty and dishevelled; his face was swollen and the ill-fitting wig had slid to the side of his head.

The world's most-hated terrorist—in the flesh.

Beena instinctively took half a step back as the other two moved forward, forming a loose arc around the car's boot. Wicket joined them, gliding between Rup's legs and staring inside.

Latif's mouth opened and he started to speak. A thin, whiny voice gurgled out.

'Please, don't hurt me. Don't kill me … please! I can make you rich. I'll give you whatever you want.'

The teens were taken aback—their eyebrows rising as they glanced at one another. Not the first response they expected from the world's most dangerous terrorist. Threats to life and limb, pain and torture, maybe—but not a snivelling mess. And certainly not this pitiful specimen.

While they digested the sight before them, the first response was from Wicket—a low growl. Rup stared at the whimpering man and then glanced at Afzal.

'Is this pathetic man really Latif?'

Afzal nodded vigorously. 'Yeah. The very same guy parading in the jail suite in his fluorescent string undies. When the going gets tough, I guess the cowards reveal themselves. Latif's no tiger, only a scaredy cat.'

Beena grabbed the water bottle from Afzal.

'We stopped to give you a drink. To keep you alive.'

'No! Please! I wanna go home.'

Rup's jaw hung open. 'I ask again, did we capture the right guy? Or did we snatch the decoy instead?'

'As pitiful as he seems, that's Latif. The man with the small, limp dick.'

Latif peeked at Afzal, his bleary eyes lighting up with recognition. 'You? You know me. I can make you rich—and get you whatever you want.'

Beena studied the bound, quivering man. 'We don't want anything. Now, drink water like a good boy.'

Latif studied the water bottle. 'I heard you talking …'

Beena glared at Afzal. 'I told you.'

Rup grabbed the water bottle and shoved it in Latif's face. 'Open your mouth, scumbag.'

'I don't want to die. I can tell you things. Secrets. About the attack in Mumbai that nobody knows. Our plans in Kashmir. Or how I alerted American intelligence about bin Laden. They paid me a lot of money for that. I have a brand-new Range Rover. You can take it. Anything. Please don't hurt me.'

Beena folded her arms. 'This is simple. We won't hurt you if you drink. But we promise nothing if you refuse. In fact, Wicket doesn't like you, so maybe we can test whether she likes to bite. She's hungry.'

'Please no more drugs.'

Afzal grabbed the coward's hospital gown. 'Drink!'

Latif was sobbing now. 'Please! I don't feel good. My feet are swelling up.'

'I've had enough.' Beena darted back into the car, then re-emerged with a strip of cloth she'd ripped off the bottom of a uniform shirt. 'Rup, hold him down.'

The man in the boot wriggled, his eyes bulging with fear. Rup reached in and clasped his head tight. Once Rup had him stationary, she gagged their prisoner's mouth with it. She stood back to admire her work.

'Plan B. Done.'

Rup scanned the surroundings. 'So, what do we do now? Do we drive back down south like our original plan?'

Afzal walked a few paces from the car, surveying the horizon. 'I don't know. We didn't study the maps around here. Never in a million years did I think we'd end up north of Rawalpindi.'

'I'm sorry about driving in the wrong direction. This is all my fault.'

'Nothing we can do about that now,' huffed Beena. 'We'll figure it out. We must.'

Afzal nodded, his face grim. 'We gotta rethink our strategy and keep a clear head. Like Bee said, we can't argue about stuff because that's when things fall apart. But first things first. We can't hang around here.'

'Yeah, let's get off this street and find a place to regroup.'

Wicket rubbed her body against a morose Rup's legs, her tail wagging, trying to cheer him up. Rup patted her on the head. 'Well, the dog's happy that Latif's quiet. That's progress, even if it's small.'

Beena examined their surroundings. 'Maybe there's a silver lining to this mess. No one would expect us to drive north, so all the intel and fortification will be concentrated near the southern borders.'

Afzal nodded—and then shook his head in disbelief. 'Abbottabad. We're in fucking Abbottabad. This is fucked up. I had it all planned to cross over to Jammu through Sialkot. But now?'

'We found an alternate plan to silence the asshole in the boot. We can figure one out for getting back to India from here. Once we find a place to settle and reorganise, we can use Rambo's phone to check the maps. One step at a time.'

Rup pointed at some dark buildings. 'What if we check that place out? It looks dark and deserted.'

'Agreed, but I'm driving. I don't want to end up in Siberia next,' said Afzal grumpily.

Beena started back for the car. 'Come on. We can't camp out here. We've got work to do.'

# 15

## Raising the Dead

Beena stuck her head out the window to study the night sky. 'I can hear it, but I can't see it … wait. There it is. There's a helicopter. I can see its lights.'

'Shit. I bet they're looking for Latif. And for us.'

Afzal switched the radio on, changing channels. 'Nothing on the news about Latif. You think the decoy is still doing his job?'

Beena pulled her head back inside the car. She pointed to a grey box on top of the dashboard. 'Try the military radio. Could be they're not making this news public yet.'

Afzal leaned over and the device crackled to life. Official ISI and military messages were going back and forth, some in Urdu and some in English. Afzal listened, his expression turning to shock.

He turned to the others. 'They're talking about someone called Russel being kidnapped. Everything on the military band is about the search for Russel. Shit! It must be him. Maybe a code name?'

'Russel? What else are they talking about?' asked Rup.

'The airports are being monitored and they're setting up roadblocks. The country is on lockdown. And the borders down south have extra security.'

'Russel?' Beena mused. 'You mean R-S-L? As in short for Rasheed Saeed Latif. Interesting code name. They don't want the actual situation to be known.'

'Ha! That must be it. R-S-L. You're a genius, Bee!'

Rup sniggered from the back seat, staring out at the neighbourhood. 'He's the opposite of what we expected, so it should be L-S-R, not Russel.'

Beena turned around and gave him the death stare and Afzal quickly changed the topic. 'Good call, Bee, on the military radio. I'm glad we picked up a military vehicle. We'd have been running blind without this.'

Rup was peering into the darkness. He pointed to a large house. 'That's the place I saw. It looks abandoned and has high walls around it for privacy.'

Beena inspected the building, her eyes narrowing. 'Looks like a haunted mansion. Maybe they're trying to keep something in, not strangers out. Did you think of that?'

'I don't think so. The gate is open and busted up and the wall is crumbling in spots.'

'We've got no choice—it's too hot for us to be on the road right now.' Afzal slowed the car, scrutinising the structure. 'Rup, you're right. It might make a good place to hide as long as no one's there.'

He cautiously pulled the car into the deserted-looking property. The rear wall was missing and there seemed to be open space beyond. There were no other vehicles in the compound. Afzal turned the engine off and got out. Beena and Rup followed.

Afzal surveyed their surroundings to check for cameras or other people in the compound. He gestured at the boot. 'Bee, you stay here with him. Wicket will warn you if anyone approaches. Rup and I'll inspect the inside.'

She frowned. 'Why can't I go?'

'Sure, if that's what you want. I'll stay here with Wicket and you two can check the house out.'

'I thought you'd be more insistent on making me stay with the car.'

'Why? There's no safe place in a district like this. It's just as dangerous outside.'

'Hmm … I hate it when you're right.'

She spun on her heel and left, following Rup.

The wide doors at the entryway to the building were fragments. They looked as if they'd been blown off, leaving a gaping hole. The interior was dusty and full of shadows. Beena and Rup crept inside, warily checking the rooms.

Uneasy, Afzal leaned on the car and scanned the building. Most of the windows were broken. The walls were punctured with bullet holes, and one large opening with blackened edges that attested to some sort of fire.

After a few minutes, Beena and Rup hurried back out. Rup's eyes were wide, and he was panting. 'The place is a mess, but it's empty.'

Beena chuckled and bumped Rup with her elbow. 'I'm surprised you think it's a mess. It's a clone of your dorm room. And better than your apartment.'

'Why does everyone think they're a comedian?' Rup looked at them and paused, expecting an answer.

Afzal smiled. 'It's a defense mechanism. When people are scared, they tell bad jokes to take the edge off.'

'Well, based on the quality of your jokes, you must be scared as shit.'

Beena grinned. 'Let's go. We can't stand out here clowning around.'

Afzal gestured at the boot. 'We can't leave him here. He will bang on the lid again.'

'Let's take him in. We'll keep his cuffs on.'

Afzal and Rup dragged Latif out of the boot. They double-checked his handcuffs, removed the restraints on his legs and pushed him along. His eyes were burning red and looked sore and dry. The whites had gone yellowish. And the stink was formidable—putrid.

Rup wrinkled his nose and groaned, 'This bastard is smelly. How do we know the hospital cleaned his behind after his thunder and downpour?'

Afzal glared at Rup and swore under his breath. Beena chuckled and opened the car door to let Wicket out. The dog wagged her tail till she spotted Latif, at which point she let out a low growl.

'She doesn't like Latif at all,' said Beena, chuckling. 'This dog has more sense than half of this country.'

With effort, they got the bulky terrorist into a big room on the ground floor, dropped him in a corner with a thud and bound his feet again. Latif made odd noises that were doubtless more muffled pleas for mercy.

'Now what?' Rup eyes flitted around the dusty room. 'This place gives me the heebie-jeebies.'

'At least we're out of sight.' Beena's voice was more determined than fearful. 'Let's check the map first.'

Afzal pulled out the burner phone and opened a navigation app. Beena peered over his shoulder.

'We can still consider our original plan: head south through Sialkot and cross over near Jammu although it'll be riskier now, based on the military channel's chatter.'

'That's a long drive through high security blockades. Why not head straight for the border to our west?'

'It'll be as hard within JeK territory.' Afzal zoomed in to study the area to the west of them. 'I don't know much about these towns.'

He turned on the phone's flashlight and shined it around the room. 'Maybe we'll find something here to help us.'

'Like what? This busted building has nothing of value from what I see.'

Rup pulled out his phone and turned on the flashlight. The walls were peeling, cobwebs lined the ceilings, trapping dust and flies. There was a wall cabinet with its doors busted. But nothing of value was hidden inside.

So, they moved to the next room. Again, nothing.

After checking the ground floor, they climbed to the first floor, taking Latif with them, and came to a bedroom with a dusty, damaged bed against a wall. As they sat Latif down on the bed, it shifted and slid noisily across the floor.

'That's a weird noise from such a solid looking floor,' said Beena, bending down and peeking under the bed. After feeling around for a few minutes, she found loose floorboards.

'Whoa, this must have caused the noise. What have we here?'

Afzal and Rup held the flashlights while Beena lifted the boards exposing a small hidden opening. She reached in and pulled out old, tattered papers.

'Looks like Urdu or Arabic. Here, Afzal, see if you can make any sense of it.'

Afzal's eyes bulged as he leafed through the pages.

'Holy shit! This sounds like correspondence between Osama bin Laden and the Pakistani military! It seems like they knew bin Laden was in Abbottabad. Let me translate, listen to this: 'Americans suspect you're in Pakistan. Counterintelligence launched. Your location is secure for now.' I can't believe this. This looks like a Pakistani colonel telling Al-Qaeda to keep up the terrorist attacks. This is a bombshell discovery—if it's real.'

Beena jumped up and scanned the bedroom. 'Hold on. Guys, when we pulled in, I had a weird sense of déjà vu. Now I know why. We've seen this place many times on TV. I think this is Osama bin Laden's old compound. In Abbottabad.' She spread out her hands. 'Right here, in this room, is where Osama was likely killed by Seal Team Six.'

The air in Afzal's lungs emptied as if he'd been punched in the stomach. He whirled around.

'Shit! You're right. I saw bullet holes and signs of a fire. Probably an RPG.'

Rup started pacing. 'I drove us to Abbottabad by mistake— and of the thousands of buildings, we manage to find Osama bin Laden's old hiding spot.[1] Are we cursed?'

'We're fucked!' Afzal moved to the window to see if anyone was about.

Beena was back on her knees, crouching next to the hole in the floor. 'Calm down, bin Laden is dead and there's no one around. Shine your lights over here. I can feel another small box.'

She lifted out what seemed like an old tiffin box and dusted it off before opening the lid.

'Holy shit!'

'What?'

---

1 I know. I know. Don't get all excited. The author knows that this building has already been razed to the ground. But for the purposes of this story, just hang with me, alright?

Beena pulled out a handful of money. 'A secret stash of cash! A couple bundles of dollars, a few Euros and Pakistani rupees.'

Afzal collected the bundle from Beena. 'Woah! Hmm … not sure what we can do with the dollars, but the Pakistani rupees are a godsend. Buying petrol and food will be a lot easier.' He pointed at the hole. 'Is that it? Anything more?'

Beena felt inside the cubbyhole and shook her head. Afzal stuffed the cash into the backpack. As they pulled the wooden slats back on top of the hole, Wicket turned towards the dark and let out a low warning growl.

From the shadows, a raspy voice came as though in response to Wicket. 'What are three kids doing in a dangerous place like this?'

The two boys turned to shine a light on the voice. A tall, thin bearded man of about sixty stood near the doorway. His head was wrapped in a dark turban and he was wearing loose, dusty clothes.

The three teens and their prisoner stiffened, as if they'd seen a ghost. Beena, pale as a sheet, managed to stammer a few words, 'No way! How?'

The trio huddled closer to each other. Wicket slinked to Rup, growling. At that moment, they heard a thud. The teens followed the stranger's eyes towards the noise. Latif had passed out and toppled face first to the floor.

Beena's throat felt parched. She swallowed hard. 'You're supposed to be dead.'

'Ah, that. I'm not dead, I assure you.' The tall man smiled. 'And I'm not who you think I am. I'm not Osama bin Laden.'

The three looked at one another—and then back at the man in front of them. Rup found his voice. 'You could've fooled us. You look exactly like him.'

'Well, I'm supposed to. They forced me to undergo plastic surgery to look like him. And we were a rare commodity, since you can't find many thin, six-foot-four Afghans.'

Beena scrutinised him. 'You mean like a body double?'

'Yes, that's right. My name is Farouk. Perhaps you can tell me why three kids dressed in ill-fitting nurse and army uniforms, with a prisoner in tow, ended up in Osama's old house in the middle of the night?'

'Wow, a body double. They did a good job, don't you think?'

'Shh, Rup. This is not your stage.'

'But wait, if we looked off, why haven't you alerted anyone?' asked Afzal.

Farouk grimaced. 'I've no interest in helping the government, the Al-Qaeda or JeK terrorists. They took my family hostage and forced me to change my face. Then, whenever it was dangerous for their dear leader or they wanted to mislead folks about the whereabouts of bin Laden, they rolled me out. If a bomb went off, a drone found me or bullets were fired, I was the one supposed to die.'

'What? Was bin Laden not all about suicide bombings and sacrificing for the cause?'

'Bah! He didn't even believe half of it; it's a myth that he was willing to sacrifice himself to reach Allah, though he would have happily sacrificed everyone else. If he'd had a whiff about the air raid by the Americans, I would've been the decoy in this room—and dead. After bin Laden was killed, his gundas murdered my family. Now I have nothing and no place to go, and spend my days tending to goats out there in the fields to make a living. I have only contempt for these terrorists.'

Beena's heart broke for him. 'I'm sorry about your family.'

'Thank you,' said the man. After a pause, he asked, 'So, who is the handcuffed man?'

Rup shrugged. 'See for yourself.' He bent and lifted the head of the unconscious Latif.

Farouk returned the shrug. 'Don't know him.'

'What?' Beena squinted at Latif. 'Is it me, or does he look different?'

Afzal scratched his cheek. 'Hmm. His face is puffy and his eyes are slits. Seems like the combination of both white and black vials did a number on him.' Then, he looked at the man. 'You said you noticed our ill-fitting uniforms. Do you have any other clothes we can change into?'

'Yes, follow me.' He led them into the smaller room and pulled back a piece of canvas, exposing a heap of clothes on the floor.

'Great! Thank you for your help.' Afzal reached into the backpack and fished out all the foreign money along with some of the Pakistani cash. 'Please take this. It's the least we can do.'

Farouk shied away and put his hands up. 'I can't take your money.'

'We found this under the bed—it is yours more than it is ours. Please accept it as a sign of our gratitude,' insisted Beena. She grabbed the stack from Afzal and pressed it into Farouk's hands. The man examined the bundle of money in his palms. His eyes welled up and he whispered, 'Thank you.'

'No, thank *you*. Just don't tell anyone we're here.'

Farouk studied the trio. 'You kids have guts—I respect that. And don't worry, I'll say nothing. With this money, I should be able to make a better life. I will not forget your help.'

'Before you go, can you tell us the best way to the Indian border?'

'The border crossings are a bit far from here. And JeK terrorists have a stranglehold in this district.'

'How about the crossing near Chakoti?' asked Beena.

'Ah, that's a tough one. That's a JeK stronghold. Rough, narrow mountain roads to even get to Chakoti and lots of guards at the border. Over half a dozen for each shift, and it's a narrow bridge. But … hmm …'

'Half a dozen guards?' Rup gulped. 'With AK-47 rifles as well, I'm sure. We're doomed.'

'Hold on, Rup. Farouk, what? Is there something about Chakoti that can help us?' Afzal asked.

'I'm not sure if it helps, because the Chakoti border is still dangerous. But I know they change the guards at the bridge at 10.45 a.m., 6.45 p.m. and 2.45 a.m. The evening and overnight guards are tough and well-trained because that's when they must be most vigilant. But the cushy job is the 10.45 morning shift. This is the easy going, privileged group; ill-trained and often late getting into position. If you were trying to cross, try around 10.45 a.m., right around the change of guard and maybe there's an opportunity.'

Afzal nodded and shook Farouk's hand. 'This is valuable. Thank you. Khuda hafiz.'

The old body double bowed his head. 'Khuda hafiz. I wish you good luck.'

He smiled and disappeared into the shadows.

~

After the commotion and blockades settled a bit, Tamir did a little recon at the hospital parking lot at Rawalpindi. It wasn't long before he found his Jeep—all smashed up.

'Fuck!' he screamed, and kicked the Jeep.

He jumped in and examined it. His boxes were still there. So was his gun. The three teens had left behind an empty red backpack, but his was missing. His journal was missing too.

After a few moments, he gathered his thoughts.

*You kept my burners and my journal. Hmm … maybe you realised the true worth of the journal and left the drugs behind. Shit! I should've tracked my phones, not the Jeep.*

He pulled out his phone and opened another tracking app. He scrolled through the menus, muttering, 'Where are the phones now?' It took a few seconds, but the app finally displayed a map with a green 'X' on it.

'There you are.' Then he zoomed out and his eyes almost popped out of his head. 'Are you fucking kidding me? Abbottabad? Who are these kids and what are they doing in JeK country?'

He paced for a minute, then took the boxes of drugs and loaded them into the stolen pickup. He gazed with a puzzled expression at the gun. Then he pounded the hood. His theory about military brats seemed wrong now. This was something much deeper.

*Were they nerds hired by competitors, trying to break the code in the journal?*

He banged the front of the pickup. It didn't matter. They were as good as dead when he found them and that was that.

Tamir climbed into the pickup. Abbottabad was a bit of a drive, but he intended to floor it all the way. He wouldn't even stop to take a piss.

~

Qadir paced the length of Commander Imran's office. He was now sure the kids were behind the kidnapping. But he couldn't prove that to Imran's satisfaction who was in charge while his own commander was recovering in the hospital.

Imran tapped his foot impatiently. 'Qadir. You must stop fixating on this. My nephew suspects that terrorists have kidnapped the kids from the gurudwara to trade for prisoners being held in India. He believes they'll make their demands soon. It's only a matter of time. The teens have no link to Latif, but we can use this situation as a form of leverage with the Indian government.'

Qadir shook his head. 'Sir, I'm positive the kids kidnapped Latif, not the other way around. You saw the trio on the security video from the hospital.'

'That hazy video doesn't mean anything. You can't prove these are the same kids—the big guy in the video doesn't even have a turban. And the girl is wearing a hijab. Given the heightened activity we picked up, we're sure RAW agents have nabbed Latif.'

'But this seems like too much of a coincidence. Three Indian teens missing inside Pakistan and Latif is now kidnapped?'

The commander swung around his desk, strode forward and stopped right in front of Qadir—close enough for him to smell the man's aftershave.

'You're not hearing me, Qadir. Let me be crystal clear. Don't you dare fuck up my nephew's investigation.' Imran pointed at the office door. 'Forget Latif. Your role is to find those kids as soon as possible. No, make that faster than "as-soon-as-possible". Got it? You keep my nephew informed of every little thing—especially if the kids do somehow have Latif. He oversees the Latif case. Not you. Is that clear?'

'Yes, sir.'

Qadir turned on his heel and started for the door. Imran bellowed behind him, 'Find those kids. That's an order. Wrap it up, fast.'

Qadir tipped his head to acknowledge the order, then returned to his office.

# 16

# Revenge Fantasy

Latif wouldn't stop moaning. The squirming and muffled whining was getting on their nerves.

Beena jerked her head towards Latif. 'Guys, we need to plan our next steps in private. Can we plug his ears?'

'Forget about him listening to us—I can't listen to his whining anymore. Let's shift him to the next room. Two birds, one stone,' replied Rup.

The boys dragged Latif to the adjacent room, tied his legs, checked his cuffs and left him there. Then the three sat on the floor around a makeshift table, which was an upside-down wooden crate.

Afzal continued fidgeting and watching the doorway. Rup raised his eyebrows at him. 'His feet are tied and his hands are cuffed. Where's he going? C'mon, we need to plan the border crossing.'

'Let me check on him once more. You guys start, I'll be right back.'

'You alright?' asked Beena, concerned.

'Yeah, I'm fine. I just don't want anything else to go wrong.'

Afzal cautiously entered the room holding Latif. The prisoner was squirming. He stopped as the teen walked over. The muffled whimpering increased in volume. Afzal walked over, knelt and pulled the gag out of Latif's mouth.

'I want to ask you something.'

The prisoner moaned, 'What do you want to know? I'll tell you everything. Please let me go. I'll pay you—as much as you want. Just tell me … give me a number.'

Afzal stared at him for a moment. 'Why do you do it?'

'Do what?'

'You know. Terrorism. Delhi, Mumbai, Kashmir, the children's hospital.'

Latif paused, examining Afzal, assessing him. 'It's my job.' He said it as though it was the most natural thing, the most obvious.

Afzal blinked at the prisoner. 'That's not something you fill out an application for. Most would assume you were sending a message, or that you enjoy seeing people suffer.'

'That's not all. It's hard to explain—there are many parts to it.'

'Try me. What you did was unthinkable, so I'm trying to understand why you did it. We're taking you to face justice in India, but I'm starting to realise that some people may not see it the same way I do.'

Latif suddenly came to life his eyes wild and face straining.

He chortled, 'Take me to India? You kids are Indians? Is that why you kidnapped me? You and your stupid friends will be dead within a day. The army and the JeK are searching for you. You're already dead but you don't know it yet.'

Latif's bluster was returning.

'Maybe. But you're not going to survive either. Imagine the shame of being kidnapped by a bunch of kids from India.'

Latif ignored Afzal. 'And if you're not dead, I'll trade you to release good friends from Indian prisons. I have a dozen top-level JeK commanders there. Once they're home free, I'll take brutal revenge. You and your families will get extra special treatment.'

'We'll see. Look at your pathetic self. I'm not exactly quivering with fear.'

Although Afzal was matching Latif's bluster with his own, his blood had run cold listening to threats from a man who had murdered so many without remorse.

Latif studied Afzal's expressionless face. He paused and, changing tactics, went back to moaning.

'Can you please untie me? Or loosen my feet? This swelling is getting worse.'

'I know. Your face looks like a bloated seal.'

'Help me then.'

'Why did you kill so many innocents in Mumbai?'

There was a pause as Latif collected his thoughts. 'Power. Influence. I was born to lead, and I like the prestige. It's a business, like everything else.'

'That's the first honest thing you've said,' Afzal said. 'But why kill innocents? For a business, you could start a construction company and get money and influence.'

'Construction? What's the fun in that? Every time one of my guys walks into a businessman's office, they wet themselves, afraid of what I can do to them and their family. They scramble over the table to gift me money. That's power. Money isn't the objective. Power is, and power only comes from fear. Islam is a great tool for me to create fear and gain power. You can do whatever you want if you have both.'

'And you don't care about the lives you destroy? How about the young men or children you've brainwashed to commit these horrible crimes?'

'Why should I care about the ants I step on? They're insignificant. You let me go and I'll show you what power can do. I can get you whatever you want, make you whoever you want to become.'

That thought sent a swift shudder through Afzal's veins. But he kept up his bluster.

'Yeah, right. When you were out of your element, you exposed your true self. Your only power is being a cowardly, snivelling slob.'

Latif didn't respond. He observed Afzal, as if sizing him up. 'You look familiar. I have seen you before.'

'What?'

'You look like someone who used to work for me in Kashmir, to recruit naïve youngsters and do other stuff I can't talk about.'

'What a vague statement. Interesting ploy, trying to create a connection as if you know me. You don't, and this game won't get you anywhere. We're taking you across the border to India. You will pay for your crimes.'

'The road is still long. You three will be strung up within a day, I promise you that.'

'Silly, empty threats. We saw how scared you were when we opened the boot of the car. We should've taken a video to share on social media, but I'm sure we'll have more opportunities to broadcast your cowardly nature.'

Latif was quiet again. His shoulders slumped; he jangled his handcuffed wrists.

'Let me go and I'll make it worth your while. What do you want? Money? Fame? A big job? Women?' He added slyly, 'Boys?'

'You don't have anything I need. What I want is friendship. Trust. Respect. A future of my own making. A life worth living.

That's what I want. And I already have those. You can't give me anything.'

Latif looked up, repulsed. 'Friendship? Trust? With those kafirs in the next room? Never happens. They're meant to be your slaves. And respect? I'm more respected than you'll ever know.'

Afzal stood up.

'For all your talk of power, you're weak. You will have to be reborn a thousand times to be deserving of friends like the ones I'm fortunate to have. And, no, you don't have respect. People might fear you, but no one respects you.'

He shoved the gag back into the squirming Latif's mouth. Then he turned and left.

~

Afzal settled back down on the floor at the makeshift table, a faint smile on his face. Beena shot him a look. 'Why are you smiling? What did you do back there?'

'We talked. That's all. It was a good talk.'

She let out an explosive snort. 'You had a good talk with Latif?'

'I didn't say I liked what he said. I just learned a few things.'

Rup leaned forward, close to Afzal's face, studying his eyes. 'No, you're happy about something too. Spill it, buddy.'

'Well, okay. I know it's hooey, but I never realised how much of a chip I carried on my shoulder. I let one bully convince me I wasn't worth as much as others, and it took another power-hungry one like Latif to shake me out of it. My worth is my intent and what I contribute to life. What any idiot thinks about me is not important. What's important is what I think, and what the people who care about me think.'

'No shit, Sherlock. We could have told you that. In fact, we told you this exact thing and it did not penetrate your thick, stubborn skull. We could have been spared this idiotic trip,' said Beena.

'You should skip chemistry and try philosophy, Afzal. This is deep stuff,' Rup added.

'Ha! Parv will probably not believe us, even if we get back home with this terrorist,' said Afzal.

'It doesn't matter. Parv still has to shave his head. I'll see that he does—under the big tree and in front of the entire school,' said Rup, rubbing his hands together.

'Don't plan the shaving kit yet. The crucial question right now is—how do we get home?' Beena hovered over the map.

Rup was staring into his phone, his fingers tapping away.

'Which maps are you checking Rup?'

Rup lifted his head. 'Not maps. I'm messaging my drama club buddies.'

'What the fuck? You're sending messages to your stupid friends in India? Are you kidding me?' Bee was furious.

'I thought the gang would get a kick out of seeing the bin Laden home. And they did.' Rup held the phone out.

'Are you nuts? Don't you know that the ISI can track your phone and those messages? And pinpoint where we are? Stop that!'

Rup looked like he'd been caught red-handed by his teacher.

'Hopefully, no one is tracking us yet,' Afzal laughed. 'Classic Rup. Well, what's done is done. Shut it down, buddy.'

'Okay, okay, I got it. No need to rub it in.' Rup looked over at the map, trying to change the subject. 'Let's check out that mountain road again. Looks curvy and dangerous.'

They pored over the map, making plans and taking notes. A few hours into it, they were ready to call it a night.

Suddenly, Wicket's ears pricked up.

Rup was immediately alert. 'What's up, girl? Is someone coming?'

'If Wicket is anxious, something must be off.'

Rup stood up and walked out the door with Wicket on his heels. A few short seconds later, Afzal and Beena heard him shout.

'Latif's gone!'

They rushed into the adjacent room and saw nothing but torn hospital tape.

Afzal stared at the tattered tape. 'Shit! I saw him squirming. I thought he was uncomfortable with all the swelling from the drugs.'

'Well, he squirmed his fat feet free.'

Rup scanned the room. 'I don't see cuffs here. He must still have them on.'

'He can't get far with swollen feet and in cuffs. Let's get the bastard.' Afzal started for the door.

Beena stared at Afzal without moving.

'Let's think about this first.'

Afzal hissed, 'He's getting away. Every minute we wait, the chances of us getting Latif back to India go down.'

Beena's voice wavered. 'Haven't we done enough? You just said that you don't care what Parv thinks anymore. Finding that bastard will be hard, and every minute we waste, we're in deeper shit. It's time to focus on getting home.'

'Bee has a good point. Everyone is looking for us. You saw the chopper flying around out there.'

Afzal shook his head. 'If they catch us without Latif, we lose our only bargaining chip. You overheard them talking about pressurising India. On top of that, Latif just threatened me that he would barter us for hardened terrorists jailed in India. Imagine the innocent lives they would destroy. And no way would he fail to personally come after us and our families—'

Beena clenched a fist. 'We'll figure it out. Forget about that bastard. We must get home.'

'How about all the other people killed by this bastard in Mumbai, Delhi, Kashmir? We've come further than anyone in capturing him. We must finish this. Why are you being a coward?'

Beena's face reddened. 'Excuse me? Did you call me a coward? After all I've done, following your outlandish plan and risking all our lives?'

Afzal started to say something but Beena continued, her eyes flashing. 'You don't listen to reason and you call *me* a coward. And you, Rup, messaging your stupid friends and risking our lives. You know what? You two idiots do what you want. In fact, you've been doing that all along anyway. I'm so pissed right now, I can't think straight. I need some air to clear my head.' She stormed out. Rup blinked rapidly

'Did she leave?'

Afzal snorted. 'Very perceptive.'

'We have to go get her. It's dangerous out there.'

'We must find Latif, or we lose our only leverage if this mess gets any worse. Bee will calm down and come back.'

'She's right, you know. She was only trying to tell you that you're obsessed with Parv. And with Latif. It's stopping you from realising the danger we're facing.'

'The only obsession I have is about our safety—if we don't recapture Latif, we're gonna be in a lot more danger.'

'Bee is tougher than you and I put together, but we can't climb out of this mess unless we stick together. She needs to know we have her back. If Bee decides we leave without Latif, that's what we do.'

Afzal hung his head. 'Okay, do what you must. It's the right thing for you to be with her. But I must find Latif while the trail is fresh. If we split up, we can do both.'

Rup's face hardened. 'What? No. Afzal, come with me. Bee should be our first priority.'

'She is. And so are you. Honest. But none of us will live for long if we don't get Latif back. It's best if we split up and meet back here.'

'I don't agree at all. But okay, good luck.' Rup turned and ducked out of the door, followed by Wicket. Afzal stood alone in Osama bin Laden's dark war-torn compound, with nothing but a phone for light, its battery running low.

~

*ISI leadership is filled with smart men doing stupid things.*

It wasn't the first time this thought had raced through Qadir's mind. He sighed and checked his phone. Nothing yet.

He felt tired and passionless. Tea would help. It always did. Qadir walked over to the side cabinet and switched on the electric kettle. He stood there thinking, waiting for the water to heat up.

*The kid in the hospital didn't have a turban. Are my eyes playing tricks? Or are these not the same kids?*

When the whistle blew, he poured the hot water over a tea bag and let it steep, leaning back in his chair.

His phone vibrated. It was the security footage from the Kartarpur temple. Hurriedly, he placed the tea down and opened the file. The video was a bit fuzzy, but he found a good frame and zoomed in.

'Fuck me. It's really them.' Springing up from the chair, he paced his office room. 'I knew it! But Imran is blind and won't see this as proof. He's only concerned about his nephew's career.'

He walked back and forth, staring at the images on his screen. 'Find those kids. That's my order, that's what I'll do.' Then he smiled. 'Plus, I get to prove Imran and his stupid nephew wrong.'

Then he sighed. If they were RAW agents, using the Kartarpur corridor to cross the border was maybe an easier way to infiltrate Pakistan.

These teens weren't the garden-variety, videogame-playing, time-wasting morons representative of today's young generation. Perhaps they *were* RAW agents, trained and dressed to act like normal teens.

In the back of his mind, Qadir was sure the teens would want to get back to India as soon as possible. But another part of him feared the worst, because no border had reported any unusual activity. After rummaging, he unfolded a large, detailed map of Pakistan and spread it out on his desk.

He spoke out loud, tracing his fingers across the paper. 'Let's see. The nearest Indian border from here would be Sialkot, southwest of Rawalpindi. But why has there been no activity there? Or on any of the roads to Sialkot?'

He paused for a moment and smacked the table.

'Wait, the better question is where *has* there been unusual activity? These are smart kids. We must find the activity to find them.'

Qadir jumped back onto his computer. His machine couldn't keep up with his furious requests for information. With renewed energy, Qadir scrolled through screens of information, reading internal ISI wires for any unusual reports over the last two days.

He read through them.

*Jeep drove through poppy fields and smashed through a barn near Kharian. Helicopter pilot ejected in Chakwal; helicopter crashed due to unknown issues. Fishing boat capsized outside Karachi harbour. Abandoned Jeep near the Rawalpindi military hospital, signs of drugs inside, bullet holes in the windshield. JeK claims responsibility for children's hospital attack—*

Qadir stood up straight, eyes shining with excitement. *Abandoned Jeep at the hospital? A Jeep in the news twice? That sounds too much of a coincidence. Is it the same Jeep that drove through the poppy fields? I bet it was.*

Then, out of the blue, a thought struck him.

*If they abandoned the Jeep at the hospital, what new vehicle did they take Latif in?*

On a hunch, he dialled his boss's office. The assistant picked up.

'Hey. I was calling to see how the boss is. It's awful what happened to him in the hospital, getting drugged and all.'

'Yeah, he's better now and will be released in a few days. Can you believe it? He was there purely for a minor operation.'

'I'm sorry to hear it. Glad to know he's being released soon. I assume someone picked up his car from the hospital?'

'Hmm, I don't know. His driver is on leave, so the boss's been enjoying driving himself around.'

'Please share my regards. Thanks.'

Qadir rushed to his computer and signed into the official military intranet.

*No one missed his car because no one even realised it had been taken.*

He looked up his boss's vehicle in the car tag database and clicked the track button, still putting the pieces together in his mind.

*Where are you, my dear car? Please, please don't be in Rawalpindi hospital, or I'll have to start over. But if you're somewhere else, the kids are driving you.*

After an agonising minute, a result jumped up on the map. Blip, blip, blip. The coordinates winked back at him.

'Abbottabad?' Qadir whispered. 'Freaking Abbottabad?'

# 17

# Fire in the Hole

For the first time since they'd left India, Afzal was terrified. He paced the small room that had once held Latif, his palms clammy and his mind in a haze.

'How could I have been so stupid? I've put everyone, including my family, under a major terrorist threat with my moronic plan,' he muttered.

He stopped, smacked his head and approached the makeshift table, sweeping everything into the backpack. 'Get a grip, Afzal. Everyone's safety depends on you. Stop moping and get a move on. Okay, let's see. Latif has swollen feet, so he will be hobbling. I must find tracks that look like shuffling feet.'

Afzal hoisted the backpack and cautiously stepped out of the house. He switched on his phone's flashlight and examined the ground.

*Which way did you go, you whiny bastard? Come on, give me a clue.*

It didn't take long for him to find scuff marks, as if someone had been dragging their feet. The tracks led towards the rear of the courtyard. He followed them for another ten minutes. They went into the fields nearby.

*Does Latif know someone around here?*

Suddenly, Afzal heard hard boots crunching on rough ground. Twin flashlights appeared and he crouched low, turning off his own. Peeking around, he spotted two soldiers on foot patrol. He wanted to backtrack, but the sweeping beams of light were getting close—too close. He was pinned.

Then it hit him.

He reached into his pocket and fished out a fistful of Pakistani rupees. Pausing, he assessed how the wind was blowing and eased a little to his left.

Soon the soldiers were close enough that he could hear them talking. One said, 'These nightly patrols are a useless waste of time. No one has been caught trespassing near the military compounds here.'

It was time. Afzal held up the fistful of money and opened his hand. The wind caught the notes and it swirled away from him, blowing towards the two soldiers.

Before the second soldier could respond, the first one exclaimed, pointing. 'Is that—!?'

He ran and picked up some bills. 'Thousand-rupee notes! There's more here. The animals must have gotten into another bin Laden stash.'

The second soldier grinned. 'This night patrol is paying off—literally.'

With the excitement of young children getting birthday presents, they ran around, trying to track down every note blowing in the breeze. Afzal darted out of hiding, peering at the ground. He hoped to pick up the trail again. It was a long shot, but his only play.

He glanced back to check on the soldiers. They were engrossed in searching for the notes. He bent closer to the ground.

*Where did you go? Come on, reveal yourself to me.*

Suddenly, without warning, an animal darted in front of him. Its fur brushed his leg and Afzal jumped, suppressing a scream. He turned to flee, but he tripped over the animal in the dark and stumbled to the ground.

As he fell, he curled into a ball, putting his hands up to defend himself from an attack. Instead, he felt the animal sniff, lean in and lick his forearm. He spread his palms to see a familiar white smudge on a shining face.

'Wicket, you fool. You scared me!' he whispered. The dog slobbered all over him. 'I've never been so glad to see you. Now where are Bee and Rup?'

It was low, but he heard Beena hiss, 'Will you stop rolling around in the dirt and get over here? There are soldiers all over.'

Her voice had come from behind a mound of earth not far from him. He shuffled over, staying low. Beena popped up to give him a hug.

'I'm glad you're here.'

Rup snorted. 'Afzal, you should've come with me.'

'I'm sorry, Bee, about what I said. And Rup, you're right. Friendship and trust are more important than anything.'

'Friends before anything else,' Rup said solemnly.

'We're all here, so at least we'll be together when we're arrested.' Afzal glanced towards the soldiers.

'Shh,' Beena said. 'Enough with the *Sholay* dosti drama. There are half a dozen soldiers afoot patrolling this area near the military base. We've been playing hide-and-seek, waiting for the patrol to thin out before we returned to the compound.'

They watched the panning torch lights for a moment.

Rup broke the silence. 'I wonder what Farouk's doing now?'

'I don't know, but I hope he's safe.' Beena looked at Afzal. 'I knew you'd come.'

Afzal let a small smile slip. 'I was hoping I would run into you too. But to be honest, I was following Latif's tracks. They're easy to follow since his hobbling gait leaves a distinct pattern on the ground. He's still out here, undetected. If the soldiers had found him, we'd have heard a big commotion.'

Rup waved his hand. 'He's gone, buddy. Forget about Latif.'

'If you're dead set on leaving right now, I'll come along. But I still think we should recapture Latif—he's still handcuffed and drugged. Without Latif as a bargaining chip, we may lose more than our lives. The worst part is that Latif plans to swap us for jailed terrorist leaders. And who knows what the ISI plans to do if they capture us instead.'

The two of them didn't say a word.

Afzal continued, pointing, 'I saw his tracks right there. He's close by—my guess is within a hundred metres. He's making a beeline for those open fields.'

Beena sighed, 'You're like Wicket after a potato chip. Can't let it go, can you?'

'Listen, it's not about me and Parv anymore. This is much bigger than my ego or my patriotism being doubted. This is about a mass murderer. I was sick to my stomach talking to him for five minutes. People like him destroy not only lives, but entire generations. Even if I die trying to bring this terrorist to justice, it'll be a life well spent. Thirty minutes is all I ask. If we don't find him, we leave immediately. What do you say?'

Afzal stared expectantly at Beena.

Beena glanced at Rup.

Rup looked at both and shrugged.

Beena exhaled sharply. 'You can be a convincing asshole when you put your mind to it. I think we should leave right now, but since you have tracked him to the open fields, let's give ourselves fifteen minutes to find this bastard. Not thirty, but fifteen.' She extended her hand. 'Deal?'

Afzal ignored her hand and gave her a quick hug instead.

'You both are the best friends in the world. Fifteen minutes.'

~

Latif's head was still cloudy from the drugs and his feet were painfully swollen. To make matters worse, he saw multiple sweeping lights in the woods.

*Those bastard kids are still after me.*

Crouching behind a large rock, he tried to catch his breath. His hands were still cuffed, but the gag had loosened a bit in his mouth. He spat it out and cleared his throat. With difficulty, he forced his eyes to focus on his feet. They looked puffy and bloated, like a pair of large medical gloves filled with water. He was having difficulty balancing himself. Way worse than he expected.

He glanced at the sky.

*Can't focus. I need these drugs out of my system as soon as possible or I'm screwed. If I lie down with my legs raised, it may reduce the swelling. And the drugs will subside. Think! Where can I lie down for a bit without being found?*

Faintly, through the darkness, he heard goats bleating. He managed to get to his feet and lumber towards the noise. After a few minutes of painful movement, he found the source of the sound—a small, fenced-in plot of land with around half a dozen goats. In one corner, there was a small lean-to with hay and supplies to milk the goats.

Latif trudged along and reached the small structure. He balanced himself on a thin column, sat down gingerly and lifted up his swollen feet onto a bale of hay.

*I should be fine in an hour, and then … sweet revenge. More of my friends will join me from Indian prisons. We'll have fun then. This unpleasant situation just might be a blessing in disguise.*

~

The trio watched the soldiers.

Afzal gestured towards them. 'They aren't looking for anyone; they're on a routine patrol. We'll wait for them to move away and then we follow Latif's scuff marks. He's close, I can feel it. Once we grab him, we get in the car and beat it.'

'A few more minutes,' Beena said, watching the soldiers.

But Wicket had other ideas. She'd smelled something and was intent on chasing it. Rup placed a hand on her head. 'Stay here, girl. Be quiet.'

Beena covered her face and groaned, 'Why are we still lugging that dog around? She's going to be the death of us.'

Afzal was staring at the soldiers. He got up and dusted himself off.

'Alright, the soldiers are far enough away. I hate sitting around, and the fifteen-minute clock is ticking. We must get back before they find an unknown military car in the compound or Latif raises an alarm.'

'Which way should we go?'

'Follow the shuffling feet. This way.'

Afzal set off in the direction he had pointed. Rup and Beena followed. Wicket wagged her tail, brushing against Rup's legs as she cantered along. After a few minutes, she emitted a low rumble and animatedly started sniffing the ground. Just as Rup tried to settle her down, she shot off into the distance.

Beena raised her eyebrows. 'You think she has his scent?'

'Possibly. Wicket doesn't like the man. And he stinks, so it should be easier for her to track him.'

Afzal cupped his phone's light. 'She's following the faint scuff marks on the ground. They are barely visible, but I'm sure they are his. I bloody hope she's not chasing a rabbit. Come on!'

At that instant, they saw a set of bright lights shining in the distance, sweeping and panning across the landscape.

'Shit. More guards. We've got to find that jihadi in ten minutes or get the hell out of here.'

They scampered and found Wicket a few metres ahead of them. She loped along with purpose, nose brushing the ground, sniffing furiously. The three jogged close behind, crouching as low as possible. After a few minutes, Wicket led them to a fenced-in field, then flew inside with a burst of speed.

Rup's eyes were watering, and he held his side as if he had a cramp. He panted, 'Where's she taking us? Do you still see the tracks? Where are we in relation to the compound?'

'Too many questions, Rup. I can't see any tracks. The ground seems harder here.' Afzal scanned the ground nearby as he tried to catch his breath.

'The dog likely stumbled on something useless. Probably a squirrel. We can't afford to babysit this silly animal anymore. We must leave now—and if Wicket wants to hang out here, we leave her,' said Beena.

'Don't be melodramatic, Bee. I'm sure she's searching for Latif.'

They saw the dog's faint silhouette in the distance. Rup whispered across the darkness, 'Wicket, what did you find?'

Instead of rushing back to him, the dog stayed where she was and growled softly. They dashed over and found her snarling at a pile of hay under an open lean-to.

Beena got to the dog first and caressed her neck to calm her down. Then she glanced up, took a step back and let out a low whistle.

She pointed triumphantly at what Wicket was growling.

Lying on a pile of hay was Latif, asleep. His feet were up on a bale, cuffed hands on his tummy and he was snoring, oblivious to everything around him.

'I can't believe this,' panted Rup, leaning down and patting Wicket's head.

'Wow,' Afzal checked his watch. 'Wicket's a proper hero. A tracker and a stickler for keeping time. Fourteen minutes on the dot. I wasn't sure we'd catch Latif in time and was already preparing a speech to extend our deal for ten more minutes.'

'How do we move him into the car without the soldiers catching on?' asked Beena, swiftly getting to the practical side of things.

Rup winked at Beena. He reached into his pocket and pulled out a box of matches.

'Hay burns quite well.'

Beena rolled her eyes and said, 'For every problem, you open a box of matches. Fire won't draw those soldiers away. It will only attract them here.'

'Precisely my point. The fire will attract the soldiers,' said Rup. 'We first wake the bastard and then we light the place up. The flames will get him on his feet and moving pronto. The soldiers are still a bit far off—by the time they come here we'll be long gone and they'll be watching the wrong place.'

Afzal cracked his knuckles. 'I'm in. Let me get Latif up and ready. Once we're ready to move, light it up.'

Beena sighed. 'Okay, worth a shot. Seems like the better plan among many terrible ones.'

Afzal approached the pile of hay, shook Latif's shoulders and then smacked him on his head.

'Up, you tub of lard.'

Latif opened his eyes, still foggy in the head. His face drained of blood when he recognised them. 'You again? Please, I can't bear this anymore.'

Afzal hoisted him up and stuffed his mouth with a handkerchief. 'No escape for you, you fat bastard. Time to move.'

As Latif was yanked to his feet, Wicket ran over and grabbed his hospital gown. She tugged on it, growling. Beena watched the dog do her thing and smiled.

'Actually, I take back what I said. I'm starting to like this dumb mutt. She has the right attitude about the wrong sorts of people.'

Rup pulled Wicket away. Then he lit the match and threw it on the hay. 'Move fast. It'll go up quick.'

But they couldn't move Latif fast enough. As they goaded him, he whined through his gag until the lean-to exploded and shards of wood rained down on them. Then, even Latif picked up speed. Rup goggled at the huge fire now crackling behind them.

Beena ran, covering her head. 'What the fuck did you do?'

'Nothing! I just threw the match on the hay!'

'Must have been dry wood hidden under the hay,' panted Afzal.

'Doesn't matter. Move! With some luck, we might make it back to the compound if this fire distracts the soldiers.'

Rup put his arm around Latif's waist and prodded the sluggish prisoner to move faster. Afzal pushed from the back while Beena corralled Wicket, who was frantic after the loud blast. With new purpose, they made for the compound.

They saw a four-man patrol rush towards the fire and crouched behind some bushes. The soldiers sprinted towards the inferno, paying no attention to anything else outside their path. Once the patrol was gone, they got up and pushed on towards the bin Laden building.

Running into the compound, they opened the boot of the military car. As they tried to shove Latif inside, he resisted, turning around and looking at Afzal, an odd glint in his eyes. He moaned through the gag, indicating a desire to speak.

Afzal reached over and took it out. 'What?'

Latif licked his dry lips. 'Okay. I'll make a one-time offer. Let me go now and I'll make sure you get back home safe. If anyone else captures you, there are no guarantees we won't trade you for my friends.' He jerked his chin towards Beena and Rup. 'And to show my sincerity, I'll include your two kafir friends in the deal.'

'I can't trust you as far as I can throw you. Which isn't far,' Afzal smiled mirthlessly. 'I would never make any deal with you. You're coming to India, and you'll face the wrath and the justice of my people.'

Before Latif could speak again, Afzal gagged him. They stuffed him into the boot, shut the lid and quickly piled into the car. Beena took the driver's seat.

'It seems the recapture has terrified Latif.'

'I think you're right, Bee,' Afzal said. 'And it's time to get home. Head for the Chakoti border. We'll take the shortest route but through the low-traffic back roads.'

Bee cranked the ignition and the car roared to life.

'Let's hit it.'

# 18

## Second Blood

Beena rubbed her eyes. It was well past midnight and she'd been driving for a while. She looked over at Afzal's phone. 'We have the right destination, right? You still think this is the shortest route?'

Afzal nodded, watching the navigation. 'Close enough. The major benefit is that these side roads aren't busy. We should be coming up on Muzaffarabad soon, then we'll swing east towards Chakoti. Keep your eyes peeled for trouble.'

Rup yawned from the back seat. 'So we can't take a quick nap?'

'Says the man who lost our money and drove us down the wrong road—all because of a nap. Not to mention you blew up a pile of hay a few hours ago. You're turning into a proper pyromaniac, Rup. My ears are still ringing,' grumbled Beena.

Before Rup could retort, she braked suddenly and they all jerked forward. Their headlights lit up a military vehicle parked across the road, almost blocking it. In front of it stood two soldiers, waving them down.

'Shit. It's a bloody checkpoint. Farouk had warned us. Still need a nap, Rup?'

'Nope. But looks like the game is afoot. Time to see if Mr Decoy's credentials are the real deal. And time for me to earn my keep.'

As he spoke, Rup fumbled around in the darkness of the backseat. Afzal craned his neck to see what Rup was doing.

Beena groaned, 'Earn your keep? You're not going to do a stupid voice, are you?'

'Of course I am.'

'Don't do anything stupid, Rup. We can't have them finding what's in our boot.'

Afzal glanced at him, worry etched onto his face. Rup smiled, tapping an ID card on the front seat.

'I got this. You're on my stage, dear friend.'

'I hate it when you're overconfident.'

Beena pulled the car up just short of the improvised roadblock and stopped. One of the two soldiers approached the driver's window and shone a flashlight into the car. Its weak, yellow light filtered in.

As Beena rolled the window down, the soldier said, 'No one informed us of any military transports travelling at this hour.'

Before Beena could respond, Rup cleared his throat from the shadows of the back seat. He spoke, sounding like a tired old man, 'This is an urgent, priority-level military mission and there's no need to inform anyone. We don't have time to answer twenty questions.'

Latif thumped on the walls of the boot and the soldier stiffened. His flashlight swerved towards the back.

'What is that?'

Rup replied in a bored voice, 'Our prisoner, of course.'

'What? A prisoner? In the boot?'

'You should know better than to ask about things that don't concern you.'

'We're following orders.'

'I know, I know. You're being a good soldier. Let's get this over with. Here is my ID,' said Rup, holding up the card. 'Check it and let us through. As I said, we don't have time to waste.'

The soldier smacked the base of his flashlight, trying to coax more light from it. 'Damn, this stupid torch needs new batteries. I can't see your ID from here. Please give it to me.'

Rup handed the ID to Beena, and she passed it to the soldier though the window. Rup continued in the same old man voice, 'We're late and must deposit our prisoner in a secure location. Hurry up.'

The soldier checked the card with his flashlight. He glanced back at his colleague and turned back to the voice in the back seat.

'Please get out of the car, sir.'

'What?' Rup was indignant.

'Please, sir. We must search every vehicle. Strict orders.'

'Orders from whom? This is absurd. And get that light away from the inside of the car. These are confidential documents.'

'Out,' the soldier repeated.

Beena and Afzal stepped out. But Rup stared at the soldier from the back. 'Are you really going to make me do this?'

'Sorry, sir. Orders.' The soldier opened the back door, gesturing for Rup to come out.

'Okay.' Rup stepped out with a swift fluid motion, pulled the hat down on his head and strode forward towards the soldier, who pulled back a step. He pushed the man's flashlight down, stood nose to nose with the persistent soldier.

Rup hissed through clenched teeth, 'We've gathered vital information from our prisoner that we must deliver ASAP. It has been a long day. Don't make me lose my patience.'

'Where are you going?' the soldier asked, taking another step back.

'That's top secret.' Rup stepped forward to close the gap once more. The soldier's face was level with Rup's chest, which bore the name and designation tag on the uniform.

Soldier number two wandered over. 'What's the problem?'

'This major here is traveling with a nurse, a dog and a prisoner in the boot. It's strange,' he replied, looking sideways at his fellow soldier.

Rup stretched himself to his full height, stared down upon the soldier and, gesturing towards the boot, growled, 'Only a few minutes ago, we completed interrogating this traitor. Now we're on our way to interrogate another witness about the escape of a prisoner from Rawalpindi.'

The soldier glanced at the boot, the ID card in his hand and then at Afzal and Beena.

Rup continued, 'My nurse is an expert in administering specialised drugs and my young officer there is an expert in interrogation techniques. Don't ask me about the dog. We save her for when they're hardcore and don't want to talk, even with the drugs. Let's just say that when she takes the first testicle, they always talk.'

The second soldier flinched as if part of his dinner had come back up, and unconsciously bent over a bit. The first soldier glanced at the ID once more and glanced at his companion for support. Finding none, he turned around. 'We're sorry to delay you, Major. Have a good night.' He stepped back and saluted Rup for good measure.

'Thank you. You as well.' Rup waved his hand, turned and climbed back into the car. Beena and Afzal followed his lead.

'Now what?' Beena whispered.

Rup pointed at the keys. 'Let's go!'

As they passed the soldiers, Rup waved a salute at them. The soldiers stared and saluted back awkwardly.

After a couple of minutes, Beena said, 'Shit. That was close! My heart is still racing. And that voice? It was creepy coming out of you.'

'It's my grumpy old man voice. Afzal has heard it. I changed it slightly to become an angry, grumpy old man.'

'And that weak flashlight helped. The game would've been up if they'd seen your face!'

Beena asked, 'And where did you come up with that story where Wicket is a testicle-mutilating machine?'

'A confident delivery makes any story believable. You learn all kinds of stuff in drama and improv club.'

Beena glanced at Wicket, who was leaning happily against Rup, her tongue dangling from her mouth. 'This softie of a dog looks like it had a lobotomy. I mean, have you ever seen anything less testicle-mutilating than that?'

Afzal interrupted, 'Guys. This little episode has got me thinking.'

Bee groaned. 'Uh, oh. Afzal is thinking again. That means we're screwed.'

'No, seriously. This car is a problem. Those soldiers knew who in the army is supposed to be going where. They definitely track these cars. We thought an army car might be excellent cover but, in fact, we're exposed. I think we should find a new one.'

Rup, lounging in the back with Wicket, said, 'No way, dude. It's got us this far. This is a good car and the back seat is mighty comfortable.'

Looking at Afzal, Beena nodded. She said, 'You have a point, Afzal. With the increased level of security, roadblocks and a slightly brighter flashlight, someone will figure out we're impostors. Especially if we are dressed as military officers and nurses.'

Suddenly, Beena noticed a set of fast-moving headlights in the rear-view mirror. They seemed to be getting bigger. 'Hey, is it me or is the car behind us driving fast?'

Rup peered out the back window. 'You're right, it does seem to be nearing rapidly.'

'I hope it's not Qadir,' Afzal said.

Beena glanced in the mirror. 'What should I do?'

'Drive normally. They can go around us.'

The lights grew quickly as the vehicle drew close, its front grill reflecting the dull red of their tail lights. Beena tightened her grip on the wheel. 'Go on. Go around us,' she said, stretching her hand out the window and gesturing for the car to pass.

The headlights disappeared momentarily, as the car drove up right behind them. Then it abruptly accelerated and rammed them in the rear. Their car shook and metal screeched. Rup yelled, grabbing Wicket with one hand and the roof with the other.

Beena gritted her teeth. 'Shit. Who have we pissed off now? They want to play rough? Okay, let's do this.'

The beams behind them reappeared as their pursuer seemed to tap the brakes. Then, as if nothing had happened, the mystery vehicle pulled out and sped up alongside to overtake them.

'What? He's going to coolly pass us after ramming a military car in the ass?'

But whoever was driving the strange car had other ideas. The vehicle didn't overtake them. When the pursuer reached their rear quarter, he turned sharply and clipped their car. It was a classic pit manoeuvre, and it worked perfectly.

Their sedan spun out of control, metal and rubber grinding. Beena struggled to keep the screeching, whirling car on the road, but it was futile. They crashed headlong into the roadside ditch, a cloud of dust rising into the air.

Beena cranked the keys. The ignition clicked, but the engine stayed silent. She thumped the steering wheel with the palm of her hand.

'Shit! This car is done for.'

A voice boomed from the car behind them. 'Get out with your hands raised. Don't try anything stupid or you'll be shot dead.'

'Fuck, it's not a cop. It sounds like Rambo!' hissed Afzal.

The three friends emerged with their hands held high. The strange vehicle turned out to be a battered pickup truck—the same one that had chased them earlier, looking a bit discoloured and a lot worse for the wear.

The driver's door flew open and Tamir stormed out. 'You little shits are impersonating military officers? The balls on you. Where's my journal?'

Afzal nudged Beena. 'Rambo looks high-strung. And his first concern is the journal?'

She whispered, 'If we hand it over, he'll kill us right here for sure. We must rattle him and throw him off to have any chance. Follow my lead and bring a bit of crazy out.'

'What are you two whispering about?' demanded Tamir.

Beena shot back, 'I was just saying that you don't like us pretending to be army officers but you're okay with me impersonating a nurse?'

Tamir paused for a moment and studied Beena, his eyes

narrowing. Then he stepped forward and shoved the gun into her face, its muzzle pressed against her cheek. He leaned forward threateningly.

'You being smart with me?'

Beena felt the cold metal on her face. Fear shot through her, but she put on a brave face. 'Well, yeah. I am smarter than you. What do you want?'

Still jabbing the gun at her face, he growled, 'Where's my journal? Or do you want a bullet in your brain?'

'What journal? I don't know what you're talking about.'

'I think you do. You abandoned the drugs with the Jeep but took the backpack with the journal. You obviously knew it was more valuable.'

Beena raised her eyebrows.

'We took your backpack because it had working phones, you dumbass. What does this journal even look like?'

Tamir glared at Beena and took a few steps back, still pointing his gun at her. 'You think you can fool me? You stupid brats better tell me where my journal is, or she's going to get it in three …'

'Okay, okay,' said Afzal. 'You don't have to be violent. Our backpack got damaged. So, we took your backpack and the phones inside; the rest we emptied in Abbottabad. We didn't see a journal, but we can take you to where we dumped the contents of the backpack.'

Before Tamir could respond, they were interrupted by more lights bouncing down the road. 'Don't make any stupid moves,' he said, keeping his gun steady. 'Probably some peasant running something illegal in the dark. You three stay right here till they pass, then we can talk about taking me to my journal.'

But the new vehicle coming down the road didn't move past the standoff. It pulled up metres short of them and the doors swung open. A man's voice boomed from the shadows, beyond the blinding headlights.

'Put the gun down and take two steps back.'

Tamir squinted turning to address the voice. 'You aren't police. I can tell.'

'You're right. This is an order from the Pakistani army.'

Beena nudged Rup and whispered, 'I think those are the soldiers from the roadblock.'

Rup put his hands up, shaded his eyes and asked, 'You sure?'

Beena nodded vigorously.

Rup took two bold steps forward and to the side, stepping away from the lights. He pulled his hat down and thundered, 'Havildar, arrest this man.' The old man voice had returned. 'He crashed our car and was forcing us to take him to our next interrogation so he could rescue the prisoner. He's a traitor to the country.'

'Wha …?' Tamir gawked at Rup, with a confused expression.

The two soldiers stepped forward, their weapons aimed firmly at the drug dealer. The first soldier barked, 'Drop your gun and get on your knees.'

Tamir inspected the two guns pointed at him. He kneeled on the road, placing his gun on the ground. The first soldier rushed forward and kicked the gun away, keeping the drug dealer at gunpoint. The second soldier stood a few metres away, his pistol steady.

'Listen, they're lying—they're not even military—and they have an important journal …' Tamir looked at the soldiers and gestured at the trio, his words a jumble.

The first soldier interrupted him. 'Ha! I've already checked their ID. Enough of your lies. Do you have ID?' He was clearly a stickler for process.

Beena glanced over at Afzal and flicked her head at the pickup. Afzal nodded and both looked at Rup.

'Go get our stuff,' Rup said quietly. 'I'll take care of this.'

Sticking to the shadows, Rup marched over to the two soldiers. He stood with his back to their vehicle, his silhouette framed by the bright lamps illuminating the drug dealer on the ground. 'The nation owes you a debt of gratitude,' he said, glaring at Tamir. 'This asshole wrecked us and our car has stalled. We've been delayed—I'm confiscating his pickup as an emergency measure. And as punishment.'

'No fucking way! First you steal my Jeep, and now this? This isn't going to happen again, asshole. Not again!'

The first soldier kicked Tamir. 'What Jeep? This is a military car, you idiot. And no swearing at an army officer. Where's your ID?'

Tilting his head slightly to one side, the second soldier added, 'This is highly unusual.'

Rup nodded. 'Not just unusual. It's treasonous. RAW spies kidnapped a top-level officer and we're working hard to ferret out the traitors who did it. But the damn infiltrators are trying to fight back. Are you telling me you don't want to help our country?'

'No, not at all. That wasn't what we meant, sir.' The first soldier glanced at his colleague and at the man on the ground. 'Is he part of that mess in Rawalpindi?'

Rup let his eyes drift to the drug dealer. 'We think so, yes.'

Tamir started to say something, but the soldier kicked him again.

'You're making a mistake,' wheezed Tamir. 'Do you know who I am? Who I have connections with?'

'Shut up. You interfered with a military operation. And I haven't yet seen an ID.' The soldier glanced at Rup. 'We'll take care of him for you, sir.'

'Thank you.' Rup patted the soldier's shoulder.

As he turned to leave, the second soldier said, 'One moment, sir.' He reached into his pocket and extended an ID card.

'You forgot this. We waved at you to stop, but you left in such a hurry.'

'Aha, my ID. Where's my head? I was too focused on interrogating the traitors. Thank you for bringing it. You will go far in your career.' He grabbed the ID from the soldier.

Meanwhile, Afzal and Beena tightened Latif's gag and dragged him out from the car's boot. The soldiers watched them lead the handcuffed prisoner to the pickup. They studied his blotchy skin and his drugged, bloodshot eyes. His face had swollen so much that his eyes were almost shut.

Latif tried to yell at the soldiers, but his gag kept him from saying anything intelligible. The second soldier shivered and spat on the ground. 'Bloody traitor. Is he Chinese? I can see you are experts at working on prisoners who don't want to talk.'

Rup chuckled, 'I told you, my assistants are the best.'

'Glad it wasn't me. Did the bastard talk?'

'Sang like a bird now that he only has one testicle. He should've talked sooner and maybe he would still have been able to have children.'

They tied Latif up and loaded him onto the bed of the truck. Beena ran back to the car, got Wicket and helped her into the front. Afzal grabbed the rest of their belongings, including the backpack. As he loaded it into the pickup, Tamir shouted, 'Hey, that's my backpack. I'm going to kill the three of you nice and slow. You see if I don't make you suffer!'

The first soldier rapped Tamir on the head with his pistol. 'Enough with the threats. That's a camouflage backpack used by the military. One more peep from you and you'll regret it.'

The drug dealer grimaced. Beena chuckled and piled into the pickup.

Rup stood straight and put both hands behind his back. 'Excellent work, havildar. You will be commended with bravery medals. But now we must rush.'

He slid into the passenger side of the pickup as Afzal jumped into the driver's seat. Without delay, they started the pickup and tore away from the scene.

The trio and Wicket sat crammed into the front bench seat while Latif bounced around in the bed like a loose load of lumber on the unkept roads. The mountains glowed in the soft orange of a sunrise.

It felt like a new day.

~

Qadir threw the floorboards across the bedroom. The long drive to Abbottabad had not improved his humour, and the fact that he might have just missed the teens made him angry and frustrated.

He paced the room and called the two soldiers over. 'Okay, so they took off in a pickup. But are you sure they had a prisoner with them?'

'Yes, sir. In the boot. And a dog for interrogation.'

'A dog? For what now?'

'Interrogation.'

Qadir dismissed them with a wave of his hand and sat down on the bed to think.

*So, they have Latif. But why had they come north when it was easier to go south to escape? And what's this about a dog being used for interrogation? This is getting weirder.*

Then it hit him. If they were RAW agents, the trip north made sense. The move would be hard to anticipate—everyone expected them to go south and exit east via Sialkot. American forces had shown it was possible to slip into Abbottabad. Maybe the Indian Air Force planned on using the same tactics to airlift them out of there.

Qadir chewed his lip. It was a crazy idea, but possible.

*What would I do now if I were them?*

He ruled out an American-style rescue by the Indian Air Force. Relations between India and Pakistan were already tense. Moreover, since the Osama bin Laden raid, Pakistan's upgraded radar system would detect any such air intrusions. They already had Latif, so Qadir doubted they had any other objective but to get home.

*No, it must be via land, not air. They'll make a beeline to the closest border to return home to India.*

With a burst of energy, Qadir re-examined the map, tracing his fingers across the marked roads and towns close to the border.

'Chakoti,' he whispered, tapping a spot on the map. 'That's it. That border town is where they will make their play. No other viable exit point for hundreds of kilometres.'

He continued to trace his finger on the map.

From Abbottabad, they would have to drive through Muzaffarabad and then up the Midnight Pass to get over the mountains. That is the only road to Chakoti.

Qadir surveyed the mountainous terrain surrounding Chakoti. 'Bad idea for me to drive up the pass. That narrow road is a slow and tough ride, and I might not catch up to them in time.'

Then he stood and smacked the map on the table.

'If I can make it to Chakoti before them, I can drive down the pass and towards Muzaffarabad and intercept them. I can trap them on the narrow road where they'll have nowhere to run!'

Brimming with confidence, Qadir made a call. 'Get me a chopper. Make sure you bring extra fuel.'

Then he made another call to arrange for a vehicle. He would show everyone, including his commander, that he was right.

'Once I capture these Indian agents running amok in my country, I'll be the hero of Pakistan. These idiots will have no choice but to pay me respect and promote me. This is your career-making move, Qadir bhai!'

# 19

## The Midnight Pass

Qadir's chopper landed in one of the few level areas high above Chakoti—a small clearing covered in tall grass. Around them, large mountains loomed menacingly and the Jhelum flowing in the valley separated Pakistan from India.

Qadir said to the only other passenger in the helicopter, 'These three kids have surprised me with their resourcefulness. It might be overkill, but I might need a good sniper before this is all said and done. Keep your comms on, your rifle oiled and your scope dialled in.'

The soldier tapped his long rifle, nodded and touched his cap.

Qadir hopped out of the chopper and hurried towards a black SUV at the edge of the field. He got in, started the car and drove out, feeling determined.

The Midnight Pass, connecting Muzaffarabad and Chakoti, was built decades ago. Even with recent improvements, it was a narrow and dangerous road. Buses infrequently plied the road to transport passengers and cargo. The local government had tried to maintain it, but few used it.

Qadir drove faster than the recommended limits. He knew the road well; he'd chased more than one suspect over this pass. It took a few hours, but he made his way up and over the apex of the mountain pass.

As he sped towards Muzaffarabad, the downward trajectory seemed to propel him toward the end of the mission. He was going to show those pesky teens that they'd crossed paths with the wrong man.

~

Wicket lay spread out across Beena and Rup's laps, panting happily. Beena had to push the dog to the side before she could punch Rup in the arm.

'Um, why am I squeezed in the middle of this stupid seat?'

'The bench is only so big. Someone must sit in the middle.'

'And who decided that it has to be me!?'

'We should take a break before Muzaffarabad,' said Afzal, ignoring their bickering. 'We have a new car—well, a pickup truck—which blends in better, but now we need to get out of these uniforms.'

After finding a quiet, woodsy place to pull over, the three teens piled out of the truck. Beena changed into a loose-fitting women's salwar-kameez with a grey hijab covering her hair. Rup and Afzal opted for the faded kurta-pyjama combination that men usually wore in these parts. All of them topped off their clothing with full-sleeve woollen sweaters.

After checking Latif's bindings, they covered him with the tarp. Afzal said, 'Come on. We're getting closer, but we still have a long way to go.'

Afzal started the pickup and they resumed their travel, stopping only once on the outskirts of Muzaffarabad for diesel, food and water.

The way up the mountains quickly grew steep, curving in unexpected places. The road was rough and patchy and with no guardrails protecting vehicles from the steep ravines, the narrow pass grew even narrower with each turn.

As they wound up the mountain, Afzal's eyes were glued to the road that seemed to be getting worse by the kilometre. He clutched the steering wheel, his knuckles white as he squinted ahead.

'This road is certainly not for the faint of heart.'

Hairpin bends and moss-covered boulders made the road slippery in some places, while in others, it was arid and crumbling. Most of the time, the mountain pass was scarcely wide enough to accommodate two small vehicles. That was usually fine—until a large vehicle came along which was something every motorist dreaded on roads like this—the inevitable standoff, where it became a dangerous game of chicken.

The going was slow. As they approached tighter curves, Afzal said. 'This road is nuts! I don't think I can keep this up.'

'With your driving skills, I'm not too optimistic either. Let's hope we don't run into any big vehicles.'

Beena's words must have been prophetic—or a curse. At the next turn, they saw a big black vehicle in the distance.

Afzal sighed. 'Just my luck. I may be able to squeeze through.'

'Nod, say hello, then ask them to back up. Don't overthink it,' Beena said pragmatically. 'I'll drive from this point onwards.'

'Yes, please. I'm sweating bullets here.'

'You'll be fine,' Rup added, patting a nervous Afzal on his shoulder, and then he noticed something. 'Hey, I think he's driving a lot faster than we are.'

The black SUV accelerated further. Afzal stared at the oncoming behemoth and the dust cloud it kicked up, eyes wide. 'It feels like he sped up when he saw us!'

'Hmm, there's not much space, and we're unfortunately on the abyss side of the road.' Beena spun around to look to their rear. 'Quick, you need to put it in reverse.'

But before Afzal could react, the black SUV was already on top of them. He slammed the brakes to avoid a head-on collision with the vehicle, which skidded to a stop barely a few feet in front of them.

'What's this maniac doing?'

The driver of the other car leaped out. With a gun aimed at the pickup, he shouted, 'Put your hands up and exit the vehicle! Now!'

Rup squinted at the man. 'Is that Grumpy? I thought we lost him in Lahore. How'd he catch up to us?'

Beena screamed, 'Forget that, Rup—put it in reverse, Afzal! Back it up!'

Afzal hurriedly engaged reverse. Then he floored it. The pickup truck retreated, tires squealing, as Afzal swung the steering around to navigate the curves. About forty metres into it though, he miscalculated a turn and the vehicle's rear slammed into the side of the mountain.

'Great driving. You crashed into a stinking mountain!' Rup had Wicket curled up in his lap, shaking.

In the crumpled bed of the truck, the tarp restraints had come loose and Latif was panicking—slithering around like an injured snake. Afzal gripped the wheel, his hands trembling.

'Well, I erred on the side of the mountain and not the thousand-foot drop. Sue me!'

Beena snorted. 'You erred right into it, all right.'

A set of tires screeched. The SUV pulled up. Qadir stepped out again, his gun steady and pointed straight at them. 'Get out, hands raised where I can see them. No more funny business.'

'Bee, any ideas?' whispered Rup, nudging her.

'No. But a cop is better than being caught by a drug dealer like Rambo,' Beena replied. She fastened the backpack on her shoulders. With raised arms, the three exited the crashed pickup, Wicket trailing behind them.

'We're unarmed. Don't shoot,' said Afzal.

The tall man motioned with his gun. 'Keep your hands where I can see them. Where's Latif?'

Beena pointed towards the back of the pickup and Qadir walked around the crumpled vehicle. He whistled, staring at the handcuffed Latif in the truck bed. 'Son of a bitch. You could've killed him when you crashed.' Qadir shook his gun at Rup. 'You, big guy. Help him out of there and put him in the back of my SUV. This donkey's spawn needs to be returned to his prison cell. I don't want to listen to his radical, self-indulgent bullshit, so make sure his gag is good and tight. I don't want to hear a peep from this asshole.'

'I'll help Rup. He's hard to move,' said Afzal, motioning towards the truck bed.

'Go on. Make it quick,' Qadir said and looked at Beena. 'In fact, you help too. Then I can see you together all at once'

The three teens unloaded the terrorist and dragged him over to the black SUV. Latif tried to talk, his bulging eyes staring at Qadir, but all he managed was a couple of gurgles. He fought hard while being led towards the cargo space behind the SUV's rear seat. His words were muffled but somehow intelligible.

'No, not the boot. I can't … please.'

Afzal tightened the gag. Rup shoved Latif and he tumbled into the cargo hold with a thud. He pulled down the hatch with a loud thump.

Qadir eyed the kids and holstered his gun. 'Don't get any ideas. If you try anything, I'll shoot you dead without a second thought. You, big guy, sit in the back with the girl.'

He then turned to Afzal. 'And you—you drive.'

Rup looked at Qadir, then at Wicket. 'The dog will want to sit with me.'

Qadir put his hand on the butt of his gun and growled, 'Any sudden moves and I'll shoot it.'

'Please, don't. She's a good dog and will be no trouble at all. She's special, part of our team.'

'Don't try to bullshit me about your interrogation dog like you did with those gullible soldiers.' The grizzled ISI agent saw the surprise in their eyes. 'Yeah, I've been tracking your movements. Now shut up and get in before I shoot your kneecaps and haul you in.'

They were silent. Beena and Rup got into the back seat with Wicket. Afzal climbed in the driver's seat while Qadir got into the front passenger seat.

He observed the young man. 'So, are you the leader?'

Afzal didn't say anything. Qadir exhaled. 'Fine, let's get back to civilisation. You kids have given me enough trouble as it is, but now you can help turbo-charge my career. Drive.'

Afzal started the SUV and put it in gear. He manoeuvred around the crashed pickup and started driving back down the Midnight Pass, away from the Chakoti border.

'We'll be in Muzaffarabad soon. In the meantime, would any of you care to tell me what this was all about? And where's the red backpack? You seem to have switched it.'

None of the teens spoke.

'I knew you three were trouble the minute I saw you in Kartarpur. I didn't know RAW even hired such young people.

Maybe ISI needs to rethink our hiring methods.' He paused. 'So the question is, why did you kidnap this turd? And how could you imagine that you'd get away with it?'

By this time, Latif had spat his gag out—the insult had brought him back to life. He craned his head over the rear seat, glaring at Qadir. 'Hey you! I will not be lugged around like a suitcase or insulted like that. I know you're ISI, so you know exactly how important I am. Untie me. That's an order!'

Qadir glared back. 'Yeah, I do know who you are. That's why you're still tied up. Not nice to be out of your comfy jail cell with all those luxuries, is it?'

'How dare you—let me out of these bindings! That's an order! I'm Rasheed Latif. I deal with ISI idiots like you every day.' His voice cracked, betraying his effort to sound menacing.

'Yeah, I guess that means you get special massages every week too. The ISI knows everything, you pervert. I've no respect for terrorists who kill children in my country. Put this turd's gag back on and shut him up.'

Beena reached over and picked up the gag. Qadir kept his gun pointed at her as she stuffed Latif's gag into his mouth.

'Why are you pointing that gun at her?' protested Afzal.

'Because it'll make you and your big, dog-loving friend think twice before doing something stupid.'

Afzal kept his eyes on the road and his mouth shut. Then he saw another vehicle coming up the narrow road—a beater of a car, leaving a thick, smoky trail behind it. Qadir noticed it too.

'Pull over. Let that clunker go past.'

# 20

# The Fickle Nature of Luck

Tamir checked his phone, which showed the location of the last burner phone. 'Midnight Pass? What are you doing there? No matter, that's my backyard. Got you, you bastards.'

Now he was free to chase them down. Convincing the soldiers that he wasn't a traitor hadn't been easy. It had been even harder to get them to understand that three teenagers had fooled them. He promised the soldiers that he wouldn't say a word about how they let three kids, who were impersonating army officers, escape and they let him leave to track them down.

Tamir stole another vehicle—an old car with bald tires. The engine thumped violently as if skipping a beat. It was burning oil, leaving a trail of smoke hanging in the air behind it.

He hoped it would hold together long enough for him to catch the teens. The mountains loomed high ahead of him. He briefly surveyed the neighbourhood to see if he could swap his beater for another car, but couldn't find any better options.

'Screw it. I don't have time to waste. It's do or die!'

The drug dealer focused on the broken road in front of him, pushing the clunker to its limit as it groaned up the windy road. But as risky as the road was, he had a larger concern consuming his mind.

*If I don't find the journal, I'm a dead man.*

The journal was filled with information that could bury a lot of key people in his organization as well as in the government.

Extremely powerful people. The kind of people that didn't believe in forgiveness.

Tamir took a deep breath to calm his nerves.

*Just find the kids, get the journal and then you can enjoy killing them all. It's them or you, Tamir … them or you.*

Taking a curve too quickly, Tamir over-corrected on one section of the road. The car's rear tires spun fast, causing the back end to drift sideways. He lost control and the car jerked sideways, glancing off the mountain's wall. It felt like a light tap, but the deep rumbling sound told otherwise.

He glanced in his rear-view mirror to see a heap of mud and rock spilling down on the pass behind him. 'Shit. *Bach gaya saala!* That's one hell of a rockslide,'

After another thirty minutes of struggling to keep the smoking, overworked wreck on the road, he spotted a black SUV coming from the opposite direction. He slowed down his furious pace a bit.

By the time Tamir approached the oncoming vehicle, it had already pulled over. His free hand gripped his gun, his eyes were peeled for any potential threat.

As Tamir passed by, his gaze met the driver's—a nervous-looking teen wearing a faded grey kurta-pyjama and an old sweater. He glanced at the passenger in the front seat—a tough-looking older man in a suit and in the back, a young girl and another teen boy.

With a dog.

It was the same fucking dog.

Those were the same fucking teens!

Tamir slammed the brakes. The clunker screamed to a shuddering stop.

*I should've checked the locater app more frequently. Why are they coming back down?*

As Tamir turned, he saw the older man waving furiously at the driver to keep going.

~

Qadir pulled his gun.

'Go! For some reason, that guy has recognised you. Get us the heck out of here.'

Afzal pressed down on the pedal. Qadir opened the window and aimed his gun at this new threat—an old smoky car turning around on the road behind them.

At the next turn, Afzal almost drove the large SUV over the edge. Qadir glared at him. 'You trying to kill us?' Afzal gripped the steering and concentrated hard on the road. Rup clasped Wicket tight and Beena seized the door handle. 'We know this guy. He's a drug dealer who's pissed at us because we stole his Jeep in Lahore. He'll likely kill us if he catches us.'

'Then you better pray your friend can drive better than he is now,' said Qadir, watching the old relic of a car speed up behind them.

A shot rang out and everyone inside the SUV except Qadir flinched. He chided them, 'What are you ducking for? He's shooting at dust from a distance. It would be a one in a million shot if he hit us. Plus, even if he makes the shot, ducking won't save your brains or your ass.'

Nevertheless, Rup's head had noticeably shrunk into his shoulders, like a tortoise. Afzal felt the SUV fishtail underneath him as they barrelled towards another steep drop to the edge of the pass. He jerked the steering wheel and the rear tires drifted. One dipped over the edge before restabilising.

Latif screeched as the cruiser lurched back onto the road. 'Oh, Allah, I don't want to die!'

Turning a corner, Afzal wrestled with the steering. Qadir reached out to steady the wheel when Afzal abruptly slammed hard on the brakes. The car jerked to a stop, flinging everyone forward.

'What the hell?' roared Qadir, peering through the cloud of dust surrounding them.

A pile of boulders and dirt blocked the pass ahead. They couldn't see the road on the other side—it was impassable.

'Shit!' The ISI agent pounded the dash. 'Stay down, stay down!'

Leaping from the car, he ran to the back, taking aim at the approaching vehicle.

About twenty feet from them, it skidded to a stop. A cloud of dark smoke and dust rose; all they could make out was a hazy silhouette hopping out from the driver's seat and taking cover behind the beater.

This high in the mountain, there was a persistent breeze, so the scene cleared up within a minute or so. The dust settled to reveal Qadir standing behind the SUV, ready to fire. The driver of the other vehicle was not visible, but his voice rang clear.

'Drop your gun.'

'No fucking way. I'm an ISI agent transporting suspects. I'm not afraid of a pissant driving a piece of shit car.'

'ISI? I'm not a moronic soldier falling for a stupid, made-up story about ISI agents or soldiers with interrogating dogs.'

*Does everyone know about the dog interrogation story?*

'You don't know who you're messing with. I'm Qadir Khan from the ISI.'

'And I'm Barack Obama. ISI, my ass!' He fired a warning shot. 'Shut up and drop the weapon!'

'I don't think so.'

Qadir took aim at the hazy shape behind the car and pulled the trigger, but the only sound was a *click*. The ISI agent glared at his gun.

*Shit. Of all times.*

Tamir saw the man disappear behind the SUV. He fired, sending a burst of dirt flying only a few feet in front of Qadir.

'Ha! It's over. Your gun is jammed. I don't know you and I've no desire to kill you—yet. Just hand over what's in the SUV. Well, and the SUV too, and you won't get hurt.'

'Not going to happen.' Qadir ejected the magazine, slid it back and took aim once more. *Click*, but no bang.

Another shot rang out. This bullet almost hit his foot. Tamir laughed loudly, enjoying his upper hand.

'I have a fantastic view of the petrol tank from here. Throw your useless gun over the side.'

Another shot. It buried itself in the road a mere inch from Qadir's toes

'Damn it! That was supposed to put a hole in your foot. Yield, or the next shot will find the petrol tank.'

Qadir gritted his teeth. He tossed his pistol over the side of the pass and watched it disappear.

'Come out from behind the SUV. No sudden movements. Are the keys in the car?'

'Yes.'

'Good. Now climb to the top of the rubble.' Tamir emerged from behind the wreck he was driving, aiming his gun at Qadir. For a moment, Qadir stared at them from the base of the rockslide. Then he turned, headed for the rubble and climbed.

'Qadir is out and Rambo is back in the saddle. He's nuts and will kill us,' Afzal whispered. 'What's our play now, Bee?'

'We should try to bluff our way out of this. And don't give him his journal. That's the only thing keeping us alive,' said Beena.

Walking towards the SUV, Tamir waved his gun at Afzal.

'Move over. I'm driving. Idiots driving this road are likely to end up at the bottom of the mountain.'

The drug dealer backed up until he was in front of the clunker, then used the bumper of the large SUV to nudge it over the side of the pass. They heard the eerie sound of the rusty wreck coming apart as it fell.

Tamir yelled at Qadir, 'Sorry, but I can't have you following me.' Then, he swiftly turned around and floored it, driving back up towards Chakoti.

Standing on top of the rubble, Qadir could only watch as the assailant drove off—with his career-making teens and Latif. He stared until he could no longer see the dust trail.

*What is it with those kids? It would be easier to catch the Yeti.*

His heart sank as reality set in—he'd had the three teens for a brief moment but had now lost them. To a stupid drug dealer, no less. He could feel the mission slipping away from him.

'Bastard,' was all Qadir could muster under his breath.

Still cursing, he took out a phone from his pocket and dialled.

'Hey, it's me. Ask the pilot if he can pick me up on the mountain pass.' He listened carefully. 'No? Why can't—fuck. Alright, understood. I'll see if I can find a relatively flat spot with enough room for him to hover overhead. Will call you back. Thanks.'

Then he clicked off and started walking.

# 21

## The Long Walk of the Grumpy Man

'I can't believe he shoved the car down a mountain. You think it smashed to bits?'

'With all that's going on, that's what you're focused on?' whispered Beena.

'Shut up!' Tamir bellowed, irritation dripping from his voice.

The cabin remained quiet for a few kilometres.

Then a voice from the cargo area whined, 'Please let me go. This is no way to treat a leader of JeK! I can make you rich. I'm tired and in pain.' Latif had managed to spit the gag out again.

Wicket snarled at Latif.

'Everyone shut the fuck up! Someone gag the babbling idiot in the back. And you better keep that mutt quiet too, or I'll finish what I started outside that chai shop.' He brandished the gun in his right hand to emphasise his point. 'I must make a phone call. Be quiet.'

He took out his phone and pressed a speed dial button. 'It's me, Tamir. I'm driving up the Midnight Pass and there's a problem. I could use your help … yeah, I left a man at a landslide blocking the road … near the Rahim point curve … good. No loose ends. I'll settle the payment when we meet. Thanks.'

'Well, *Tamir*, who did you call?' Beena's voice was low and steady.

Tamir frowned. 'Don't call me Tamir. I'm not your friend. And why do you care who I called?'

Afzal jumped in. 'Because we're surprised at the good phone connection in such a remote mountain.'

'Drugs and terrorism. Big business out here. And modern technology makes business easier.' Tamir smiled and tapped his phone, showing off. 'Like how I tracked you to this road.'

The three shared a look. Beena flicked her eyes back on the driver. 'Drug business ... so, you called another dealer?'

Tamir shook his head with a wicked smile. 'Nope. Jihadis.'

Rup gulped. 'Shit. What are you going to do with us?'

'You'll see. But you can be sure it's nothing good. No more talking.'

It didn't last long. In the cargo area, Latif tried to talk again.

'Our prisoner makes up all kinds of stories,' said Beena. 'He'll say anything to escape.'

'I figured that out. I'm not stupid.'

Beena thought hard and fast, then she leaned forward. 'If you're as smart as you look, then you must have already figured out my mission. The ISI planted me in Chinese territory to infiltrate their inner circle. And this traitor in the back is my mission. I must make it to the border with him for an exchange.'

'Everyone's always jabbering about something, telling fantastical lies.' Tamir squinted at Beena in the mirror. 'And you may look Chinese, but you sound Indian. Your story needs work.'

Beena shrugged. 'This is an important operation with a lot of money involved.'

The drug dealer's ears perked up and he glanced over his shoulder. 'Money? How much?'

She smiled at Tamir in the mirror. 'Three million. Dollars, not rupees. We'll give you one million if you help us.'

'Three million dollars? Ha! You're full of shit. Don't try to con me. Now shut up.'

Beena sat back in her seat calmly. 'Your loss. In any case, you shouldn't be driving on these dangerous roads without your seat belt. And don't hold your gun while driving. You could set it off.'

'Shut up, will you? I've been driving these roads for years, even at night,' growled Tamir. 'I must look for my exit—that damn path is small enough to miss.'

~

Qadir had been walking for an hour—following the assailant, his SUV, the three teens and Latif. It wasn't what one would call a high-speed chase, but he was inching towards his quarry, one step at a time.

Along the way, he scouted for a wide spot without a wall of stone that would prevent the helicopter from hovering, but was unsuccessful. He was thirsty and tired, and the thin mountain air made breathing difficult. He tried to maintain a consistent pace and take steady, calm breaths.

Once in a while, he glanced at the sun to gauge how much daylight was left. It wouldn't be long before darkness fell.

A plume of dust in the distance gave him a flicker of hope. A Jeep was coming down the mountain.

Just in time.

Qadir stopped and held his hand out.

The Jeep zipped down the pass, getting closer. It rolled to a stop a few feet short of Qadir. The window slid down and two men looked at him, eyes full of scrutiny.

Qadir smiled. 'Hello. Will you give me a ride to Chakoti? I'll pay you well.'

The driver nodded and jerked his head, signalling for him to get in. Qadir climbed into the back seat and got comfortable.

'How long to Chakoti?'

'Not Chakoti. Muzaffarabad.'

Qadir shook his head. 'That's the wrong way. I must get to the border near Chakoti. As I said, I'll pay you.'

'Muzaffarabad. We have orders to take you there.'

'Orders? Listen—'

As if on cue, the front-seat passenger wordlessly produced a pistol and pointed it at Qadir.

Qadir slumped back into his seat. 'I see. Well, the road to Muzaffarabad is blocked—a bad rockslide. You can't drive down this pass until the debris is removed.'

The driver laughed. 'We know all about the rockslide. Your role is to help us clear it. Consider it your last task before we go down to Muzaffarabad.'

It only took ten minutes to cover the distance that had taken Qadir over an hour to walk and they reached the pile of rubble. He was back to square one.

Looking up in disgust at the small tower of rubble, the driver pounded on the dash. 'This rockslide is way bigger than what we were told. It'll take more than a few hours to clear this up, and I'm in no mood to help this bastard.'

Qadir shrugged. 'I told you so.'

'Shut up. You will be moving those rocks with your hands, then we'll see about your *told-you-so* attitude.' The driver glanced at his companion. 'Some of these boulders are too big. I'll call for some machinery.'

'You do that. I got to piss,' said Qadir. Without waiting for an answer, he opened the door, hopped out of the Jeep and started climbing the large heap of rocks.

The driver leaned out his window and yelled after him, 'Hey, where are you going?'

'I told you, I got to take a leak.' Before the two men could react, he'd disappeared over the top of the pile.

'What do we do? We shouldn't let him out of our sight,' the passenger said.

'Bring him back. Bastard's playing games with us. I need to call the boss about this rockslide.'

'Who climbs to the top of a pile to piss?'

The other opened the door, unholstering his gun, and climbed out. With one cautious eye on the unsteady rocks, he began to climb the pile, his gun at the ready.

Inside the truck, the driver watched his partner climb the debris. 'This bastard is playing games with us.' Then he dialled and listened to the phone ring. It continued to ring until it went to voice mail.

The passenger made it to the top, but there was nobody there.

'Shit! He's gone!' he shouted, looking around.

It was the last thing he remembered.

Hidden behind a boulder lodged in the debris, Qadir leaped out and conked the man in the head with a large stone. He went down like a sack of flour and rolled to the bottom of the mound.

Back in the Jeep, the driver jumped out as he saw his companion fall to the bottom of the rock heap. He grabbed the rifle, rushed over to the base of the pile and idiotically started scrambling up, but only made it a quarter of the way. Qadir appeared at the apex and, testing his bowling arm, launched a rock about the size of a cricket ball. The stone hit the Jeep's driver smack on the forehead. Blood flowed, and he dropped to his knees at the base of the mound.

The man shook his head, his eyes looking glazed. As he struggled to stand, Qadir sprinted down the rubble pile and slammed into the surprised man, knocking the rifle from his hands.

The driver had no chance against Qadir's training. He pulled the pistol from the driver's shoulder holster and it was over. Both got to their feet.

Qadir kept the gun pointed at the driver's face.

'You should've had this handgun drawn when you came after me. It's easier to handle compared to a big rifle.'

The driver glared at Qadir, angry at being disarmed and angrier still at the lecture.

'This isn't personal. Even though you were probably ordered to get rid of me, I've nothing against you. It's just work.' Qadir slammed the pistol butt on the driver's head.

The driver staggered, then collapsed. Qadir stared over the cliff, then turned to face the unconscious driver. 'You'll have one hell of a headache when you wake up, but you'll be alive.'

Grabbing the driver, he dragged him away from the edge. 'You'll never know how close you came to dying today. You can thank me later.'

Qadir pulled the clip from the driver's gun. He made sure it was full and then stuffed the firearm into the belt of his trousers.

He then made for the parked Jeep. As it rumbled to life, he turned it around and began the drive back to Chakoti. The drug dealer may have gotten a head start, but somehow, he had to get those kids and Latif back.

22

# Mysteries of the Universe

Tamir drove smoothly around the sharp curves on the Midnight Pass.

Meanwhile, Afzal examined the SUV. Strapped into the passenger seat of a car driven by a gun-toting drug dealer on a narrow, twisty mountainous road gave him few options to escape.

That's when he noticed something slide out from under his seat as they navigated one of the many sharp turns. His eyes sharpened. A potato chip. He bent and picked it up with two fingers.

'Guess that guy was addicted to junk food,' Afzal said, as he raised his hand above his head, giving everyone a clear view of the chip. 'No way was that guy from ISI. They're health nuts and don't eat crap like this.'

Wicket's nose twitched, sitting up on Beena's lap. She began to whine.

'Keep her quiet,' growled Tamir.

Afzal moved the morsel in front of Wicket's nose and winked at Beena. The dog had her eyes fixed on the chip, her head tracking every movement.

With a slow, deliberate flick, Afzal tossed the potato chip into the air. What followed was no surprise. Beena let go of Wicket and the dog lunged over the seat, following the trajectory of the morsel—and leaped right between Tamir's hands, straight into his lap.

The sudden bulk and momentum of the dog jolted Tamir. Wicket's rear feet jammed against his face as she searched for her treat. His gun clattered to the floor between his legs.

'Fuck!' Tamir screamed, trying to shove the dog away, but Wicket was already between his feet, sniffing for the chip. While he grappled with the dog, Afzal reached over, grabbed the wheel and twisted it sharply to the right.

The SUV swerved hard and slammed into the side of the mountain. The impact was so forceful that all airbags deployed with a deafening bang. Stunned silence followed the loud crash.

After a moment, Afzal stirred, pushing down at the deflating airbags. He glanced over—Tamir had been knocked out cold, his unconscious form wrapped around the steering wheel.

In the back seat, Beena shook her head, blinking. 'Afzal, you still with me?'

'Yeah,' Afzal grunted, rubbing his face. 'Who knew airbags threw such a punch?'

Afzal leaned down to grab Wicket, still between the driver's legs. As he did so, he noticed something—a dull grey glint between his seat and the centre console. Tamir's gun. He picked it up and stuck it in his waistband.

'Is Wicket okay?' groaned Rup as he tried to sit up.

'Wicket is fine. She even got the chip.'

'Great plan, Afzal. That was genius.' Beena eyed Tamir and chuckled. 'I did warn Rambo about his seatbelt.'

A groan sounded from the trunk. Latif was not happy about the crash. Wicket sniffed around, hopeful for a second chip.

'How is it that we were buckled in our seat and still got shaken up, while a dog loose in the car is fine?'

'Mysteries of the universe, buddy. Mysteries of the universe.' Afzal pushed Wicket out.

Beena and Rup followed. 'Man, we should join a derby considering the number of vehicles we've destroyed in the last few days. No one is going to believe we crashed into a mountain twice in one day.'

'We must keep moving before this maniac wakes up. Looks like we're walking from here on to the border—over that mountain.'

'Up the mountain? I think you hit your head too hard. We should continue on the road. You are not thinking straight.' Rup stared at Afzal.

'The road is dangerous and we'll be seen and picked up. If we go straight over, it'll be no more than ten to twenty kilometres to the border. It's just over this mountain.'

Rup looked up at the mountain rising above them into the sky. 'I'm not sure we're even looking at the same mountain.'

'Let's go before Rambo wakes up,' Afzal pleaded.

Rup sighed. 'Alright, fine. But I'm telling you now, I don't like it.

~

After an hour of hiking uphill, Rup's nostrils were flared, trying to inhale desperately needed oxygen. Beena was in better shape, but she too showed signs of fatigue. Afzal was gasping, sweat beading on his forehead.

Latif could not move his feet. Rup had to drag the out-of-shape terrorist along to keep the group moving.

'I won't make it. Just leave me here to die,' he sighed like a side actor in a B-grade movie making a play for sympathy.

'Move your feet, you lump of lard, or I'll really will leave you for that ISI agent to deal with. It seemed like he didn't like you much.' Beena shot a menacing look at the prisoner.

'Once we climb to the top, I say we push him downhill. He'll roll nicely into the gorge below,' Rup suggested cheerfully

The terrorist's pace quickened and the group continued forward.

~

After a short while, Tamir stirred and peered around, dazed. 'What the hell …?'

His memory returned and suddenly he was wide awake.

*Shit! That stupid dog. I should have killed it when I had the chance. I'll skin those kids alive … if only I had brought my handcuffs …*

Tamir moved his legs gingerly and checked himself. Once he was sure he could move, he forced himself to clear his mind. He needed to think.

*They can't have gone too far. This is my territory and I know this place better than anyone. I've friends I can call on. Just gotta find them.*

Tamir checked his supplies and realised that the kids had taken his gun, so he reached into his boot and extracted one spare phone and a snub-nosed pistol. *Ha! Still in the game.*

With a jolt of energy, he got out of the car. Pain shot up through his right ankle and he screamed, almost toppling over. Leaning against the door, he massaged his foot, scanning the area. It didn't take him long to spot their tracks—they had headed up the slope. *Smart kids.* The road wasn't safe; they were taking the shortcut to the border.

Tamir stood up and put weight on his foot. A bit better. He turned and limped up the mountain with determination. He'd only been out for thirty minutes. They couldn't have gone too far ahead.

*Gotta give it to those kids; it takes guts to set out on foot up here. Mountainous jihadi territory isn't for the faint-hearted.*

~

Qadir pressed down on the accelerator, tapping the brakes as he screeched around the corners. As he barrelled up the narrow road, he kept an eye out for any side paths that the drug dealer might have taken, perhaps to one of the small mountain villages.

'Those three bastards are the luckiest people on the planet, or they are some of the best RAW agents I've run into,' he muttered, shaking his head.

His car swerved around a tight corner, and he came upon a sight. His brand-new Toyota SUV was on the side of the road, wrecked, its front almost embedded inside the mountain wall. Blueish-black smoke wisped out from around the crumpled metal frame.

'What the hell?'

Qadir jumped out of the Jeep to inspect the crash scene. There were no signs of gunshots or bullet shells, no signs of a struggle or blood.

Qadir crouched and examined the ground around the vehicle. All signs pointed to one thing—they'd headed up into the mountains.

*An expert move. Three teens with a prisoner and a dog would be an easy mark on a narrow, open road. Those bastards were trained well.*

Qadir scowled at the mountain looming over him as if it was one of his incompetent supervisors. He checked his gear, including his weapons and set off on foot to follow their tracks up the wild mountain.

'I'm getting too old for this shit.'

# 23

## The Local Wildlife

Exhaustion set in. The trio's pace slowed.

Rup had wrapped his arm around Latif's to support his weight while Afzal pushed from behind. It was as though they were moving a stubborn cow.

Beena inspected the narrow trail. 'It looks like we are getting close to the summit and we'll soon start to head downhill. Should be easier then. But it'll be dark in a few hours, so there is that.'

Latif leaned against a tree and said, 'Look, I know you're not going to kill me. You kids don't have the balls. I'm exhausted and I can't take another step. How about this? I can make a video confession about the whole Mumbai incident.'

Beena glared at him. 'That's not all what we want. We want you to face justice, not for a so-called 'incident' but for all your terrorist attacks across India. Stop whining and move.'

Latif resisted and Afzal gave him a violent shove. 'When we get you to India, our cops will know how to extract a good confession.'

Rup threw the chubby terrorist's arm off and bent over with his hands on his knees. He was wheezing.

'I can't lug him anymore, I'm exhausted. Can't believe we got him this far up the mountain.'

'We've just got a bit more to go, Rup. Then the next phase is downhill.' Afzal stared down at the valley. India lay beyond the river. This trail seemed to lead down into the valley, as they'd hoped.

Latif plonked himself on the ground. 'I'm done.'

'Get up!' Beena put on her best threatening face and took a step towards their prisoner.

'No.' Latif cracked a tiny smile. 'Face it, kid, it'll be easier getting over the border without me. You did your best, but it's over. You failed.' He sized Beena up for the first time and sneered. 'You're weak, little girl. You don't have what it takes— or know what it means to have to kill someone for what you believe in. That's why you'll never get me off this mountain and over the border.'

Beena stared back, her eyes bright and her face flushed. 'We don't kill because we're better than you. And we want you to answer for your crimes. Death is the easy way out, after all.' Her voice was terrifyingly flat. 'And we'll get you over the border if that's the last thing we do. Rup, move over. I'm dragging this piece of shit myself.'

Both the boys eyed Beena. Her nostrils were flared and she was trembling with anger. Rup reached over and put his arm on her shoulder. 'Bee, we got this. If this is the last act the three of us do together—so be it. We'll tow him over. I promise. Just give me a few minutes to rest.'

Afzal put his arm on Beena's other shoulder, his eyes glistening. 'You are the best friends anyone can ever hope for.'

'All for one, one for all,' said Beena in a low, calm voice, her eyes focused on the prisoner. 'Even if hell freezes over, we're getting this mass murderer across to India.'

Rup glanced up abruptly and grabbed Afzal's arm. 'Shh! Did you hear that?'

'What?' Afzal looked around.

Rup hushed him. 'Listen.'

A strange sound drifted over a small ridge behind them. Beena spun towards it. 'What is that?'

'Some kind of animal?' whispered Afzal.

Carefully, Beena turned to take a closer look. 'Seems to be coming from beyond this thicket. A wild animal? What kind of dangerous ones are found in these parts? Lions or leopards, maybe? Shit, we need to keep the gun handy.'

Wicket wagged her tail and trotted to Rup for a pat. He smiled. 'Well, Wicket doesn't seem to care. That means it's not anything dangerous.'

Afzal studied the dog. 'You're right. Wicket's alerted us before when danger was around. But just to be sure, I'll check the noise out.' He jerked his head towards Latif. 'You two watch him.'

Afzal moved like a ninja towards the thicket, before dropping to a low crouch and disappearing into the bush. After a short while, he popped back up.

'You won't believe me if I tell you. Come see for yourself.'

'Believe what?'

'You better not be playing around with us. My feet hurt and I don't think I can bear any of your juvenile pranks right now.' Beena shuffled over to join Afzal.

Rup addressed Latif. 'Alright, Shamu. Up. Time to take in some of the local wildlife.' The terrorist was yanked back onto his feet. 'Move. And keep quiet. I'm not in the mood for your bullshit.'

When Beena and Rup got to the thicket, they caught sight of the mystery wildlife.

A horse and a donkey. Grazing in a clearing beyond the thicket, oblivious to the world. All three giggled.

Afzal pointed at the animals. 'Something to help us carry this idiot so that he doesn't slow us down. This is a sign. As I've been saying all along—the gods want Latif to face justice in India!'

Beena pursed her lips. 'Afzal, I'm not so sure. Those animals are loaded and clearly cared for. Their owners are definitely close by and the only people hanging around up here are drug dealers and terrorists. We'd be adding another target on our backs if we steal them.'

'Not if we hurry. We need the donkey to move this asshole. And we can take turns riding the horse. It'll take us to the border in half the time. C'mon!'

Rup was on Afzal's side. 'I don't think I can lug him for much longer—we need help and this donkey sure looks good. Bee, no more doubts.'

Afzal patted the horse's neck, then checked its load.

'Holy crap! There are all kinds of supplies in here.' He grabbed some paper carelessly stuffed under a strap. 'This looks like a hand-drawn map.'

Suddenly, Wicket's demeanour changed. The hair on her back stood up and she growled.

'Someone's coming!' Rup covered Latif's mouth.

Beena hissed at Latif, 'Keep quiet or there will be hell to pay.'

The teens hid in the thicket and peered uphill in the direction of the noise. Afzal removed the gun from his waist and held it in his hand. They crouched, eyes peeled.

They didn't have to wait long. A grizzled man emerged, in camouflage attire and a rifle slung across his shoulder. He waved angrily at the animals, hollering, 'I stop to take a dump and you wander off?'

Afzal tightened his grip on the gun and stepped out from behind the tree, warily sneaking up behind the man. Focused on the stranger, he didn't pay attention to what he was stepping on—which turned out to be a dry twig.

A sharp crack pierced the quiet mountainside.

The stranger spun toward the sound. At the same time, Afzal lifted the gun and shouted, 'Hands up!'

The man blinked, looking at the group, and reached for his own weapon. Afzal responded by shooting at the ground in front of the stranger. The man flinched and Afzal said, 'The next one won't miss. Hands up!'

The man raised his hands, scowling at his captors. Rup raced over behind the man.

'Bee, get some rope off the mule.'

In no time, they had the sullen man tied to a tree on the rugged mountainside.

Latif broke his silence. 'That man is a mujahideen warrior, like me. He won't take this lightly. I'm sure his companions heard those gunshots. My deal still stands if you let me go now. But once they catch you, the deal is off—and they'll skin you alive.'

Beena scoffed. 'Still going on about the deal? You're petrified, aren't you? Good. You should be. See that river down there? We'll be back in India before they find out anything.'

'Ignore him,' Afzal said. 'Just hoist him onto the mule.'

Rup and Afzal worked together to drape the handcuffed prisoner over the donkey's back. They used more of the rope to secure him so he wouldn't slip off.

'No! Just leave me here. You can tie me up with him. I promise we won't chase after you.' Latif was in tears now.

'Shut up, for god's sake.'

Afzal studied the map he'd taken from the horse. Beena abruptly snatched it from his hands and stuffed it back.

'We can look at maps later. I don't want to be here when this guy's friends arrive.'

'Good thinking as always, Bee,' said Afzal, grabbing the reins of the horse and directing it down the trail.

Rup and Beena worked together to move the donkey. But the animal stayed put—spooked by the growling dog. It was fidgeting and almost kicked Rup as he tried to push the animal along.

'Hey, Rup, careful. Don't push the donkey's rear unless you want to be kicked in your balls. Push the sides,' Beena said, chuckling. 'Donkeys kick so hard you won't wake up for days.'

'Don't push the ass of an ass, especially when it has another ass on top. Got it,' Rup chortled.

'C'mon, guys. We don't have all day.' Afzal was already on the move, leading the horse.

Rup grabbed the reins and Beena pushed the animal from its side and, after a minute or two, it moved in the desired direction. Once in motion, they urged the animal onward, following Afzal and the horse.

# 24

## The Best Roti Sabzi Ever

Tamir struggled to climb up the mountain. His ankle was recovering after the accident, but it still hurt. Once in a while, he had to stop and stretch to ease the tension in his legs.

He surveyed the orange-tinted sky. There was barely a cloud, which meant it would likely be a chilly night. That was good. It would be hard for those kids; not acclimatised to the mountain cold. Tamir followed the rapidly thinning trail, cursing them. How could these kids be moving so fast?

Suddenly, a sharp sound reverberated in the distance. He flinched.

Gunfire.

*It had to be the kids. Those clowns have left nothing but destruction in their wake. The sound isn't too far away. But who was firing and why only one shot?*

Adrenaline gave him a burst of energy and direction. He checked his gun and hurried towards the sound.

~

Darkness crept in. They'd had little sleep since crossing into Pakistan. The lack of rest along with the physical exertion of hiking in thin air over a mountain was catching up with them.

Afzal urged the horse forward. Rup led the donkey and Beena paced alongside to make sure Latif didn't slip off.

Afzal turned to look behind them. 'I don't believe Rambo is following us. Do you think he went down the road instead of up the mountain?'

Latif surprised everyone when he answered, 'Don't worry, Tamir will find you. This is his backyard. You won't make it to the border. I guarantee it.'

Beena shrugged. 'Your guarantees are like your deals—worthless. Maybe Rambo will follow, but he won't find us. I'm more worried about the terrorist gangs at this point.'

'I'm all for pushing on,' said Rup. 'The more ground between us and any of them, the better.'

Afzal stopped. 'Bee, can you help me? We need to make sure we're going in the right direction. Let's study the map in the horse's saddle pouch.'

Afzal flicked on the flashlight, shielding the beam. Beena blocked the light on his left. On the other side, they used the horse as a screen. When he was happy that the light was contained inside the triangle, he focused on the map—pointing at specific spots.

'These markings at various points seem like tunnels. Some are on the other side of the river.'

Beena focused on the markings. 'That tunnel is interesting, since that spot is already inside India. Are they using it to sneak deeper into Indian territory?'

'Shoot, you know what that means? That man we tied up must be a jihadi. Maybe they were planning to sneak into India to do who knows what.'

'We stopped another attack before it started? I can live with that.' Beena couldn't hide the pride in her voice. Her face became serious. 'Wait. Tamir is still frantically trying to find us and his notebook, and because we have their stuff, terrorists will be hunting us, too.'

'At least we got rid of that ISI agent.' Rup sounded hopeful.

Beena patted the horse's neck. 'If the terrorists were planning to sneak into India, what are the animals carrying?'

'We took off so fast, we never checked. Maybe it's time to have a look.'

Beena nodded. She held onto the horse's reins as Afzal opened the first pouch. He took out a set of binoculars.

After digging more, he pulled out a water canteen. He opened it and took a long swig, then passed it along.

Rup exhaled noisily, wiping his mouth with his sleeve after taking a big gulp.

'Shit, I forgot how thirsty I was.'

He stooped down and gave some to Wicket, who lapped up the water.

'You're right. These animals were gifts from the gods, complete with supplies. Let's see what this donkey is carrying.' Rup fought with a knot on the donkey's load.

'Guys, there's food in this pouch. Jackpot!'

At the mention of food, Rup stopped wrestling with the knot. His eyes became huge at the sight of something to eat.

'Well, don't hog it. Pass it around.'

Afzal handed over the food, large pieces of naan wrapped tightly around what seemed like meat and vegetables. Beena grabbed the offering. 'Just what we needed!'

Rup took a huge bite from his wrap. As he chewed, he mumbled, 'Oh, mama. That tastes good. I think that's the best roti-sabzi ever.'

'Coming up the mountain was the right call, from a nutritional perspective.'

'It's amazing what a little water and food can do. Here, Wicket. You have some too.'

They all laughed as Wicket devoured the food in big chunks. 'What about me?' Latif whined.

'Shut up!' yelled the three teens in unison.

Rup went back to wrestling with the knot on the donkey—this time winning. He opened the flap, peeked inside and took a sharp breath, waving furiously at his friends to come over.

'What's wrong with you, Rup? The naan choking you?'

Wordless, Rup gestured at the pouch, eyes big behind his glasses. Beena peered inside and saw a dense loop of colourful wires attached to a several grey bricks and electronic modules. She stepped back, alarmed. 'Shit. They look like explosives connected to a timer. It doesn't seem switched on, but don't make any sudden moves. Shut the flap carefully and don't touch it.'

Afzal gasped, 'Bombs? We've been lugging around bombs!'

Atop the donkey, Latif struggled against his restraints. His eyes were wide with terror. 'Bombs? No, don't leave it in the pouch. Get me off this mobile landmine!'

Beena hissed, 'Stay still and shut up or you'll set them off.'

Rup exhaled heavily. 'We should unload this pouch and get as far away as possible. We don't know when they'll go off.'

Beena shook her head. 'We can't do anything in the dark. If you didn't notice, there are several wires here. And one snakes around the belly of the donkey, like a safeguard trigger. I'm sure the terrorists didn't mean to blow up a donkey. We need daylight to sort this out.'

'These dudes were planning to do some terrible shit in India,' Rup said.

Afzal locked eyes with Latif. 'I suggest you learn how to keep perfectly still atop a swaying donkey.'

Latif did not respond, staring at Afzal long and hard. The boy scowled. 'What? You got something to say?'

'Alright, Bee. Time to show off your Manipuri mountaineering skills. You should take the map and lead us down to the valley,' said Rup.

Beena couldn't keep a small smile from escaping. 'I'm not sure if that's a jab at my skills, my mountainous heritage or a compliment.'

'All of it, buddy. All of it.'

# 25

# The Bridge-Tunnel Plan

Tamir gritted his teeth and kept moving in the direction of the distant gunshot—stopping occasionally to check for tracks. His head was still a bit cloudy from being knocked out by the airbag, but he tried to think things through.

*That swollen man in the back said he was Rasheed Latif. Is that possible? He didn't look like Latif. Doesn't matter, he could be valuable.*

He pulled out his phone and opened the app, but there was no sign of his burners.

*They must be turned off. Damn, six months of burner phones used up in one week.*

Tamir stopped to examine the ground for any sign of the teens.

*Shit! There it is. Dog poop near a bush. This crap is the only useful thing that stupid dog has done for me. Aha, and beside it tracks of someone struggling or being pushed.*

He was closing on their trail. The fat prisoner was slowing them down. Tamir grinned. A fresh spring in his step, he walked on, until he heard rustling sounds in the bushes ahead.

Tamir paused again, straining to understand the noise. The branches on a bush were shaking violently. Then he heard a man groan. Tamir inched onward.

It was a bearded man, gagged and bound to a small tree.

Tamir scoped out the area before he approached. The man's eyes widened when he saw him—he mumbled and strained against his binding. Tamir knelt and removed his gag.

'Did those kids do this?'

The man coughed and spat. 'Three of them with a mangy dog! They got the drop on me. They stole my horse, mule and important supplies. One of the kids nearly shot me!'

'Yeah, I believe it. More than you know. Was there a big man with them?'

'Yup. He was tied up too.'

'If I free you, will you help me catch them?'

'You bet your ass. I need those animals. Well, I need the load they carry. Hey, I know you. Tamir, right? We met a few times when you visited my boss. I am Nadeem.'

The man nodded his thanks as Tamir cut the rope.

'I remember you now, Nadeem. I called in a favour from your boss a while back. Nearly called him again to search for the kids.'

Nadeem shook his head, massaging his hands to get circulation back. 'The boss doesn't need to know yet.'

Tamir inspected the man. 'Alright, when we catch them, you'll be rewarded.'

Nadeem said, 'My friends should have been here by now.'

'You have friends here?'

'Yep. Bastards are late as usual.'

The terrorist stood up. Tamir followed.

'Will it take long to round them up, d'you think?'

'No. We've some important work across the border, if you know what I mean.'

Tamir took his phone out and opened his tracking app.

'Let me figure out where those blasted kids are. While I do that, you find your friends. Tell them there is a reward when we find those kids.'

'Okay.' The terrorist rushed off.

~

The food and water had lifted their spirits. Beena led the way now, studying the map. 'According to this sketch, there are a couple of tunnels from this side all the way across the border. Maybe one of them will get us home. The official border crossing is a bridge—one of these tunnels is close to it. Let's head for that tunnel. The bridge can be our backup if the tunnels don't work.'

Afzal nodded. 'Makes sense, Bee. What's our fastest route?'

She focused on the map. 'I'm not sure where we are. And it's hard to read in this light. I say we use the bridge tunnel.'

'Bridge tunnel? That sounds weird.' Rup chuckled. 'Bridge tunnel. Jumbo shrimp. Pygmy elephant.'

'You know what I mean,' she snapped. 'You focus on the weirdest shit.'

'I can't help it.'

'Please focus on our precise location instead.' Beena groaned and continued, 'Because without that, we really can't figure out how to get there.' She halted, thinking hard.

'Does this mean we have to turn on Tamir's phone and use the GPS?' mused Afzal aloud.

Beena turned to Afzal. 'Are you nuts?'

Rup looked at Afzal gravely. 'Phones can be tracked, Afzal. You can't be too careful.'

It was Rup's turn to receive Beena's icy stare. 'Oh, *now* you get it—after sending fifty messages via WhatsApp?'

'Look, we know Tamir found us by tracking his burners, but we have no choice.' Afzal took out the phone. 'What say, Bee?'

'Ugh, fine. Maybe the risk is low if the phone's GPS is turned on only for a short time. Alright. Two minutes? That should be short enough to be safe.'

Afzal took a deep breath. 'Okay. Two minutes.'

'I'll time you ...'

Afzal pressed the power button. 'Don't start counting yet. GPS is offline while it boots up.' His fingers hovered over the phone. 'Come on. Why do these things take so long?' Finally, the home screen flickered on. 'Start counting!'

Beena nodded and started mouthing silently. His fingers tapped furiously, bringing up a map on the small screen.

'There. It's up!'

Afzal glanced at the paper map and back to the screen.

'Okay, we're good. Powering off! I know where we are. How long was that?'

'One minute, twenty-two seconds. Not bad.'

Afzal held the map and pointed. 'We're right here. That bridge tunnel of yours is in this direction.'

'How far?'

'Fifteen kilometres. Maybe less. I'm sure the terrorists are looking for these animals, there's no time to waste. C'mon, let's move.'

~

Tamir watched the terrorist leave. Then he flipped his phone open again, and checked his phone tracking app.

Nada. He checked his favourite messaging channels, including the ones the local drug dealers used. There were a few notes about opium activity in Afghanistan and other conspiracy theories in Pakistan. One jumped up and caught his eye.

*JeK leader Rasheed Latif missing and presumed kidnapped by Indian RAW agents.*

Tamir whistled. 'Damn! The bloated prisoner was telling the truth. He *is* Latif! But the kidnappers? They're only kids, not agents.'

He sat on a log of wood and considered his options.

*Better not tell Nadeem and gang about Latif yet. Once we dispose of the kids, I can rescue him. I'm sure there will be a reward or some favour I can call in later.*

Suddenly, his phone buzzed. A red dot blinked on the tracking screen. 'Holy shit! Those morons have turned my phone on.'

He took note of their location; they seemed to be making a beeline down the mountain. He looked up when he heard a rustling sound behind him. A group of four terrorists appeared along with Nadeem, armed for the hunt. Tamir stood up, stuffing the phone into his trousers and nodding at the new additions.

'Good, Nadeem. I want the big prisoner alive. He could be useful.'

'Those kids are going to pay. In blood. As long as the prisoner doesn't get in the way, I don't care about him.'

'They also have a notebook I need. After that, do what you want with them.'

'I'm only concerned about my animals. We'll take care of those two kids, especially the girl.'

'Deal. And as I said, there's something for all of you when we find them. You know me; I can deliver.'

The terrorists nodded.

Tamir continued, 'You have a gun? This little one won't cut it.'

'Guns? That's something we have in plenty.' One of the terrorists reached into his knapsack and handed Tamir a locally-made pistol.

'I prefer German guns, but this should do,' Tamir said. He slid a magazine in, pointed at a branch and eased off two quick shots. Leaves scattered in the clearing. 'Good enough. Now we track them with this.' Tamir held up his phone.

Nadeem tilted his head. 'What do you mean?'

'The kids stole a few of my burner phones. And lucky for us, one of those phones was just switched on. I know exactly where they are.'

The terrorists laughed. One of them, a short stocky man, said, 'That high-tech shit always gets you in trouble. Out here, we keep it simple. We use old-fashioned phones and only in emergencies.'

Nadeem instantly spotted hoof prints on the trail. 'We don't need any high-tech tracking. I know my horse's tracks anywhere. Let's go.'

~

Qadir hated the mountains. They were isolated and the weather could get chilly at night. He should be shivering, but he'd been working so hard to track his prey that he was generating excess body heat. He felt a cold bead of sweat trickle down his back. Not good.

He checked the surroundings again. The trail was well-used. Finding fresh tracks was tough but not impossible. The dog had left faint markings in a few places, but the clearer trail was from someone being pushed and dragged.

*They came this way. But how far behind am I?*

At that instant, two sharp gunshots rang through the clear mountain air. Bam, bam! Qadir squinted uphill in the direction of the sound.

*Shit. Sounds like a handgun. Now what did you three do? Alright, time to stop messing around. I need to hunt you like you're the best RAW agents ever to infiltrate Pakistan. Because that may well be the case.*

~

'Leave me here. I'm of no use to you.'

Latif's voice was halting and soft. He spoke like a recording, programmed to repeat over and over. Afzal's was the opposite— confident, loud and firm.

'Your future, what little of it is left, is in India. We're almost there. Your gag is off so you can breathe in this high altitude— we don't want you to wheeze to death yet. Keep quiet, or we'll stuff it right back in.'

Beena smiled. 'A bit more than *almost there*, but close enough. Fifteen kilometres through strange, mountainous terrain, that too in the dark? That will take us … hmm … maybe eight to ten hours? But we should be able to make it by 10.45 a.m., just when the guards are changing shifts.'

The voice from atop the donkey was panicky. 'Ten hours? I can't ride this beast for another ten minutes. Get me off this thing.'

Wicket responded to the fat terrorist with a growl.

Rup groaned. 'Oof … ten hours … that's a serious hike on a good day for me. And this isn't one of those days.'

Beena laughed. 'It'll be good for you—toughen you up.'

'Will think of a good comeback later, after I steal some of Wicket's energy.' Rup's voice held traces of the exhaustion they all felt. They smiled as they watched the dog, still full of energy, sniffing every rock on the trail.

Suddenly, Wicket's ears perked up, responding to a faint crack in the distance. Beena glanced at her and whispered, 'Was that a gunshot? We need to keep moving. This place is crawling with bad guys.'

They continued down the faint trail, the faint gunfire injecting more urgency into their gait. After a while, they came to the crest of a small hill. Far down in the valley, through the foliage, they could see faint lights glimmering on both sides of the river—and a straight row of bright lights connecting them.

Afzal said, pointing excitedly, 'That must Chakoti and the bridge over the Jhelum! I can see India. We're close!'

They stopped for a minute to gaze at the scattered lights near the valley.

'Those lights are Indian soldiers. We'll hand Latif over to the nearest one as soon as we cross the border.' Afzal was back to his usual self, planning three steps ahead.

'I just want to set foot on Indian soil,' Beena said wearily. 'Then I'll worry about how and where to turn over this sack of shit.'

Suddenly, Latif chimed in, looking straight at Afzal from his prone position on the back of the donkey. 'Aha! Now I remember where I've seen you before. You look very similar to Rizwan Sheik. He helped me launch an attack in India some ten years ago.'

Afzal turned. 'What did you say? Rizwan who?'

'Yep. Rizwan Sheik. I've been racking my drugged brain all this time. Except for a cut on his forehead and a limp in his left leg, Rizwan could have passed for you. He was killed because some treasonous relative leaked his information to the police. What a shame to have a traitor in the family rat you out.'

Before Afzal could respond, Wicket growled at the trail behind them—her ears perked up and her hackles raised.

'Someone's coming,' Rup whispered. The colour drained from his face when he spotted something.

'Guys! Someone's coming!'

# 26

# Bullets, Flesh and Blood

Looking at the moving lights, Beena whispered, 'Everyone, keep quiet. Afzal, gag him, will you?'

Before he could, Latif bellowed, 'I'm over here. Help!'

Afzal grabbed Latif's head and stuffed a rag into his mouth, but it was too late. The lights stopped scanning and focused in their direction, drawing closer. Afzal watched them for a second. 'Fuck, they heard the bastard.'

Suddenly, shots rang out. The sound of a bullet whizzing past startled them.

'Duck, take cover! On the ground!' hissed Beena, pulling them down. The three friends hit the earth and huddled close.

Machine guns sent a hail of bullets over them. They heard a few of them thud into nearby trees. The horse and donkey strained at their reins. Rup crouched on all fours, crawled over to the animals and pushed them behind a large tree. He gestured urgently, whispering, 'Come! Take cover here.'

Afzal and Beena started to drag themselves over, when a bullet zipped overhead and showered them with leaves. Wicket yelped and jumped up. Rup shuffled over to calm her down, whispering, 'Wicket, shh. Lie down.'

Suddenly, a thump sounded—the sickening sound of a hard bullet striking soft flesh. There was a sharp gasp of pain followed by a low groan.

'Bloody hell. That hurts.' Rup clutched his left shoulder and collapsed with a painful shudder.

Afzal's face turned white.

Beena crawled swiftly over in the darkness towards Rup. Shaking, Afzal followed her—his entire body sweating in spite of the cold. Tears welled up in his eyes as he leaned over. 'Oh shit, shit. I'm so sorry, Rup. I shouldn't have brought you guys into this mess.'

The burst of bullets stopped abruptly. The silence was ominous.

'I think they're reloading,' Beena said, as she felt Rup's shoulder—he winced at her touch. 'Goddamn it, Rup. You're hit and there is blood seeping out.'

She looked grimly at Afzal and checked the other side of Rup's damaged shoulder. 'You're lucky it didn't hit your neck. We need to stop the bleeding.'

Afzal was in tears. 'Why did you get up to move the animals? That damn bullet should have hit Latif. How are you, Rup?'

'Sorry, I wanted to make sure Wicket was safe.'

Hearing her name, Wicket nuzzled Rup and licked his forehead.

Afzal stared into the quiet darkness, his face grim. 'They know we're around here. We don't have much time to slip away.'

'How do we outrun these guys? And with Rup injured—!'

Afzal warily scanned the area. Lights were bobbing and sweeping in the distance. They were closer than before. He said in a low voice, 'They're coming, maybe four or five of them. It's only a matter of time before they find us.'

He paused, looking at Rup's bloodied shoulder and then at Beena. 'I know how we can escape. I'll draw them away and run in the other direction. You guys keep moving towards the border; I'll get them to follow me.'

Rup shook his head and struggled to raise himself. 'No, no. We stay together. I'm fine, I can keep up with you.'

'No, Rup. We can't outrun them. You're hurt and we need to stop that bleeding urgently. Our only play is to distract them.'

Beena's eyes brimmed with tears. 'Afzal, no. Don't leave us.'

Afzal's face was set, eyes glistening. 'Head straight for the bridge with those animals. I'll meet you at the border before tomorrow's shift change. I promise.'

Beena and Rup both cried, 'No!'

Beena reached out and grabbed Afzal by his tunic. Afzal firmly pried her fingers open, releasing her hold.

'Bee, tend to Rup's wound. If I'm late, don't wait for me. Reach home in one piece and get justice for your aunt. Now go!'

With that, Afzal spun and sprinted into the darkness.

Beena and Rup watched their friend disappear into the night. Rup turned to Wicket. He patted her head as she stared at him with big bright eyes.

'Go with Afzal, girl. Keep him safe, okay?'

To Beena's amazement, Wicket turned and ran off, following Afzal into the dark.

Stumbling through the rough terrain, Afzal had tears in his eyes. The guilt of plunging his friends into life-threatening danger overrode his fear of being caught. In the dark, all the guilt and insecurity he had been experiencing came to a head. There was no denying that his stupid ego had placed his dearest friends in life-threatening danger.

In addition, the name Rizwan Sheik throbbed mercilessly in his brain, like a jackhammer pounding away—changing everything in an instant. But this wasn't the time to think about what Latif had said. This was the time to lead the men with guns away and give Rup and Bee a chance to escape.

As he lurched through the dark thicket, Afzal powered on the burner phone. Right then, he heard someone rushing through the brush—directly behind him and fearing the worst, stopped and hid behind a tree. But to his surprise, Wicket came hurtling right up to his hiding place.

'Wicket!' he breathed; the dog wagged her tail. 'I've never been happier to see you. Come, let's go!'

They continued running and then suddenly, it hit Afzal.

'Your barking is a nuisance, but right now, bark as much you'd like. Wicket, speak!'

To Afzal's surprise, the dog barked. Then she barked again, her playful eyes shining—visible even in the low light.

'Good girl. Keep it up and come with me.'

He swiped the phone around, turning on its flashlight. With the light, barking dog and cell signal, there was no way they could possibly miss him.

~

Rup and Beena were still in shock, watching Wicket speed after Afzal into the dark woods.

Beena watched as the unknown lights paused, shifted direction and started to move in Afzal's direction. They'd taken the bait. He'd bought them time to make their escape.

She checked the animals for injuries. They had calmed down.

Beena supported Rup as he struggled to mount the horse, using his good hand to haul himself up. She untied the animals and pulled them forward, moving as fast as possible, taking the trail leading straight towards the bridge over the Jhelum.

After a few moments of intense silence, Rup gave voice to what they were both thinking. 'That's the bravest thing I've ever seen anyone do.'

Beena blinked back tears and looked away. 'Yeah. Let's hope it doesn't get him killed.'

# 27

# The Leopard's Den

Qadir followed the tracks to the tree to which the trio had tied the terrorist. Daylight was gone, and he turned on his phone light. He spotted frayed ropes and footprints on the ground. It appeared as though a small army had wrestled here.

At that instant, gunfire sounded in the distance. A lot of it.

*Bloody hell! This is getting out of control. It's time to bring in the big guns.*

He flipped his phone, dialled and waited impatiently. When it was answered, he barked, 'Hey. I need you to pick me up from this mountain. I'm sending over the coordinates. There's a small clearing close by where you can hover.' He listened to the short answer. 'Good. See you shortly.'

It took thirty minutes, but the chopper eventually found Qadir. It hovered in the sky and dropped a rope ladder. Qadir climbed up with practised ease, buckled in and put on the headset.

'Nice to see you boys again. Thanks for coming.'

'We didn't want to miss out on all the fun. Ready?'

'Hell yes. I've been tracking the three suspects, but looks like locals are involved now. Likely mujahideen. I need eyes in the sky to find them. Hit the spotlight.'

A large lamp mounted under the front end of the helicopter powered on. It shot a blinding column of light down the mountainside, illuminating everything in its path with a harsh glare.

Qadir spoke into the headset again. 'We're looking for three teens and a fat idiot. They'll be walking right towards the border. Keep an eye out for locals, too. I heard gunfire in that direction. JeK is likely involved.'

'Understood. Where do you want to check first?'

'They're making a dash for the Jhelum border bridge. Let's prioritise our search on trails that head straight down there.'

'Got it.'

The pilot propelled the helicopter, keeping the bright spotlight on the trail.

~

They stopped about a kilometre from the shooting. Beena stuffed Rup's shoulder with pieces of cloth and finished by tying her scarf tight across his shoulder. 'This should control the bleeding. Don't make any sudden moves and bust the sling, okay?'

Rup nodded, gingerly feeling his shoulder with his hand. That's when they heard a distant whir. Beena looked up and saw the airborne threat. A bright eye-in-the-sky scanning the mountainside was coming straight down the trail towards them.

She gritted her teeth. 'That must be Qadir and the ISI. We're fully exposed here—there's no way we can outrun a chopper.'

'But where—'

'Come on. I've an idea.' Beena pointed towards a small rock overhang on the side of the trail. She tied the horse under a small tree and reached over to help Rup dismount. He gestured at Latif as she tied the donkey right next to the horse.

'What do we do with him?'

'We can't untie and dismount him in time. Let's get him centred.'

Latif flopped around, looking ready to slump to the ground any minute as they tightened his knots and adjusted his position. Satisfied with the result, Beena ran back to the horse. She returned with a prayer rug and covered Latif with it.

'Let's hope that works. Come on, let's get out of sight.'

Beena and Rup climbed underneath the overhang and packed themselves in tight, away from the edge. All they could do was watch the beam of light cutting through the trees, heading straight towards them.

~

The pilot skimmed the treetops as he manoeuvred the craft, following the trail down the mountain which led straight to the border bridge. After a few minutes, the pilot's voice rang in Qadir's headset.

'We have something. Hard to see clearly but looks like locals moving who knows what on a couple of pack animals.'

Qadir raised the binoculars and zoomed onto where the light shone.

'Hmm … unless you also see a mangy dog with them, those are not our targets. They're on foot and dragging a fatso. Let's keep looking.'

'Gotcha. Man, that damn donkey is awful fidgety. Looks like it's lugging a pretty heavy load.'

'Exactly why drug smugglers and terrorists use them. Stubborn as hell but can carry a lot of cargo.'

The pilot snorted. 'Yeah, but that poor animal is about to buckle!'

Afzal felt exhausted. He'd left his friends thirty minutes ago, managing to cover a good distance. Hopefully enough for Rup and Beena to escape. Now it was time for him to lose his pursuers.

The first thing he did was shut off the phone. Then, he whispered, 'Wicket, come here.'

The dog loped over and sat at his feet, wagging her tail.

'Good girl. No barking. Okay?'

Wicket stared at him, unblinking and still as a statue. Afzal shook his head. 'What am I even doing, talking to a dog? Rup has me believing she understands what we say.'

Suddenly, she turned and emitted a low growl. Afzal spun to follow her gaze; lights were moving in the bushes.

'Come on, we need to hide.'

Afzal tugged at her coat and started jogging away from the lights. Wicket stayed close to him. It was dark, and the surroundings were hard to make out.

After a few hundred yards, Afzal tripped on a rocky protrusion and stumbled. As he flailed, his fingers brushed against some dangling vines—he grabbed them tightly and jerked to a halt, swaying side to side, panting.

'Whoa lucky. Running in this darkness is tricky.'

As he struggled up, he noticed that Wicket had stuck her head into the vines and was sniffing furiously. She pulled her head out and stared at him, her ears pulled down.

'What is it, girl? We don't have time for games.'

A crash in the thicket nearby jolted him. The flashlights were bouncing around in the dark. On a whim, he crouched down and peeked through the leafy curtain to check what Wicket was sniffing at. It was a tiny cave, dark and hidden well by a rock outcrop and the surrounding shrubbery.

'Good job, Wicket, get in.'

He patted her rump and Wicket shot inside like a bolt. Afzal followed, crawling on his hands and knees through the small opening. The floor was damp and cool. A heavy, acrid smell hit his face. His fingers jumped to cover his nostrils.

'Ugh … smells like concentrated piss.'

Afzal turned, trying to look around. The cave was pitch dark except for a slight sliver of light streaming in through the leafy vines at the entrance.

*Must be some kind of den. Shit! Like for a leopard?*

He felt for Wicket—she was lying quietly on her belly, her paws spread out in front of her. Only her bright eyes were visible.

Light beams glinted through the dense curtain. He stiffened, but in any case, it was too late for a plan B. Movement was visible outside—only a few feet away. Afzal held his breath as footsteps approached. He felt Wicket tense up, her body coiling, and moved closer, running his hand gently over her fur.

They waited. It felt as if their pursuers were trudging around for an eternity. Afzal felt sweat bead his face, his heart beating like a drum.

Suddenly, Wicket raised her head, her ears pricking up. A pair of familiar boots came into view through the bushes at the cave's entrance. It was Tamir. He was standing right outside.

Fear jolted through Afzal. His body shivered; he felt paralysed and unable to think or move. He'd never experienced emotion so real and extreme.

No Bee. No Rup. He was all alone.

Afzal reached out and hugged Wicket, pulling her closer. She stayed still and silent, her eyes shining straight at him. He was grateful she was close by. Without her, his fear would have been a lot worse.

He promised himself that he would never forget this moment. The name Rizwan Sheik, dropped so casually by Latif, made Afzal realise the true worth of what he had and what he stood to lose. And if he got out alive, he would lead a life everyone could be proud of.

After a few never-ending minutes, Afzal heard one of the men call out to Tamir, 'This thicket is too dense. With the rocky terrain here, there aren't any feet or horse prints to follow. I don't think they came this way.'

'How can that be?' roared Tamir. 'We all heard that stupid dog, saw the phone GPS coordinates and their flashlight. They were right here!'

Another voice insisted, 'They must have gone in another other direction.'

'Those idiots don't know these mountains; they could be lost and wandering all over. We must keep searching.'

The voices faded as they moved away from the cave. Wicket licked Afzal's palms and stood up. He gazed at the bright-eyed dog and gave her another pat on the head.

'You did good. Now let's get out before whatever lives in this cave comes back and makes a meal out of us.'

28

# Dangling Over Nothing

Following Wicket, Afzal crawled gingerly out of the cave. Once in the open, they moved away from Tamir and his friends. But walking off-trail over a dark mountain is difficult. This was a harsh environment, one that turned everyday tasks into dangerous affairs. That included finding one's bearings.

Afzal scanned his surroundings but, in the inky darkness, couldn't see properly beyond his arm. A shape could be anything—an animal, a hole, a clump of bushes or a pool of water. And he dared not switch on his phone light.

'Come Wicket,' whispered Afzal. 'We need to get back to Bee and Rup.'

Wicket barked when she heard Rup's name.

'No, Wicket. Shh … quiet!'

Afzal froze in place, listening. To his dismay, he heard faint voices that seemed to be getting louder. A flashlight blazed through the foliage. Then another. And another.

'I told you the dog is around here. I will skin them alive!' A loud voice, unmistakably Tamir's, shredded the silence of the night.

Afzal looked around in desperation.

*The way back to the cave is blocked. We need to find another path.*

Afzal moved away from the lights swiftly, following Wicket through the thick underbrush. They would've sprinted, but the terrain and rocks prevented it. *At least Rambo and friends have to wade through this too.*

As they pushed through one section of thick brush, Wicket stopped abruptly. Afzal stopped as well, trusting the dog's instincts. Feeling a breeze on his face, he peered around and saw nothing—until he glanced down and noticed he was on the edge of a sheer drop. If he'd taken another step, he would've fallen into a ravine. He stepped back, heart pounding.

Not too far away, Tamir yelled to the other terrorists, 'They must have been hiding. Spread out and see if you can find the horse or the donkey's tracks.'

The lights widened their arc, continuing to move closer. Afzal stared down at the abyss. A dark void lay in front, and a pissed off drug dealer advanced from behind. Fear clouded Afzal's mind, but he forced himself to calm down and evaluate the situation.

'Breathe, man. Breathe,' he whispered to himself, steadying himself, his back towards a small knotty tree barely held up by its roots, protruding over the edge.

Inching sideways along the jagged edge of the cliff was the only way, but it was risky in the dark. One wrong step, and he would fall.

The lights were almost upon him. Time to move. Or die. Or both. He felt the rough bark of the tree trunk and peered down.

*Wait. Maybe there's another option …*

'Wicket, come here,' he whispered.

Wicket trotted over, wagging her tail. Afzal crouched down and picked her up, cradling her against his chest with his left arm. Then, with his right hand, he grabbed the tree's protruding root and tugged, testing its strength. He sat on the edge, hooked his feet over and cautiously climbed down the cliff face—holding onto the root with one hand and the dog with the other.

*Shit. This is stupid. This is sooooo stupid. What am I doing?*

Afzal scraped his shoe frantically across the rock face, feeling for some purchase. The root gave way a bit, dislodging dirt and a few pebbles showered onto his head. Wicket squirmed in his arms, shaking off the sudden rain of debris. Gingerly easing his grip on the tip of the root, he stretched to find a slightly large stone protruding from the rock wall. Hopefully it would support him for a few minutes.

Afzal felt another root jutting through the face of the cliff. He shifted his weight onto the stone, balancing about a metre below the edge of the ravine, and leaned onto the wall, grabbing the new root. Wicket shifted closer against his chest, her nose nuzzling into his neck.

A beam shone over his head, fading into the void. Wicket tensed up in his arms and he whispered into her ear, 'Shh, Wicket, shh. I got you.' He held her closer against his ribs, feeling her rapid heartbeat through his clothes. The dog's breath was warm against his neck in the cool night.

Tamir and the terrorists were nearly on top of him. He heard one of them say, 'Are you sure it was the same dog? I don't see anything.'

'Shut up! I'd recognise that stupid bark in my sleep.'

More lights flashed over the edge of the cliff, scanning the area. To his right, more dirt and small rocks tumbled over the edge. Wicket was starting to feel like a small bag of bricks. His arm was getting numb and he could feel his strength ebbing.

Afzal forced himself to breathe. His right hand held tightly onto the root, which was slowly ripping out of the cliff. If they shone the flashlight to their left and below, they'd see him.

Fresh footsteps and noises told Afzal that Tamir had joined his colleague at the lip of the cliff.

A beam of light swayed over the edge—like a pendulum. Another flashlight shone down the abyss to Afzal's left. Tamir peered down to see if he could see any bodies.

'Could be they fell over, but I'm not betting on it. These three kids are alive to cause me pain. If you ask me, they're still around here somewhere.'

A terrorist said, 'That drop is too far down for that puny flashlight. And we'd have definitely heard a scream.'

'Yeah, you're right. This is too far off the normal walking trail, which is where that helicopter is shining its light. I'm sure that's ISI, searching for the kids. We're wasting our time here.'

The stones covering the area crunched under shoes and Afzal heard them move away, bickering about what to do. Footfalls receded into the thicket.

Afzal let out a sigh. But his respite was short-lived. The root was starting to give way—showering him with even more dirt. A sharper tug would completely rip it from its base.

Afzal let go of the root and placed his right hand on the rock face. He stared up at the top of the ledge. It was only a metre away, but felt like a mile. How would he climb back with only one arm and no root for support?

'Bloody hell. We're in a bit of a pickle here, Wicket. And just how are you getting heavier with every passing minute?'

~

The helicopter pilot spoke over the comms, 'I saw faint lights a little higher up on the mountain. They seem to be in a sweeping pattern. You want to check them out?'

'Yeah. Lights up here are unusual. Someone's looking for something, or someone, with urgency. The targets are the kids. Whoever fired those machine guns is also searching for them.'

'Should I make our weapons operational?' The pilot turned to look at Qadir.

The grizzled ISI agent nodded. 'But remember what I said. Alive if possible. I want to interrogate them. If it seems they're going to get Latif over the border, shoot to kill. That's the only time you take them out. Understood?'

'No crossing the border. But before that, capture and detain.'

'Exactly. Let's find these assholes.'

~

Wicket wagged her tail and licked Afzal's sweaty face as he tried to estimate how far he had to climb up.

'Glad you're positive about this, because I'm not.' Afzal wiped his face on his shoulder, then stared back at the ledge above them. 'That's the longest metre I've ever seen. How are we going to get up there?'

He clenched his teeth. It was time to climb.

Feeling around with his foot for another toehold, he found a small one, barely protruding, a bit higher than he would like. His flexibility was stretched to the limit as he tried to step up onto it.

'I sure as hell should've done more squats,' he whispered to Wicket, 'and maybe some yoga.'

He hooked his foot and pushed hard, lifting himself slowly. Once secure, he moved the other foot, searching for purchase. He found a spot and braced himself. Now he had to shift his free right hand but could not use his left to hold anything.

Afzal scanned the rocky wall. In the dark, it was hard to see, but he spied what he thought was a crack. If he were to live, he had to be sure it was something he could grab. If Afzal was wrong, he and Wicket would plummet to their deaths.

'Okay, I can do this. We've no choice. Wish me luck, Wicket. For both our sakes.'

Leaning in, he darted his right hand into the crack in the stone. His fingers slammed into the opening and pain flashed in his fingers. He felt himself starting to lose balance and fall backwards. Gritting his teeth, he hung on—sweating in spite of the cold.

*Damn, that hurts.*

It was time to find another foothold. And another.

It took over ten minutes of slow deliberate movements and he was back near the edge of the lip. He lifted Wicket as best he could but was still a foot short. Then to Afzal's surprise, the dog wriggled free from his grip. She pushed on his chest to climb a little higher, then stepped onto his shoulders, placing her front paws on the lip of the abyss. She balanced her feet on top of his head, stretched enough to dig her front paws into solid ground. The dog then pulled herself up to safety, disappearing from his view. Afzal was impressed by her resourcefulness.

'Clever girl. Now stay quiet while I do the same.'

With both hands free, Afzal reached for the edge of the cliff, hoping for a protrusion to hold on to. There were none. After a few tiring attempts, he managed to find and grab onto a small embedded rock with his right hand. He then reached out with his left and dug deep into the earth, struggling to drag himself up.

But his left hand was still numb, and his fingers could not grasp the earth. He felt his grip slipping—the soil crumbling out through weak fingers. Unable to hoist his entire weight by itself, his right hand loosened its grip on the small stone.

Afzal's head swam with exhaustion and terror—he began to lose his balance and slide backwards into the ravine.

Suddenly, he felt a sharp yank on his kurta. He glanced up to see Wicket had latched her jaws onto the left-hand sleeve and was pulling hard. She growled and strained, her front paws pushing against the edge of the cliff.

Afzal snapped into focus. With renewed resolve, he grabbed the stone again firmly with his right and dug in deep with the left. With the combined exertion of both boy and dog, he dragged himself onto level ground.

Afzal rolled onto his back, sweaty and exhausted. Wicket wagged her tail and lay next to him, licking his face.

'Oh, my good girl Wicket, thank you. You're the greatest dog in the entire universe,' he panted, patting Wicket gently on her head. 'I would've been at the bottom of the ravine without you.'

He lay still with the dog on his side, too spent to move a muscle. It gave him a beautiful view of the star-filled sky. The twinkling lights had never looked so alive or wonderous.

'That was the dumbest thing I've ever done,' Afzal said out loud, wiping his sweaty and dirty palms on his tunic. He then rolled over and nuzzled Wicket. 'And maybe the best. But now is not the time to celebrate. It will be morning soon—we need to get to Bee and Rup. This is far from over. My stupid ego and stubbornness have caused a lot of problems.'

## 29

# The Red Blinking Dot

Afzal watched the first rays of daylight break over the horizon. A new day was dawning, and he was glad to feel sunlight on his face after a long night of walking in the cold dark.

'Alright, Wicket. We know where they're headed.'

On cue, the dog sniffed around a little, then sprinted off. Afzal felt drained of energy, but he pushed himself to follow. At least it was downhill. Afzal was thankful for any small mercy, and this was one. Whenever he caught up to her, she would run off again. She was enjoying a game of chase and luckily, it made the descent less laborious. They repeated this routine a dozen times. Afzal caught glimpses of sunlight glancing off the river in the valley, which meant they were moving closer to the bridge.

But then, without warning, two terrorists emerged from the bushes—cutting across the trail about ten feet in front of Afzal. They stopped and raised their guns when they saw him.

Afzal froze; his heart was pounding so hard that he was sure the men could see it beating in his chest.

*Not again. I am so close. Breathe, man, breathe.*

One of them said, 'Halt!'

Afzal walked towards them, trying hard to act casual and calm. 'Hello. Don't run into too many people up here.'

The terrorist examined him, fingering his gun. 'Are you alone?'

'Yes. Why?'

'We're looking for three kids with a man as their prisoner.'

Afzal's chest tightened. A quick thought popped into his head.

'I'm up here searching for the same people. Three kids and a prisoner. Tamir desperately wants to find them. Said he would give me twenty US dollars to search for them and fifty if I actually found them.'

At this point, Wicket came running up to them. The terrorist tightened his grip around the gun. 'Where did you find this dog? We were with Tamir a few hours ago. He didn't say anything about you.'

'She's mine. Been my dog for years. Why?' He patted Wicket lovingly as the dog leaned her paws onto his leg, tail wagging.

'You should know.'

'Oh, because they have a dog too. Well, that's exactly why Tamir asked me to come. A dog to find a dog. He said you guys heard their dog barking last night. My girl can find them quickly.'

The terrorist studied the dog nuzzling Afzal's legs.

'How do we know Tamir called you?'

'What kind of question is that?' Afzal asked, his voice raised. 'Tamir said something about ISI being involved and how they're listening to all the calls. He didn't want the phones switched on to tip ISI off—he wants to catch those kids before the ISI does.'

The terrorist snorted. 'So do we.'

'Tamir said if ISI gets to the kids first, we lose.'

'That sounds like him.' The terrorist squinted at Afzal. 'Let me see your phone.'

Afzal pulled the burner and held it out. The man examined it.

'That looks exactly like the phone Tamir has.'

Afzal nodded. 'It should. He buys them by the dozen. It even has his tattoo design on the back cover. He gave me this one last month. Or was it two months ago? I can't remember. Anyway, he wanted to be able to call me when he needed special jobs done. Like today.'

The terrorist appeared to relax. 'Alright. He told us the same things about ISI too.'

'Are you going to see him again later?'

'Yes. Why?'

'Here, take my phone. Tamir told me to return it, for security reasons. I already have my instructions to find the kids—I don't need it anymore.' Then he switched on the phone and handed it to the terrorist.

'Fine. We're off now,' said the terrorist, pocketing the device.

'Why don't you guys search down the marked trail? I'll follow my dog to search that difficult terrain over there.' Afzal pointed to the right of the trail.

'Why in that direction? You think the kids are there?'

Afzal hung his head, as if embarrassed. 'I took the easier trail downhill since Tamir told me they were heading straight for the border, but I've not seen them yet. My dog desperately wants to go up there, so I'm going to trust her nose. She's usually right, so I might make those fifty dollars after all.'

'Hold on. Why don't we go search up there and you continue down the same trail?' asked the terrorist.

'No, no. My dog thinks they are somewhere in that direction, and it will be easier for her to track them. You take the marked trail,' said Afzal.

The man narrowed his eyes, and raised his gun slightly to emphasise his point. 'No. We will go that way. You and your dog continue down this trail.'

Afzal shrugged and put his palms up. 'Hey, no worries. But just give me a cut if you do find them there. Okay? Good luck.'

'Luck has nothing to do with it, kid.' Then both men walked towards the thick bushes.

Afzal did not linger around. Wicket ran off leading the way and he followed right behind her. He glanced back once to make sure the two had indeed continued in the wrong direction.

'Happy trails, fellas! I'm surprised he didn't ask how I'd contact Tamir without a phone.'

~

As daybreak came, Tamir huddled with his grizzled terrorist companion, Nadeem. He grumbled, 'We were so close to capturing them during the night. I'm sure of it. Now the trail has disappeared. They could be anywhere.'

'Splitting up this morning was a good idea. As three separate teams, we're covering a lot of ground. We'll get them,' Nadeem said, sounding calm.

'You should be nervous. You know what will happen if that load you were moving is lost.'

'Everything we do, we risk our lives. It's the way of things in this region. But I'm confident those three kids will be caught. The word is out.'

A whirring engine interrupted further conversation.

Tamir stopped. 'That damn helicopter again. We need to look like we're locals taking a break. Let's squat. Don't look up.'

'Alright. I could rest my feet for a couple minutes.'

Nadeem found a rock and sat down on his haunches. Tamir did the same. The helicopter zig-zagged over the sky above them.

As he squatted, Tamir's phone buzzed deep inside his pocket. He fished it out and the tracker app's map appeared one more time.

The red dot was blinking again.

'Holy shit. Their phone is switched on. They're not far away at all.'

Nadeem squinted at the blinking dot, his forehead creased. 'Why would they turn your phone back on?'

Tamir laughed. 'I'll tell you why. Because those dumb idiots got lost last night. They were so far off the trail—that's why we weren't able to catch them. They don't know where to go and they're using my phone's GPS. We got them!'

The grizzled terrorist scratched his beard. 'Hmm ...'

Tamir showed his companion the location of the red dot. 'They're not far. Let's go scoop them up.'

The tired men rose and set out towards the blinking red dot on the tracker app.

As they walked, Tamir asked, 'Should we call the other two teams? Tell them to join us near this spot?'

'Not yet. No calls. Not secure. Let them continue their search until we are certain about the kids. Don't worry—once we catch the kids, we'll text them.' Apparently, Nadeem had his methods.

'You guys need to discover burner phones. They're helpful,' Tamir said.

'Maybe. But to find a few annoying kids, we need local search teams, not technology.'

'Don't underestimate these three. They're incredibly resourceful. Trust me, I know.'

As they bore down their target, Tamir watched the red dot glide over the map. They fell silent as they came closer to their quarry. The thought of finally capturing the troublesome teens and retrieving their lost assets was electrifying.

Creeping down the rough trail, they were almost upon the blinking dot. Up ahead, they heard pebbles crunching underfoot and branches rustling. Even obscured by the dense foliage, they could see motion.

Tamir and Nadeem drew their guns. After exchanging a quick nod, they jumped out and shouted, 'Freeze! Put your hands up!'

Two people dropped their weapons, turning around with their hands reaching for the sky. To everyone's surprise, it was the younger men, staring back at Tamir and Nadeem in shock.

'Why are you pointing the guns at us?!'

'We tracked my phone to you.'

'What do you mean?'

'Do you have a phone on you? I gave strict instructions not to carry any because they can be traced,' said Nadeem.

The terrorist took out the burner from his pocket. 'You mean this phone?'

Tamir took one look at the device, lifted his head and howled at the sky like an enraged beast. 'Fuuuuck!'

'How did you get that? Did you find it lying somewhere?' Nadeem asked, watching the man closely.

'No.'

'How did you get it then?' roared Tamir.

'Your friend, that local kid with a dog, gave it to me.'

Tamir strode over to the two terrorists, his face barely a few inches from the man with the phone.

'I don't have any friends here with a dog. You let them escape?'

'No. There was only one kid. This local boy Tamir hired to help with the search, boss. With a dog. To find the other dog.' The two peered beseechingly at Nadeem over Tamir's shoulder.

Nadeem snorted. 'The kids gave your phone to our men to fool your red dot. That was pretty smart. See? This is why I don't use high-tech stuff.'

Tamir glared at the younger man, his face red. 'You dumb asshole. I didn't hire any kid. But you let one of them give you my phone and then simply walk away?'

'He said he was part of the search, too. I thought he was working for you. He had your phone and knew all the details of the search.'

'This is unforgivable.'

The drug dealer locked eyes with Nadeem, who sighed and nodded almost imperceptibly. In one fluid motion, Tamir reached over and drew a knife from Nadeem's waist. Then, his arm snapped forward almost like a whip, the sharp blade slicing across the younger man's throat.

A clean cut.

The man sank to his knees, clutching his throat in a futile attempt to stem the flow of blood, his eyes wild. He gurgled, struggling to breathe, as the leaves beneath him grew red.

After a few moments, he collapsed on the ground, dead.

Nadeem locked eyes with the second terrorist. The man was shaking with fear. 'Let that be a lesson to you. If we don't retrieve the load from those animals, a whole lot worse than that will happen to all of us.'

Then he turned to Tamir, who was cleaning the blade. 'Including you.'

'If I don't find my journal, there's a long list of people who will want me to die horribly,' said Tamir, handing the blade back.

Nadeem nodded to the young terrorist. 'Text the other search team to quickly get to the border. We need to intercept them—immediately.'

# 30

## So Close, Yet So Far

Beena and Rup skipped the actual trail but kept close to it as they went down the mountain. They made slow progress with a loaded horse, Rup's bleeding shoulder and a donkey hauling an obese man. If that wasn't difficult enough, the drone of the helicopter kept them scrambling for cover.

However, by morning, they'd made it to the base of the mountain, near the bridge. Beena surveyed the area for a place to hide and found one under a few thick trees. 'This is a good enough spot, both to hide and check the bridge out. We've about an hour before the change of guards.'

Rup grunted a reply. Beena looked up at him sharply.

'How is your shoulder holding up? You look like an uncooked ball of dough after losing all that blood. We absolutely need to retie the bandage. Don't want infection setting in.'

'Well, my arm hasn't fallen off yet. All things considered, I'm doing good. Hurts like hell though. And my ass is numb from sitting on this horse.' Rup's voice was dry and raspy. 'I could use some water.' He gingerly got off the horse, holding onto Beena for support.

'There's a bit left in the canteen.' Beena said. She popped the cap off and offered it to Rup. 'Go easy though, okay? It has to last a few more hours. We're not home yet and you need to preserve your strength.'

Rup grasped the bottle. 'If you hadn't forced me to ride the horse, I'm sure I would be dead by now. Thanks, Bee.'

Beena rolled her eyes. 'Men and their stupid egos. Drink up now, you goof.'

Rup smiled weakly and took a small swig. 'Oh man, who knew warm water could taste so good?'

Beena walked over to the donkey and cupped some water in her hands for it to drink. She gave the remainder to the horse. Then she riffled through the saddle pouch and fished out the binoculars. 'It's time to have a good look at that bridge and the tunnel entrances.'

After finding a suitable spot, she lay flat on her stomach and peered through the binoculars. Rup carefully lay down on the ground next to her.

'What do you see, Bee?'

'I see our tricolour at the end of the bridge. Oh, what a great sight! Hmm … Farouk was right about border security. Lots of guards on that stupid bridge.'

'Check for the tunnels. You see any of them?'

Beena refocused the binoculars as she scanned the horizon.

'Okay. Let's see if I can find … damn. I think that's one of them. But if that's a tunnel, it's stupid small. It looks like a rabbit hole from here. And further away than the bridge.'

'Small and far? That's a terrible combination.'

'No way to get a loaded horse and donkey through. We may crawl through on our bellies, but I don't think this fat shithead will fit. The tunnels are a no-go.'

The sound of the helicopter caused them both to flinch.

Beena pursed her lips. 'That damn helicopter does not seem to need any fuel. It's been circling for ages. Keep your head down.'

They fell silent and waited, listening. The sound grew louder until it flew directly over them. The roar of whirring blades was deafening.

As the noise receded, Rup said, 'We're close enough to see our flag, but it looks impossible to cross over without getting caught, with the ISI buzzing over us. The tunnels are out and Pakistani border guards are crawling all over that bridge. Plus, terrorists with AK-47s are chasing us from behind. And where the hell is Afzal? This really sucks.'

'I was hoping he'd be here by now.' Beena spun around to stare at the mountain behind them. 'We can't wait here long. You're turning pastier every passing second and need medical treatment right away. Afzal better hurry up. In the meantime, we need to deal with our slight problem of how to get across that bridge.'

Rup shrugged. 'Simple. At the right time, we draw the guards' attention to something else, like in the movies. Create a diversion so we can cross over.'

'That's a good idea. But what type of diversion?'

'That's all I got,' replied Rup with a weak laugh, closing his eyes.

Beena ignored his levity. 'I need more, buddy. But, before we do anything, we should call Afzal and see where he is. We need to time everything correctly. We still have one last burner phone.'

'Won't Rambo be able to track us if we turn it on?'

'I think he will, especially after the fiasco where you got shot. I can try to turn off the GPS, although that might make no difference. But we have to risk it to guide Afzal here. We don't have time.'

Rup nodded. 'Turn off the GPS. I like that a lot. Clever idea.' Then he added, 'See, I just gave you a compliment and didn't throw out another idea to stomp all over your suggestion.'

'Shut up and stop being so sensitive.'

'Please,' Latif cried, interrupting their conversation, 'get me off this thing. Haneef and I have over twenty million dollars stashed away. I'll give you all of it. Please let me go. I can't be taken to India.' He was sobbing, almost sliding off the donkey.

'Even twenty billion dollars wouldn't cut it, you murderer. You can see the end of your road, don't you? I bet the tricolour on the other side of that bridge is giving you a migraine,' snapped Beena, getting up from the ground.

'Twenty million—that'll be a welcome donation to the victims' families.' Rup smiled at the prospect while Beena forcefully secured Latif to the donkey again. Then, she dug the burner phone out from one of the horse's pouches. 'Here goes.' She took a deep breath and switched it on, quickly turning off the GPS. Then she tapped speed dial. After a few rings, a brusque voice answered, 'What?'

Beena nearly dropped the phone. It wasn't the voice she was expecting and she blurted, 'Who is this?'

'Aha, my final missing phone,' said the voice. 'You know who this is. You're a smart girl—you said so yourself. And you should know I'm coming for all of you fuckers. You'll never cross the border; this, I promise you. When I catch you three, I am going to slit everyone's throats for all the trouble you've caused me. And you better have my journal.'

Beena snapped the phone shut and stared at Rup, who was lying ashen-faced on the ground.

'Shit, shit. Rambo answered Afzal's phone. And he's pissed.'

'How did he get Afzal's phone?' Rup asked and then his eyes widened. 'That means he caught Afzal. Oh no.'

Beena gritted her teeth, thinking hard. 'No, I don't think so. He said he was coming for all three of us. That didn't sound like he has Afzal.'

'I'm so worried about him and Wicket.'

Beena fell silent and paced for a minute. Then she said, 'We can't do anything about them. I need to focus. It's about 10.00 a.m. right now. The guards change at 10.45 a.m. and, according to Farouk, that's go-time. I hope he's right about the entitled and lazy guards.' She glanced back at the mountain. Then she swung around and stared at the bridge. 'About 200 metres. Forty or fifty seconds … eight or ten minutes …'

'What are you mumbling about? And why are you doing math?'

Latif's whine interrupted them again. 'Get me off this beast. I need to pee.'

Rup sighed. 'A miracle! He's said something normal for once instead of making dumb threats.'

'Ignore him. We got genuine problems to solve here.' Beena continued to survey the area, using the binoculars to look at the bridge, the guard's stations and the surrounding mountains.

She stretched, cracking her neck. 'Okay, I have some work to do. I also need to survey the lay of the land, check out the guards and also figure out a way through. Stay with the horse, protect your bandage, keep an eye on Latif and stay hidden.'

'Not that I'm in any position to move. What are you going to do?'

'I'm going to implement your diversion idea; the one you saved for last. Something that would make my uncle proud.'

'Will you be gone long?'

Beena studied Rup's ashen face and forced herself to smile reassuringly. 'Not long. But be ready to move in forty-five. That's blast off time. Okay?'

Rup nodded wearily. 'Got it. Forty-five minutes. But we can't leave without Afzal and Wicket, okay?' He paused and swallowed hard. 'Bee, I'm afraid I won't last much longer.'

Beena swallowed hard too, her eyes welling. It was exactly what she had been dreading—Rup was deteriorating, and rapidly. But she had to give him a boost. 'Whine again and I'll kick your ass so bad that Sister Aisha's ruler will feel like a balm. Chaat dinner awaits us in your haveli, my friend. You're going to be fine.'

'Okay,' he said. But he seemed unconvinced.

Beena checked his forehead.

*Damn, he's fading fast. Afzal better come soon, and this last-ditch plan better work.*

# 31

# The Bridge Over Jhelum

Rup's eyes opened when he heard Beena sneaking back. She collapsed in a heap next to him, sweaty and out of breath. Putting one finger to his mouth, she whispered, 'It's almost time.'

'Oh good, you're back. I was worried. Did you see any sign of Afzal or Wicket?'

Beena's face went glum. 'Not yet. No sign of them. I was out and came close to screwing up. I think the border guards almost saw me. That was the hardest two hundred metres out and back I've ever had to deal with.'

Rup continued to look up the slope, a worried expression clouding his pale face. His eyes were sunken and unnaturally bright behind his glasses.

'There's no sign of Afzal yet. You were gone a while. Did we miss the window?'

She glanced at her watch. 'No. Don't worry. We've about fifteen minutes or so left.'

'I kept watching for Wicket and Afzal. I was sure they'd be here.' Rup shivered and hugged himself.

Beena knitted her eyebrows together. 'Why are you so sure about that?'

Rup nervously chuckled, his eyes bright. 'I've a confession to make.'

'What did you do now? Message the terrorists and give them our coordinates in the hope they would share that with Afzal?'

He scowled. 'You're never going to forgive me for messaging my theatre group, are you?'

'Nope, never. Now, what do you need to share?'

'You remember the bag of potato chips from the horse's saddlebags? I used that to leave a trail for Wicket to follow. She'll bring Afzal to us, I'm sure of it.'

'What? How?'

'Every so often, I dropped a chip from the horse for Wicket. I thought it would make it easy for her to find us.'

Beena patted Rup's cheek. 'That is actually kind of sweet. Naïve, but sweet.'

Then she glanced at her watch again and her expression changed to one of worry.

'Shit, it's almost time. There's movement down at the bridge and I can see the guards moving from their positions. We need to move now.'

'Wait … wait a minute. We can't leave Afzal behind.'

'We won't have another chance, and we'll all be captured if we don't step on it right now.' Beena's expression was serious, but tears glistened in her eyes.

'We still have time. C'mon, Bee. This is Afzal we're talking about.' He struggled, with enormous effort, into a sitting position.

'Damn it, Rup, I know it's Afzal! But we're out of time. He would want us to go ahead. On your horse, right now.'

But Rup's gaze was focused on the hills behind Beena. Suddenly, he jerked up straight, forgetting his busted shoulder. He pointed, his face regaining a faint flush. 'Hey! That's Wicket … and Afzal!'

Beena spun around, her jaw hanging. 'Holy shit, you're right!'

Bursting through the foliage, they saw a whirl of a dog followed closely by a lean figure in a faded grey kurta-pyjama. It was indeed Afzal—hair bouncing and limbs flailing wildly. He was sprinting down the slope, his hands pumping up and down, with Wicket leading the way.

A shot rang out, and they heard the bullet whiz by.

Beena shoved aside a branch and peered through. 'It's Rambo and company! Shit. Afzal better pick up his pace. And you, Rup, on the horse, NOW! It's time.'

About a hundred metres behind Afzal, a bunch of men crashed through the thicket into the clearing. They were running with guns extended, firing at both boy and dog. More shots rang out.

Afzal flinched, swerving as he ran. At that moment, helicopter rotors thundered in the sky. Beena and Rup saw the chopper swing around from the edge of the mountains towards the river.

'Fuck! The helicopter is also here. Everybody and their mother is chasing Afzal.' Beena checked her watch again. 'It's nearly time.' She peered towards the bridge. 'Shit, the guards are moving. It's now or never, Rup. Let's go!'

'I can't get up on the horse now—it'll take me five minutes to mount. I'll have to run, Bee.'

'Shit! Okay. Run! I'll bring the donkey and Latif. GO!'

With a surge of energy out of nowhere, Rup burst out from the hiding spot. He yanked the horse's reins, urging the animal to gallop with him, and sprinted for the bridge.

Beena wrenched the donkey along, forcing it into a canter, Latif bobbing miserably on its back. Just as she was about to catch up with the struggling Rup and his horse, Wicket appeared at her side, her mouth open and tongue flapping out.

Beena looked over her shoulder. Afzal was in full sprint, closing in fast on them. She then glanced up at the mountain behind the guards' lodge. 'What the hell? It should have happened by now!'

Rup gasped, 'What are you talking about?'

'Nothing! Shut up and run!'

He grimaced and pressed down on his shoulder wound as he hurried along. Blood was seeping out at an alarming rate. Afzal finally caught up, sprinting just a few feet behind them, as more shots rang out. He lowered his head and sped up.

'Run, run!' he panted, nearly level with them.

Just as Afzal made it to his friends, a thunderous explosion rocked the mountain behind the guards' lodge at the base of the bridge. Dirt and debris leaped up high above them, filling the air. It was as if a volcano had spewed its innards into the sky. Large stones showered down near the guards on the bridge, causing them to scramble for cover.

The shock wave from the unexpected blast almost knocked Tamir and the others over. Mouths agape, they froze in place, watching the rubble and dirt shower down from the sky.

Beena, still sprinting, shouted, 'Diversion. Don't stop. Keep moving!'

Ignoring the commotion and rubble raining down, the three teens ran as fast as they could, guiding the two pack animals straight for the bridge. Wicket ran alongside Rup, barking with excitement.

The guards at the bridge were in complete disarray and panic after the explosion. One guard shouted to the others, as he bolted off, rushing down the bridge and onto the outer road, 'Screw this. I'm not dying here!'

Beena hollered above the din, 'Twenty metres to the bridge—almost there!'

'Chase and kill them all!' Tamir screamed, appearing through the settling dust behind them. 'No one crosses that bridge alive!'

The terrorists recovered from the blast, scrambled up and continued their chase. They were less than thirty metres behind the trio. The chopper was right above them, causing fierce winds to blow the dust around.

The three urged the animals onwards, trampling right through the two rattled guards at the entrance.

'Watch out for those damn spikes!' shouted Beena over the din of the chopper's engine, hurdling her donkey over the sharp row of metal placed to keep unauthorised cars off the bridge. Rup and Afzal, dragging the horse, vaulted over the sharp ends and rushed forward.

The narrow bridge appeared in front of them—an empty open road, inviting and serene. The Indian tricolour waved at them on the other side of the horizon, as if gesturing and welcoming the trio home.

Afzal noticed a guard supporting himself on the rails, dragging himself upright.

'Careful, Bee! That guard's going for his gun!'

'No stopping! We go for broke!' Beena charged ahead, leading the donkey straight at the guard. Wicket ran with her, barking animatedly.

Afzal's jaw dropped. 'She's out of her mind.'

Still reeling from the blast, the remaining guard tried to pull his pistol out of its holster. He hands shook as he fumbled with the gun—his bulging eyes focused on the trio rushing towards him. But before his gun even cleared its holster, Beena had body-slammed him with the donkey, hammering him back into the ground with a sickening thump.

Suddenly, just as the trio had an open path to the Indian side, the helicopter plunged down from the sky. It banked fiercely, pulling up and levelling out—its screeching frame mere inches above the rails. The copter steadied itself and hovered a few feet over the bridge at the centre of the crossing—leaning forward and thundering at them with sharp, whirring blades.

A sniper was perched at the open door, peering over the dark barrel of a rifle, blocking access to the Indian side and to safety. And sitting across the sniper, glaring at his prey, was a tall, dark-suited man.

Afzal gasped, slowing and stopping alongside the three. 'Fuck! Qadir!'

Behind them, Tamir and his four terrorist companions were advancing. All of them were armed and pointing their guns at the teens.

Latif craned his neck from the side of the donkey. 'What the hell is going on? Can someone please just shoot these idiot kids?'

Qadir pressed his headset. 'Hover low over the bridge and stay right here. Keep them on our half of the bridge, alive if possible. I want to interrogate them. But there's no fucking way you let them cross over to India. Shoot them dead if they try. Understood?'

The sniper nodded.

'Good.'

Qadir stepped out of the helicopter door, sprang down and landed on the bridge with a light thud. He stood tall in the middle of the bridge between Pakistan and India, his jacket billowing behind him. Raising his arm slowly, he pointed a revolver at the three teens.

Afzal looked around and examined the gaggle of armed terrorists on the Pakistani end of the bridge, a sniper pointing his rifle at them from the helicopter hovering over the border and an armed ISI agent standing on their finish line.

They were trapped in the middle of deadly vice with no way out.

# 32

# One is Never Enough

Tamir hollered over the din of the helicopter, 'Give me Latif and my notebook. I need them both.'

'Nobody moves!' cried Qadir from the centre of the bridge. 'The sniper will take you out in the blink of an eye.'

Tamir squinted to see who the tall man at the centre of the bridge was. 'Not you again. I thought we took you to the shed. Who are you, anyway?'

Qadir flashed his badge. 'ISI. Now drop your weapons.'

Tamir muttered curses under his breath. 'Well, damn. Look at his flashy badge and helicopter. The old man may really be with ISI. But that don't mean shit now. There's no way I'm leaving without that journal.' He refocused his attention on the teens. 'Give me my goddamn journal, or I'll kill all of you!'

Nadeem, however, decided that they were well past the stage of making threats. His cargo had to be retrieved, or there would be hell to pay. A death worse than hell. So, he fixed his aim at the trio and started shooting.

The bullets whizzed across the bridge and one of them hit Latif's leg, dangling on the side of the donkey. He screamed in agony.

The sniper immediately swung into action. With an ease born from thousands of hours of training, he shifted slightly, gazing over the long barrel, took a steady breath and gently squeezed the trigger. The bullet seared over the teens and tore right through Nadeem's chest, exploding in a mist of red. He was flung backwards, dead before he hit the ground.

As he collapsed, Nadeem's twitching fingers somehow squeezed off another shot. The bullet flew over the teens' heads and right through the chopper's window, hitting the pilot. The helicopter jerked and started to wobble.

When Nadeem made his fatal decision, Tamir had also lined up his target—Afzal. He lifted his gun and pointed. In a flash, Wicket charged across the length of the bridge and leaped towards Tamir. Snarling, she locked her jaws into his hand, knocking him to the ground. His gun discharged—wood splintered at Afzal's feet.

Tamir screamed in pain as Wicket dug her jaws deep into his hand, forcing him to release his gun. He punched the dog in desperation, but Wicket wasn't in the mood to unclench her jaws.

Seeing the muscled thug hit her, Rup cried, 'Wicket! Come back!'

Over the centre of the bridge, the chopper was starting to lose control, rotors howling as they strained to keep the huge machine steady.

Qadir shouted into his comms, 'You guys okay up there?' He saw the sniper disappear. There was a flurry of activity in the cockpit and the chopper flew off, unsteady and slow.

*Is my sniper piloting that thing?*

Everyone was momentarily distracted by the noisy chopper wobbling in the air. Sensing an opportunity, two terrorists, one burly and the other short, rushed out onto the bridge to retrieve their cargo, raising their guns as they charged towards the kids.

Afzal leaped forward to tackle the approaching threat. He lunged with all his might at the burly man, tackling him by the waist. But the big man was too powerful for Afzal's lean frame, and he was barely able to slow down his momentum. They collided with Rup—all three of them went down in a heap. Rup yelled in pain as he hit the ground. Hearing his cry, Wicket released her grip on Tamir's hand and spun around. Barking, she charged back up the bridge.

A bleeding Rup was on the ground wrestling with the big terrorist. Afzal tried to pin him down while Rup struggled to wrench the gun away. However, the man was too strong for them. He shrugged Afzal off and jumped back on to his feet, still fighting for the gun with Rup. Grinning maliciously, he jabbed Rup's bleeding shoulder with his thumb, causing him to yelp in agony—Rup let go of the gun and collapsed on the floor.

Wicket came tearing up the bridge at full tilt, snapping at the terrorist. The burly man turned around, surprised at the dog's fury and staggered back. Growling and her teeth bared, the dog leaped high and rammed the man's chest with incredible momentum, shoving the flailing terrorist towards the railing. Her snarling jaws and the force of the blow caused the terrorist to lurch backwards, lose balance and topple over the bridge's rail. He screamed as he plunged down and splashed into the roaring river below—his shrieks reverberating across the valley.

Rup, sitting on the ground and nursing his wound, watched as the man was swept away by the rushing waters. He reached out and hugged Wicket tightly.

Meanwhile, the short terrorist had rushed towards the donkey, determined to regain its load. As he hurried over, gun pointed, Beena slid behind the animal. When the man drew close, Beena leaped out, staying low and moving fast. She slid under the man's outstretched arm and rammed her shoulder into the terrorist's legs. His knees buckled and he flopped face first onto the ground. The gun flew from his hands, skidding across the ground.

Furious, the terrorist sprang back to his feet, shaking his head. His nose was bloody and his chin scraped raw. 'Bitch!' he screamed, lunging forward to throw a punch at Beena's head. She weaved aside at the last moment, avoiding the blow. The momentum of the punch unbalanced the man and when he stumbled past her, Beena accelerated his momentum with a powerful kick to his back. The unfortunate man was propelled forward once more, crashing headfirst onto a lamp post and collapsing to the ground.

Dazed, the terrorist blinked hard, his mouth slack. As he pressed his palms on the ground to shove himself up, he felt the shape of something familiar. His gun! Snarling with rage, the terrorist sprung up and turned towards Beena, pointing the weapon. She recoiled and stumbled back, colliding with the donkey's haunch as the man advanced on her.

The donkey brayed, abruptly reared its behind and, extending its legs, kicked hard. Its hooves landed with brutal force on the advancing terrorist's chest, hurling him back several feet, knocking him unconscious.

Seeing his colleagues go down in unpleasant ways, the last terrorist was in no mood to play nice and whipped out his machine gun. Qadir's response was equally quick and simple: he shot the terrorist right between his eyes. The man went down with a thud—a bag of sand falling off a truck.

In all the commotion, no one saw Tamir roll over and grab his gun with his uninjured hand.

And, as the third AK-47—toting terrorist fell by his side, Tamir lifted his gun.

'Fuck you!' He pointed the weapon at Rup again, who sitting still, clutching his bleeding shoulder. 'Your antics at the chai stall are to blame for all of this. Go to hell!'

Wicket, meanwhile, sensed unfinished business with the man who had abused her. Sprinting across the bridge, Wicket vaulted towards the drug dealer once more, her bloodied teeth bared.

Tamir pulled the trigger. His gun recoiled with the shot.

Wicket's leap stopped mid-air as if she'd hit an invisible wall. She yelped loudly and collapsed on the bridge. Her eyes were bright, her body shuddering as the ground beneath her turned red.

'Wicket!' screamed Rup, extending his arms towards the bleeding dog as she lay twitching on the ground.

Qadir smoothly swung his gun around. With practised ease, he shot Tamir right through his head. Tamir collapsed on the floor, a bright red dot visible on his forehead, blood pooling around the back of his skull. The gun lay motionless in his tattooed hand.

With the last remaining threat eliminated, Qadir strode purposefully towards the teens, pointing his weapon at them. Rup sobbed, gazing at Wicket lying a few feet away, holding onto the railing as he struggled to his feet. Afzal stood next to him, tugging on his friend's arm to help him up. Beena was expressionless, her hands clenched tightly around the donkey's reins.

The ISI agent glared at the teens, his eyes flashing—then a small smile crept onto his face. 'You three are good, but not good enough.' There was a sense of victory in his voice as he gloated, 'You're real pains in the ass, but now it's finally over. Nowhere to run or hide.'

He glanced at the bank of the river on the Indian side. 'So close, yet so far away. We're still in Pakistani territory—your Indian soldiers can't do a damn thing. You fools will rot in a Pakistani prison for the rest of your miserable lives. And then you will be strung up for all to see. No one will dare risk doing something like this ever again.'

Latif shouted from his perch atop the donkey, 'You ISI idiot! Don't talk—just kill them! And get me off this blasted donkey. I've been shot, you moron! Bring a doctor here now!'

Qadir looked irritably at Latif and then at the blood dripping from his leg. He started to say something, then decided against it and simply grunted, 'Hmph.'

Afzal gently nudged Beena, as if to ask—*What now, Bee?*

Beena sneaked a glance at her watch and gripped the railing. She whispered, 'Hold on tight. Grab Rup, turn and run for home in five, okay?'

Afzal wrinkled his forehead. 'Five what? Who?'

'Four, three, two ...'

Suddenly, a deafening explosion shook the bridge. It was as if the entire mountain on the Pakistani side was erupting. Large stones and dirt soared high into the air, almost obscuring daylight. A shock wave blazed through like an unseen punch, smashing Qadir to the ground. Rubble clattered down on the bridge's surface, as the wild-eyed animals brayed and strained against their ropes.

Beena did not look, nor did she wait. She turned and yelled loudly, 'Rup, run, Rup! Afzal, get the horse. Run, RUN!' She grabbed the donkey's reins, yanked hard and sprinted. Afzal, overcoming his initial confusion and shock, seized the horse's reins. They ran across the bridge. Recovering from the shock of the blast, his ears ringing, Qadir struggled to get up. He tried to lift his gun, but the charging horse knocked him back down.

In a flash, they crossed the painted line on the centre of the bridge, stepping over the international border and officially making it back to India.

But back on the Pakistani half of the bridge, barely a few metres away from home and safety, Rup had crawled in the opposite direction. He was hunched over, hugging Wicket's limp body as tears streamed down his face.

Qadir warily got back to his feet and glared at the two teens standing over the Indian side of the bridge. He turned and noticed the lone teen crouched beside the dog, his body wracked with sobs. Qadir stooped down, collected his gun and trudged the length of the bridge, stopping next to Rup clasping a bleeding Wicket.

Anger burned bright in his eyes as he pointed his gun at Rup's head. He hissed under his breath, 'Another diversion. Smart. That was very smart. Everything you did was what a highly trained agent would do.'

He gazed down as Rup wept for Wicket, hugging the bleeding body of the animal. Then he paused, looking at the blood seeping from the boy's shoulder and the pool of blood on the ground next to the dog's body.

The gun slowly drooped to his side. Qadir muttered, 'Except for that.'

Rup sobbed, unheeding. 'Wicket …'

Qadir turned and stared once more at the donkey with Latif strapped on it and the boy's friends on the Indian section of the bridge. His shoulders sagged and he let out a big sigh.

The agent gestured with his gun. 'Go on. You have five seconds before I change my mind and arrest you.'

Rup didn't stir for a couple of seconds. He sniffled, wiped the tears from his cheeks and scooped up a limp, bleeding Wicket. Holding her close to his chest, he stood up. He stared at Qadir for a moment, then turned and walked over the border to the Indian side.

Afzal and Beena welcomed him with hugs, tears streaming down their faces.

Beena was shaking. 'I was so afraid for you. Is Wicket okay?' She kissed the motionless dog softly on its face. Afzal held a limp paw in the palm of his hand, softly massaging it and weeping.

'She isn't moving,' Rup said quietly. 'The best dog in the world. She saved my life on that bridge.'

'She saved all our lives.' Beena and Afzal hugged him tightly.

The three of them approached the Indian side as the Assam Rifle soldiers rushed to them, led by Beena's uncle.

Afzal asked Rup, 'Why did the ISI man let you go? What did he say to you?'

'Not much. He told me to go before he changed his mind. He was pissed that we were smart enough to cross over—thanks to Bee and her final diversion.'

Beena hugged her uncle tightly. 'I was taught well. One diversion is never enough. You always need two.'

# 33

# Like Parents, Like Son

The theatre group held a special meeting to present a made-up award to Rup. A couple of members volunteered to create an improvised trophy, complete with a toy camera on top to make fun of Rup's poor camera work.

Afzal and Beena made an appearance at the event to witness their friend being roasted. Along with them was their most joyful guest, a limping and bandaged Wicket. Against all odds, the brave dog had survived Tamir's bullet and was saved by the skill of an army surgeon at the border. The medic didn't normally treat animals. But this was no normal dog. This, as everyone said, was the interrogation dog.

Rup had threatened to leave the school if Wicket wasn't allowed to stay with him. Nobody thought it wise to argue with him.

The three friends then left to take care of one last item left on their to-do list regarding the capture and retrieval of Rasheed Latif from Pakistan. After a few minutes of searching, they found their target.

Parv stared at the three friends approaching. 'You look … different.'

Beena raised an eyebrow. 'Haven't you heard? We captured Latif from Pakistan and brought him back to India to face justice. That can change a person.'

Parv nodded. 'I heard.'

'And you know what that means.' Rup ran his hand over his hair, as if he were shaving it from his head. 'You tell him, Afzal. He owes you a bald head.'

Afzal stood silently, a solemn expression on his face.

Parv said hurriedly, 'I was only kidding. Hey, Afzal, I'm sorry for doubting your patriotism. I shouldn't have said those horrible things.'

'Rup, Bee, it's all right. Let it go. Parv has apologised.'

Beena ignored Afzal. 'Nope, no way. No wriggling out of this one, Parv. You said it and you were serious. A bit pissed off, but serious. I think Afzal here has more than proved his case.'

Rup added, 'Yeah, he captured the man responsible for the worst terrorist attacks in India and brought him back to face justice.'

'Exactly. If you don't have a sharp razor, I can get you one. Or a blunt one if you prefer that.' Beena grinned, her teeth flashing.

Parv's face went pale. 'You can't possibly think I was serious.' He stared at Afzal for a second. 'Shit. You still want me to shave my head?'

Afzal started to say something, but Rup snorted. 'Of course he does. We sure as hell didn't risk our lives for nothing.'

Parv looked at the three beseechingly.

Rup grinned, excitement lighting up his face. 'Hang on, I've got a great idea!'

Beena rolled her eyes. 'Oh, great. Here we go again.'

~

They were in Rup's apartment that evening, splayed out on the floor. Plates of half-eaten chaat and near-empty bottles of beer sat on the rickety upturned bucket. Wicket lay contently on Rup's lap, drooling on his jeans.

Beena turned to Afzal. 'You have been awfully quiet this evening. Scratch that—the entire day. Even Rup's stupid voices did not evoke a reaction. You should be ecstatic. What about the fact that the maps from the horse helped prevent an attack in Kashmir? Or that Rambo's journal is the biggest anti-drug trafficking catch in modern times, helping discover and eliminate several gangs and their routes into Punjab and the world? Not to mention all those documents we got from Osama's old compound proving how the Pakistani military was jolly-jolly with him. And the biggest achievement, that Latif is now sitting in a prison, soon to face justice for his terrorist crimes? So, what gives?'

Rup chimed in, 'Yeah, Afzal, what gives? Also, what's with not pushing Parv to shave his head? That was the big goal, was it not? To prove your patriotism? I thought it was what kicked all of this off—our escapade, the mayhem, our near deaths.'

Afzal slowly raised his head and gazed at the two of them sprawled on the floor, looking at him expectantly. He shrugged. 'Maybe my goals have changed. I don't know what or how to say this …'

'Say what?' asked Beena.

'Talk. Don't mime. That's my advice,' said Rup.

Wicket lifted her head from Rup's lap, looked at Afzal and made a funny noise.

'Look, even Wicket agrees. Spit it out, will ya?'

Afzal pursed his lips, his expression serious. He finally muttered, 'I should never have made that bet. Parv was right about my family. Both of you were in life-threatening danger because of my stupid, fragile ego, and I am so sorry about that.'

'Whoa. Back up. What was Parv right about? What are you even talking about?' Beena looked sharply at him.

'What he said about terrorist and traitor blood. I did not want to believe it then but turns out he was right. The man Latif mentioned, Rizwan Sheik? Rizwan was my uncle. My mother's brother. And he was responsible for planning terrorist attacks in India. So, Parv was right that I had a terrorist in my family.'

'What? I was not paying much attention to Latif's babbling, but you are telling me this Rizwan guy is your uncle? Your actual uncle? And he's a terrorist?' Beena stared at him with wide eyes.

'Yes. Was my uncle. Was a terrorist—he's dead now. He was known as Rizwan Abdul. Indian forces shot him nearly a decade ago when he was trying to execute a terror plot in Delhi that would have killed hundreds of civilians.'

'Jeez,' Beena said, slowly exhaling. 'I'm glad he's dead. But why should Rizwan being family change anything about you? You are not responsible for your uncle's actions. He was a terrible person, influenced by an even worse one. Remember how you figured out that it does not matter what anyone thinks, what matters is what you and your loved ones do?'

'I know that. I'm responsible for my life and my actions, not someone else's. But that also includes me putting your lives in serious jeopardy. I am sorry about that.'

'Afzal, we joined you. You didn't force us to come. We were all a bit nuts, but we're all back home in one piece right? So, stop with the apologies, okay? Or we'll have to shave your head too,' Beena said, jabbing a finger to his head.

'I'm with Bee. Stop with that. And your uncle—he deserved what he got.'

'I'm not that bothered about Rizwan being my uncle, but it is interesting that Parv was actually correct about one of my family members being a terrorist.'

'Interesting maybe, but not relevant.'

Afzal paused again, as if collecting his thoughts. He said, 'But this is what makes me super proud—it was my mom and dad who reached out to the authorities when they discovered my uncle's plans.'

'What? Your parents gave up your uncle?' Rup was gaping.

'Yup. And I don't see it as giving up my uncle. More like, doing the right thing. My parents' courage and conviction saved hundreds of lives that day in Delhi. No one ever found out who alerted the cops. The authorities never made anything public. I only learned the truth about everything when I spoke with my mom yesterday.'

'Wow,' Beena said. 'I faintly remember Latif talking about a treasonous family. He doesn't even know what a traitor truly means.'

'Now we know where this itch to go and capture Latif came from! It is in your DNA, straight from mom and dad,' said Rup.

Afzal smiled ruefully. 'I always believed we ran away from Delhi because of terrorism accusations. I'm aghast that I even thought that. My parents are my heroes. They quietly did what was right—no fuss, no second thoughts, with zero publicity— and moved away without big explanations. All to shield me from that baggage, so I could grow up and have a normal life.'

Rup raised a palm.

'Alright, alright. That's all well and good, but that's no reason not to play barber with Parv,' he said. 'He still needs to sacrifice his locks for misbehaving with you and Bee. Think of it as a visit to Tirupati temple where they mundan your head to seek blessings from the lord! This tonsure will be the divine blessing that Parv needs to forever cure him of his bullying.'

'You are always visualising a dramatic scene, Rup,' Beena said with a laugh. 'But I agree; shaving Parv's head will be fun.'

It took a couple of weeks of work, but Beena and Rup made Parv's haircut a must-see event for the school. Afzal had one condition before cutting Parv's hair—they must raise some money in the process to donate to a worthy cause. Parv grudgingly agreed, his way of acknowledging that what Afzal, Beena and Rup had done was indeed grand and patriotic.

The moment of the much-anticipated haircut arrived, but no one could have expected how much the whole country wanted to see the event. Thousands of people attended, as well as a swarm of mediapersons. Cameras and mics were everywhere and they captured every detail as the three took turns with the electric razor to give Parv the long-awaited buzz-cut.

In a small, dimly lit prison cell, Latif flipped the channels. Smacking the side of the small black and white television, he said, 'Damn it! Every single channel is covering this idiotic event. Is this how they live in this pissant country? They cover a lousy haircut on the news?'

A newscaster could be heard over the TV's tinny speaker: *The strange story of how three brave teens came to capture India's most wanted terrorist began with a bizarre bet where the loser had to shave his head. Today, we're at the school where the capture and return of Rasheed Latif began and one student will make good on the wager that started it all.*

'WHAT? Those scrawny little runts did this to me for a schoolyard bet?' Latif's face turned bright red. Then he picked up the TV and hurled it against the wall, busting the only thing that would have kept him occupied in the dank cell.

~

Yug rubbed Parv's bald head and laughed. 'It looks good on you. Makes you look badass.'

'Language!' Brother da Costa glanced at all the cameras around and then locked eyes with Yug till a chortle escaped his lips. 'It makes him look formidable.'

Afzal nodded at Parv. 'You're now infamous.'

'More than you both know. The prime minister's office recently contacted the school,' said Brother da Costa, looking at the trio one by one. 'Pathan, Maibam, Chauhan—you have been invited for the Independence Day celebrations as the prime minister's official guests. The folks in Delhi are anxious to hear about your bet and how it all started.'

'Holy shit!' yelled Rup, then winced.

'Language!'

'I'm sorry, Brother. It just slipped out.'

The brother's lips eased into a smile. Then he winked and whispered to Rup, 'I know what you mean. Sister Alisha said the same thing when I told her.'

Afzal glanced at Beena, his mouth wide open. 'I would have loved to see that.'

'Not me. I've faced enough danger to last a lifetime.'

'Or have you?' said Afzal, and winked.

'See, Brother? They are already planning something else that will land us all in trouble. Not to mention sore behinds from Sister Alisha's ruler.' Beena scowled.

Brother da Costa put his arm around her. 'Well, you wouldn't have it any other way. And you know what? Neither would they. You keep them out of serious trouble.'

The brother locked eyes with Afzal. 'Well, most of the time, that is.'

Till we meet again.

# Acknowledgements

Acknowledgements are like the credits at the end of a movie: almost everyone ignores them, but they're where the weavers of story magic get well-deserved hi-fives. First, to my editors, Sanghamitra and Sanjana, who waded through my verbose manuscript, handcuffed it onto a treadmill and transformed it into something readable. To my agent, Anish, a magician who convinced an actual publisher that this first-time author's story about cross-border, trouble-seeking kids was worth it.

To my friend James, who introduced me to said magician. To my wife Neema, who mightily tried to imagine I was doing 'real work', and ensured I didn't starve but also did not rip the drafts to complete shreds—could not have done it without you. Also to Gopeica and Radheica, our dogs, who inspired the true hero in the story—Wicket.

To Achan and Amma—for everything. Lastly, a shout out to Bru filter coffee—without you, this book would still be quarter-formed ideas scribbled on various Google Docs.

Thank you all for your support, love and the occasional kick in the rear. You've made this wildly entertaining journey possible.